A TELLING MANEUVER

"Ah, a waltz." Theo was delighted. The dance would provide an excellent opportunity to converse with his partner, Lady Sarah, known among the bachelors of the *ton* as "the Welsh Beauty." And she was, indeed, beautiful. She was also trembling. Her tremors were slight—had he not been holding her, he would not have noticed—but unmistakable.

What the devil was wrong? He had partnered with her a number of times last year, so his request for a dance could not have discomposed her. Perplexed, he studied her face, but her features were serene. Her reserve and . . . aloofness, for want of a better word, were daunting. They also posed a challenge. He would find out why she was so uneasy in his company. But not by asking more questions.

Expertly leading her through the patterns of the waltz, he deliberately misstepped and jerked her against his chest.

Her trembling increased, and her eyes slewed to his, meeting his gaze for the first time all evening.

He stroked his hand up her spine. "My apologies, Lady Sarah." Smoothly moving them back amidst the whirling couples, he re-established a proper distance between them. Sarah's trembling eased, and Theo had his answer.

Being near him disconcerted her. Now all he had to do was figure out why.

A Rake's Redemption

Susannah Carleton

A SIGNET BOOK

SIGNET
Published by New American Library, a division of
Penguin Group (USA) Inc., 375 Hudson Street,
New York, New York 10014, USA
Penguin Group (Canada), 10 Alcorn Avenue, Toronto,
Ontario M4V 3B2, Canada (a division of Pearson Penguin Canada Inc.)
Penguin Books Ltd., 80 Strand, London WC2R 0RL, England
Penguin Ireland, 25 St. Stephen's Green, Dublin 2,
Ireland (a division of Penguin Books Ltd.)
Penguin Group (Australia), 250 Camberwell Road, Camberwell, Victoria 3124,
Australia (a division of Pearson Australia Group Pty. Ltd.)
Penguin Books India Pvt. Ltd., 11 Community Centre, Panchsheel Park,
New Delhi - 110 017, India
Penguin Group (NZ), Cnr Airborne and Rosedale Roads, Albany,
Auckland 1310, New Zealand (a division of Pearson New Zealand Ltd.)
Penguin Books (South Africa) (Pty.) Ltd., 24 Sturdee Avenue,
Rosebank, Johannesburg 2196, South Africa

Penguin Books Ltd., Registered Offices:
80 Strand, London WC2R 0RL, England

First published by Signet, an imprint of New American Library,
a division of Penguin Group (USA) Inc.

First Printing, November 2004
10 9 8 7 6 5 4 3 2 1

 REGISTERED TRADEMARK—MARCA REGISTRADA

Printed in the United States of America

PUBLISHER'S NOTE
This is a work of fiction. Names, characters, places, and incidents either are the
product of the author's imagination or are used fictitiously, and any resemblance
to actual persons, living or dead, business establishments, events, or locales is
entirely coincidental.

To my father, Theodore "Ted" Lantz,
my first and always hero.

And to Tim Jones, my hero for the past twenty years,
and Andrew Jones, a hero in training.

ACKNOWLEDGMENTS

Many thanks to Mary Balogh for graciously answering all my questions about Welsh names and the Welsh language, and for pointing me in the right direction to obtain the information I needed about Welsh harps.

Thanks also are due to Regency military expert William "Bill" Haggart, who provided photographs of the uniforms of the 7th Hussars, explained the differences between formal and field uniforms, and helped me understand the intricacies of both so that I could describe Captain Middleford's uniform properly. Any errors in the descriptions are mine.

I would also like to thank Welsh translators Ken Owen and Glenys Roberts for their attempts to find Welsh equivalents of several English phrases.

This book would have been more difficult to write, and much less accurate, without the contributions of these wonderfully helpful people.

Prologue

London, Friday, 25 March 1814

*W*hen he was four or five, Theo Middleford discovered that ladies—or, at least, the ladies in his family—were soft, sweet-smelling, and well able to entertain him with stories and games. When he was seventeen, he discovered that his attraction to women—women who flaunted their charms and entertained him with their bodies—was mutual. And, usually, mutually satisfying. But on the morning of his twenty-ninth birthday, Theo decided that it was time to eschew his rakish ways.

Last night while he'd been enjoying the charms of a self-proclaimed widow, her husband had returned unexpectedly. Not from the dead, but from a sojourn in the country. As he'd quickly gathered up his clothes and boots, the lady had confessed her lie, then almost shoved Theo out her bedroom window onto a minuscule balcony. He'd thrown his garments and footwear over the wrought-iron railing, then, clad only in his breeches, he'd climbed over it, dangled for a moment from the railing, and dropped two stories to the ground. He was demmed lucky he hadn't broken his leg. Or his neck.

Hence, his resolve this morning to reform. But he was a young man with a healthy sexual appetite. He'd never dallied with innocents or married women, so if he gave up willing widows, too, he would need another outlet for his passion.

He needed a mistress. Or a wife.

Actually, he already had a mistress, the lovely Janet Brooks, but she was in Yorkshire visiting her mother, who was ill. Who ever heard of a mistress having a mother? Most seemed to spring full-grown onto the stages of London's theaters and opera houses. But in this respect, as in all others, Jani was different. She had a mother. She was nearly a decade older than he. And she was neither actress nor opera dancer, she was a novelist. He'd chosen her as much for her brain as for her body. He could talk to her, in and out of bed, about anything from politics to passion. She was friend, confidante, and sounding board—and she was two hundred miles away.

He could, he supposed, set up another mistress until Jani returned, but two mistresses seemed . . . excessive. Which reduced his choices to option number two—a wife.

He had to marry someday, so it might as well be this Season. But he believed in the sanctity of the marriage vows, so he needed a wife who would be friend, confidante, sounding board, and as passionate in their marriage bed as a mistress.

He needed a miracle.

Chapter One

*H*e was a rake. A damned good one, too, according to the ladies whose favors he had enjoyed. But he was a rake with principles.

As he stood in the doorway of Lady Oglethorpe's ballroom, principles or not, Theodore Phillip Michael Middleford, the Viscount Dunnley, felt a bit like a horse being auctioned at Tattersall's—or a young lady on the Marriage Mart—except that it was the ladies who ogled him. Some, undoubtedly, were studying his attire, for he was one of the fashion leaders of the *ton*. Others, however, had designs on his person. Lascivious designs. All, however, were doomed to disappointment.

Eighteen days ago, he had resolved to reform, and to find a bride and set up his nursery. He'd kept the first part of his resolution, too, although each night was more difficult than the last, and there had been times he'd felt like howling at the moon. Now he would work on the second part. Finding the perfect wife might not be a simple task, but there was no time like the present to start. And no better place to begin his search than right here—the first ball of the 1814 Season.

Not surprisingly, he had given the matter of finding a suitable bride considerable thought in the past two and a half weeks. Both his cousins and his older cousin's best friend had married in the past year, and all three couples were blissfully happy. Two of the three brides were members of a group of musical young ladies who called themselves "The Six," and since Theo liked, admired, and respected both ladies, the unmarried members of the group seemed the most likely prospects for his bride.

"Are you going to stand there all night?" The whispered words were accompanied by a sharp nudge in the back.

Theo glanced over his shoulder at his brother, Captain

Stephen Middleford, who had been in England for a month recuperating from a leg injury. "Just waiting for you, dear boy. Can you manage the stairs with your cane? Or would you prefer to lean on my arm?"

"I would prefer to be home, with my foot propped on an ottoman and a glass of brandy at my side."

Turning, Theo studied his brother's face, searching for signs of pain. "We will go home if you wish, Stephen, but I thought you wanted to get out of the house."

"I did. When you suggested that I accompany you, I thought you meant to White's, not a damn—dashed ball!"

"Why would I want to go to White's and talk with a bunch of old men I see every day in Lords, or a group of young bucks who won't say anything worth hearing, when I can come here and talk and dance with lovely ladies?" Theo grasped his brother's elbow to help him down the stairs. "I know you can't dance, but you can certainly charm the ladies with your conversation."

"I don't want to charm them," Stephen muttered.

"Well, they may wish to charm *you*. After all, you are quite an eligible fellow."

"Perhaps so, but I ain't looking for a wife. Not much point in getting leg-shackled when I will soon be back in the Peninsula, and my wife would stay here."

Stephen's answer surprised Theo. And piqued his curiosity. "You wouldn't take your bride with you?"

"If I had a bride, I'd want to take her, but I can't think of any lady I know who would want to go." Stephen nodded in the direction of a group of nearby young ladies. "Can you imagine any of them sleeping in a tent and cooking over a campfire?"

"No, I can't," Theo was forced to concede. "But Aunt Tilly followed the drum with her husband—"

"Indeed she did, but there aren't many ladies in the world with Aunt Tilly's gumption." Having survived the Ordeal By Stairs, Stephen paused to rest his leg. With a devilish grin, he opined, "We'd have much better success finding you a bride, big brother. You are far more eligible than I. You're wealthy, titled, handsome, charming—"

"Please, dear boy, spare my blushes."

"Why, I daresay you are one of the prime catches on the Marriage Mart."

"Perhaps." Nudging his brother into motion, Theo headed toward a group of chairs against the wall, although their progress was hindered by friends and acquaintances who greeted them and attempted to draw them into conversation. When they finally reached their destination and were in no danger of being overheard, he asked, "Whom do you suggest I allow to catch me?"

Stephen stopped so abruptly, he almost fell over. "Are you serious?"

Smiling at the incredulity in his only sibling's voice, Theo waited until Stephen was seated before answering. "Does it seem so implausible that I would marry?"

"Not that you would marry, no. You need an heir, after all. I just didn't realize you were considering it now. I thought you would wait a few more years."

Theo shrugged. "Perhaps I will. It may take a while to find a bride."

"Highly unlikely! You set exacting standards for yourself, but other than that, you aren't too pernickety. Unless . . . Do you look for more in a bride than birth, breeding, good looks, and a decent dowry?"

"I am more concerned about respect, friendship, shared interests, love, and passion than about a dowry."

Judging from Stephen's rather startled expression, it was not the answer he expected, but Theo didn't know why his reply surprised his brother. After several moments' thought, Stephen said, with a perspicacity that Theo found a bit disconcerting, "You are a lot like George in many ways, so perhaps you should take a page out of his book. Since our cousin has found all that and more with Beth, perhaps you should take a close look at her friends. I don't know them well, but it seems to me that they are a lot like her in many respects." Grinning, he added, "Well, except for Tina."

Lady Christina Fairchild was definitely *not* a candidate for Theo's viscountess. She was too young, too impulsive, and too much the hoyden for his peace of mind. "Surprisingly, we are of one mind. The unmarried ladies of 'The Six' were the first ones I thought of, too."

"Well, instead of standing here with me, you ought to go talk to them. And ask them to dance." Shooting him a look brimming with curiosity, Stephen drawled, "Will your first partner be Lady Sarah Mallory or Lady Deborah Woodhurst, I wonder?"

Pure vexation—he'd been debating that himself—prompted Theo's reply. "It may be Miss Broughton."

His brother smiled—smirked, really—and shook his head. "I think not."

Irritated, but not quite certain why, Theo turned on his heel and strode away. *Lady Sarah or Lady Deborah? Which one is the most likely bride for me?*

Lady Sarah Mallory wrinkled her nose at the image in her mirror and wished, for at least the thousandth time, that her figure was not so . . . generous. It was just one more way in which she was different from the other young ladies on the Marriage Mart, and there were far too many of those differences for Sarah's comfort. She was Welsh. She found it difficult to converse with people she did not know well. But most distressing of all, although she was as slender as her friends, she had far more filling the bodice of her gowns than they did. And too many men—she would not call them gentlemen—ogling the contents of her bodice. It was quite disconcerting to talk or dance with a man who could not meet her gaze because his eyes were on her bosom. It did not make a whit of difference how high her necklines were, either; some men stared at her chest even when her gowns buttoned all the way to her throat.

Evening gowns and ball gowns were the worst, of course. They were designed to display a lady's figure to best advantage. Whether she wished it or not.

Sarah most definitely did not.

But if she wanted a husband—which she did, very much, and children, too, in time—then she had to wear fashionable gowns like all the other young ladies on the Marriage Mart. Even though doing so made her miserably uncomfortable.

She would bear the torment of the ogles and leers in the hope of finding a husband this Season. And it had to be this year. Other girls might take several Seasons to catch a husband, but Sarah could not. Although she'd made her come-out just last year, she was two-and-twenty—practically on the shelf! And she was not at all certain that her mother, who hated leaving her beloved Wales, would agree to come to Town again next year.

So she *had* to find a husband this Season. But she would

not marry a man who was more interested in her bosom than in her brain.

Tugging up the bodice of her cream silk ball gown with its cornflower blue sash and trim, she turned from the mirror and pulled on her gloves. Once her shawl was draped over her shoulders to her maid's satisfaction, Sarah looped her fan and reticule over her wrist and left the sanctuary of her room.

Some days the sacrifices a young lady had to make to find a husband seemed more trouble than any man could possibly be worth.

Escorted by her brother, Viscount Llanfyllin, and accompanied by her parents, the Earl and Countess of Tregaron, Sarah entered Lady Oglethorpe's ballroom. Descending the stairway was disconcerting, to say the least. When one was the cynosure of all eyes, it would not do to watch one's feet, but the staircase was so wide that the banister was not within reach. Sarah descended without mishap, but her viselike grip on her brother's arm probably creased his sleeve.

The first person she saw, standing just to the right of the stairs, was Lady Christina Fairchild, one of her particular friends. Tina and her mother, the Duchess of Greenwich, were chatting with the Marchioness of Kesteven and one of her twin daughters. Sarah was not one of the few members of the *beau monde* who could distinguish the Woodhurst twins at a glance, but it was safe to assume that Tina was talking with Lady Deborah. The duke's daughter had exchanged cross words with Deborah's sister, Diana, on more than one occasion, and generally tried to avoid her.

Deborah was also one of Sarah's best friends. More so than Tina, in fact, although they had all made their come-outs last year and were members of a singing group known as "The Six." Deborah was one-and-twenty and would understand Sarah's feeling of urgency about finding a husband this Season; Tina, who was only eighteen, probably would not.

"Sarah!" Tina exclaimed. "I was beginning to think you weren't going to attend."

The duchess groaned and muttered something about her daughter's rudeness, then greeted Sarah and her mother. The twin revealed her identity by hugging Sarah, something Lady Diana would never do.

As their mothers settled on nearby chairs for a comfortable coze, Tina pulled Deborah and Sarah to one side. Close enough that they were still under their mothers' watchful eyes, but far enough away that their conversation could not be overheard. Sarah exchanged a wry smile with Deborah, certain that Tina was about to propose another of her mad schemes.

"This Season I am determined to snare Viscount Dunnley," Tina announced as calmly as if young ladies made such outrageous statements every day.

Deborah giggled. Sarah struggled to repress a smile. "Tina, you know you are a bit . . . impetuous sometimes. Have you carefully considered this plan? I don't think Lord Dunnley, or any gentleman for that matter, would care to be *snared*."

"I imagine," Deborah said thoughtfully, "that gentlemen who are trapped into marriage make quite disagreeable husbands. Men like to do the choosing—"

"Or," interposed Sarah, grinning, "at least to think that they have."

"I am not going to compromise him into marriage," Tina protested. "I just want him to notice me and realize that I am no longer the scrawny, pigtailed hoyden he remembers from visits to Greenwich Park."

"Who says you aren't a hoyden?" Deborah teased. "I seem to remember a time or two last Season—"

"Deb!" Tina's indignant exclamation was overridden by her friends' laughter.

"Why Dunnley? Don't you want to marry for love?" Deborah's tone made it quite clear that she hoped for a love match. Sarah nurtured the same aspiration.

"But I do love Dunnley," Tina insisted. "I have for years and years."

"You aren't old enough to have loved him—really loved him—for years and years," Sarah said. "What you feel is cream pot love. Or a schoolgirl crush."

"I have been out of the schoolroom for more than a year," Tina retorted. "And I still feel the same."

"That doesn't necessarily mean your feelings for Lord Dunnley aren't a youthful infatuation," Sarah gently pointed out. "Only that they are unchanged."

"You sound like Beth," Tina moaned, referring to the

Countess of Weymouth, the unofficial leader of "The Six," who was very fond of logic and scientific deduction and applied both in everyday situations.

"Let's apply Beth's logic to your scheme," Deborah suggested.

Tina sighed, sounding quite put-upon. "Why?"

"Why not?" Sarah countered.

"Very well. If you insist." Tina sounded thoroughly disgruntled. "Logic says that Dunnley isn't going to notice me among the crop of young ladies on the Marriage Mart. He didn't last year, so it is highly unlikely that he will this year."

"He noticed you last year. He danced with you several times." Sarah felt compelled to point out this bit of illogic in her friend's supposedly logical argument.

"True, but not nearly as often as he danced with you or Deb. And he never took me driving in the park."

"Did you keep track of all the ladies he danced with and drove in the park?" Despite the teasing tone of Deborah's question, Sarah suspected that its real purpose was to determine the depth of Tina's infatuation.

"Of course not!"

"So he noticed you, but not as much as you hoped?" Sarah asked, not at all certain where Tina's argument was leading. Nor why her friend wanted Lord Dunnley's attention. Sarah always felt gauche and nervous in the viscount's presence, and she did not like the trembly feeling she experienced whenever he was near.

"Sarah!" Tina groaned, dragging two long syllables out of the name. "You don't understand."

"I don't understand your point either, Tina," Deborah confessed. "You haven't explained very much yet."

"Look at the two of you, and then look at me." Tina flung her arms out in a dramatic gesture. "You are both tall and slender and lovely—acclaimed Beauties, in fact—and you're smart, too. I am just a squab of a girl, with dark hair and dark eyes."

"You are slender and smart and lovely, too," Sarah and Deborah said in unison.

"Not lovely," Tina contradicted. "Passably pretty, perhaps."

"I disagree," Sarah said, "but we will save that discussion for another time."

"How can you possibly disagree?" Tina's tone was pure frustration. "The bachelors of the *ton* haven't given me an encomium like 'The Welsh Beauty' or 'The English Rose.' "

"That may be true," Deborah said, "but being an acclaimed Beauty does not guarantee a successful Season. Especially if one is a bit shy."

"Very shy," Sarah corrected, speaking of herself. "You may envy my height, Tina, but I would gladly trade those extra inches for your vivacity."

"You would?" the younger girl gasped, clearly astonished.

"Indeed I would. Timidity is a formidable obstacle when one is hoping to find a husband."

"Being a twin is quite an obstacle, too. There are only a handful of people in the *ton* who can distinguish me from Diana. Even the two of you can't. At least, not immediately."

The hint of hurt in Deborah's voice tugged at Sarah's heart. "Regrettably, that is true. I am getting better, but I still cannot tell at a glance." She smiled at Deborah. "I know it must be difficult for you to believe, Deb, because your personality and interests are so different from Diana's, but your appearance is identical, as far as I can tell. And believe me"—Sarah laughed—"I have looked very hard."

The set of country dances that had been in progress throughout the conversation came to an end. "Do you have partners for the next set?"

Deborah shook her head. "I don't."

A shiver snaked down Sarah's spine. She rubbed her gloved hands up and down her arms, wondering if someone had opened one of the tall windows.

"Not yet." Tina's dark eyes grew wide, and mischief danced within.

As Sarah glanced over her shoulder to see what had caught her friend's attention, that strange, tremulous feeling assailed her. The Duke of Fairfax, the Earl of Blackburn, and Viscount Dunnley, three of the most eligible bachelors in the *ton*, were approaching, obviously intending to ask her and her friends to dance.

She hoped Lord Dunnley would solicit Tina or Deborah as his partner. Whenever he bowed over her hand or led her into a dance, a tingle radiated up her arm, and her heart raced alarmingly. Sarah did not understand why the viscount so terrified her. He was a very handsome man, especially in black and white evening attire with his tawny hair glowing like a candle's flame, and a gentleman—elegant, well-mannered, and famed for his address. As an escort or a dance partner, he was considered by many young ladies to be the ideal. Obviously, his presence did not disconcert them as it did her, nor make them tremble.

Given the sudden wobbliness of her legs, she would be lucky to walk to the dance floor without falling on her face. Actually dancing might well be impossible.

Chapter Two

*B*ored with the discussion between Fairfax and Blackburn about a bill currently being debated in Lords, Theo glanced around the ballroom and saw several of "The Six" in conversation—Lady Christina Fairchild, Lady Sarah Mallory, and one of the Woodhurst twins. Since all three were smiling, it was a good bet that the twin was Lady Deborah. Lady Diana's chatter generally did not produce expressions of pleasure on other young ladies' faces.

"Gentlemen, I see three young ladies who appear to need partners for the next set." Theo had no wish to dance with Lady Tina, but he wanted to further his acquaintance with Lady Sarah and Lady Deborah. A dance was an excellent, and quite unexceptional, way to show a bit of interest.

"Which young ladies?" Fairfax inquired. "I would rather not have my toes trod upon this early in the evening."

Blackburn scanned the groups of ladies nearby, then smiled. "Little danger of that with these three, I think." As they strolled toward the trio, he asked, "Which lady do you wish to partner, Dunnley?"

"Have to dance with all of them," the duke mumbled.

"Lest you want their mamas making comments about rag-manners and ungentlemanly behavior."

"I have no objection to dancing with all three of them," Blackburn said, greatly surprising Theo, since the earl often eschewed social events for political meetings. "They are friends of Karla's—er, Lady Elston's, so I feel certain all three are very nice young ladies."

"You are assuming that is Lady Deborah Woodhurst." Fairfax's tone made it clear that he hoped the earl was correct.

They fell silent as they approached the ladies and bowed. After greetings were exchanged, Theo asked, "Might we have the honor of partnering you three lovely ladies in the next dance?"

All three glanced to the left. Theo did, too, saw the girls' mothers, and bowed to them. When Lady Tregaron nodded, granting her daughter permission, Lady Sarah said, "We would be honored, Your Grace. My lords."

"Perhaps we should use precedence to determine which gentleman is a lady's first partner," he suggested, thus ensuring that he would be the last man to dance with Lady Tina. And the first to partner Lady Sarah.

"That should serve very well." Fairfax held out his hand to Lady Tina. Blackburn, after ascertaining the Woodhurst twin's identity, offered his arm to escort Lady Deborah to the dance floor.

Theo smiled and reached for his partner's hand. "Lady Sarah, I hope you are not too disappointed with a mere viscount."

"Of course not, my lord." She sounded flustered. Odd, that; she was known as much for her formidable reserve as for her beauty. "I doubt anyone here would describe you as a 'mere viscount.' You are one of the leaders of the *ton*."

"Perhaps." It was true, although he had never understood why the members of the *beau monde* looked to him for guidance. "But Blackburn and Fairfax—"

The opening strains of the music interrupted their conversation. "Ah, a waltz." Theo was delighted. The dance would provide an excellent opportunity to converse with his partner, known among the bachelors of the *ton* as "The Welsh Beauty." And she was, indeed, beautiful. Tall, slender, and generously—some might say voluptuously—curved, with a complexion as translucent as the finest porcelain, and vivid blue eyes surrounded by a thicket of long lashes. Her hair was the color of a raven's wing, and gleamed blue-black in the glow of the chandeliers as he led her onto the dance floor.

She was also trembling, he discovered to his dismay when he took her left hand in his right, then slid his left arm around her and placed his hand at the small of her back. Her tremors were slight—had he not been holding her thus, he would not have noticed—but unmistakable.

What the devil was wrong? He had partnered her a number of times last year, so his request for a dance could not have discomposed her. Perplexed, he studied her face, but her features were serene. Aside from her trembling, the only indication of her distress was the fact that her gaze was locked on the top button of his waistcoat. That, and her silence.

"Lady Sarah?"

"Yes, my lord?" She glanced up for a moment—perhaps as high as his chin.

"Is something amiss?"

Another darting look. "No, my lord."

He did not believe her. He wouldn't go so far as to say she was lying, but it was possible that she wasn't consciously aware of what troubled her.

Something very definitely did.

And he could not help but wonder if he was the source of her distress.

There were two ways to find out. A direct question hadn't gotten him an answer. But, he was forced to concede, she could not have answered politely if he was the problem. And Lady Sarah Mallory was always polite.

Always a bit distant.

Her reserve and . . . aloofness, for want of a better word, were daunting. They also posed a challenge.

And were as intriguing as hell.

Theo was certainly intrigued. Not to put too fine a point on it, he was fascinated. He was going to take on the challenge of finding out what made Sarah Mallory tick. To find out if her reserve was a shield hiding a passionate nature.

And there was no time like the present to start. Here and now, in Lady Oglethorpe's ballroom, he would find out why Sarah Mallory was so uneasy in his company. But not by asking more questions.

Expertly leading her through the patterns of the waltz, he maneuvered them near another couple. Then he deliberately misstepped and jerked her against his chest.

Her trembling increased, and her eyes slewed to his, meeting his gaze for the first time all evening.

He stroked his hand up her spine. "My apologies, Lady Sarah. Selwyn was dancing rather erratically, and I was trying to avoid a collision. Did you hurt your ankle when you stumbled?" He eased her backward until they were several inches apart, although considerably fewer than Society deemed proper.

"No. I am fine." She glanced over her shoulder at the young baron, who danced nearby, and turned back, smiling. "He is a very enthusiastic dancer, isn't he?"

Theo chuckled. "That's one way to describe it, I suppose." Then, knowing they would draw too much attention if they continued to stand still, he asked, "Shall we continue, or would you prefer to stop?"

She dropped her gaze and bit her lower lip before saying, "Let's continue."

Smoothly moving them back amidst the whirling couples, he re-established a proper distance between them. Sarah's trembling eased, and Theo had his answer.

Being near him disconcerted her. Now all he had to do was figure out why.

Never had a waltz lasted so long! Sarah was more relieved than she could say when it finally ended. She had been afraid that Lord Dunnley would sense her unease, especially when she'd been plastered against his shirtfront after their near collision with Lord Selwyn. And perhaps the viscount had sensed it, but if so, he was too much the gentleman to mention it.

Almost, she'd accepted his offer to end the dance after their accident. Almost. But that would have been craven, and Sarah was not a coward. She refused to succumb to her fear—or whatever it was that reduced her to a quivering blancmange whenever the viscount was nearby.

As they promenaded around the room greeting friends and acquaintances, she could not help but wish that Lord Dunnley were not such a gentleman. A man who was not so nice in his manners might have left her to make her own way back to her mother. Sarah desperately needed a few moments of quiet solitude to settle her nerves, and walking so close beside him as they dodged the groups of people scattered around the perimeter of the room was not helping to restore her composure.

"Did you arrive in Town just recently, Lady Sarah? This is the first time I have seen you, but I know your father has been here since Parliament opened."

"My mother, my older brother, and I arrived last week."

He smiled, his gray eyes twinkling. "I daresay you and your mother have been busy visiting the dressmaker, paying calls, and doing all the other things one must do when one first arrives in Town."

"Indeed we have. I think we spent every morning last week in the shops on Oxford Street or Bond Street, and every afternoon paying calls."

"I don't believe I am acquainted with your brother. Or, if I am, I don't realize he is your brother."

"Rhys is Viscount Llanfyllin. If you had met him, you would have made the connection. We look rather remarkably alike."

"In that case, I am quite certain I haven't had the pleasure."

As they maneuvered to avoid a group of Corinthians whose conversation involved a great deal of gesticulating, Sarah saw her brother ahead of them, talking with two of his friends. "Do you see the three young men about ten feet in front of us and slightly to the right? Rhys is the one in the center."

"Ah . . . there is, indeed, a marked resemblance. A friend of Howe's, is he?"

"Yes. They are members of the same catch."

"The Noblemen's and Gentlemen's Catch Club. There is a bit of a rivalry between it and the Glee Club."

"And you are a member of the Glee Club?"

"I am," he affirmed. "But rivalry or no, I count Howe amongst my friends, so I shan't hold your brother's choice against him." Grinning, he looked like a mischievous schoolboy.

Lord Dunnley could charm the birds out of the trees, Sarah thought. But beneath that charm, there was a quiet strength and a sense of purpose. In addition to being a handsome, charming, well-mannered gentleman, he was active in Lords, and she felt certain that he was a conscientious landlord and steward of his estates.

When they reached her mother, Lord Dunnley bowed over Sarah's hand and thanked her for the dance. "Will you honor me with another set later this evening?"

She had not expected his request. And with her mother smiling benevolently at the viscount, Sarah could not refuse. "I would be honored to dance with you later, my lord." *Honored, but not pleased.*

"The supper dance, perhaps? Or have you already promised it?"

Lud! What have I done to deserve such a fate? "I have not yet promised the supper dance." Under the circumstances, there was nothing else she could say, but she was unable to muster the smile that ought to have accompanied the words.

The viscount bowed. "I shall look forward to it, Lady Sarah."

Unfortunately, she could not say the same. *The supper dance!* Of all the sets he might have selected, it was the worst possible choice. Even worse than dancing another waltz with him. Of course, given the bad luck plaguing her this evening, the supper dance would be a waltz.

She wished Lord Dunnley would depart for the farthest corner of the ballroom, but she knew he would not. Not until after he danced with Deborah and Tina. They, however, were engaged in conversation with their partners. Or, more precisely, the duke was talking with Tina and her mother, while Lord Blackburn chatted with Deborah, Lady Kesteven, and Diana and her most recent partner. Sarah moved toward Tina and the duchess, hoping to join their discussion so that she would not have to make conversation with the viscount.

Stepping back a pace to make room for her and Lord Dunnley to join the group, the duke gave Sarah one of his rare, boyishly charming smiles. As simply as that, she knew Fairfax would be her next partner. And she was pleased. She did not experience shivery tremors in his presence. In fact, now that she considered the matter, Lord Dunnley was the only gentleman of her acquaintance who made her feel so nervous.

That realization unsettled her even more.

When the musicians played the opening bars of the next set, she gratefully accepted the duke's invitation to dance, although without the enthusiasm Tina showed Lord Dunnley. The Sir Roger de Coverley did not permit much conversation between partners, but it was lively and fun. When the dance was over, Fairfax escorted Sarah to the refreshment room for a glass of lemonade.

The duke did not have Lord Dunnley's striking looks nor Lord Blackburn's poise; he was of average stature, with rather plain features, medium brown hair, and blue-green eyes. Not handsome, not ugly, just ordinary. But even so, there was something about him that caught the eye, and the attention, of both men and women. Presence was the best description Sarah could contrive for that "something." Whether it derived from his rank or the man himself, she could not say; only that it was there.

She had not been aware of that presence at first. With a wry smile, Sarah recalled her first few weeks in London last year. She'd met so many people, seemingly all at once, and to help herself identify them, she'd mentally assigned them nicknames based on a unique feature or trait. "Handsome and Elegant Dunnley"; "Merry Blue Eyes Weymouth"; "Silver Streak Blackburn"; "Miss Big Green Eyes Cathcart"; "Beringed Duchess" for the dowager Duchess of St. Ives. The quiet, serious Duke of Fairfax with his unremarkable features had been the most difficult for her to remember until, in desperation, she'd dubbed him "Fairfax, The Ordinary Man." Erroneous though the description had proven to be—he was, in truth, an extraordinary man— it had helped her identify him.

Extraordinary or not, he was rather reserved. Sarah suspected shyness was the cause, not a sense of superiority due to his exalted rank, and set herself the task of drawing him out.

"Are you enjoying the ball, Your Grace?"

"Indeed I am. I enjoy dancing, although I cannot claim any expertise at it."

Astonishment made her speak more forcefully than was her wont. "You are a very good dancer. Any lady would be pleased to have you as a partner."

"You are very kind to say so, Lady Sarah."

"It is not mere politeness, Your Grace," she protested. "It is quite true."

"Thank you, my lady." He handed her a glass of lemonade, then motioned toward a nearby table. "Would you like to sit down for a minute?"

With a nod, she acquiesced. He escorted her to the table and seated her, then sat beside her. "Do you ever wonder," he inquired rather diffidently, "why gentlemen ask you to dance?"

Surprised by the question, she took a moment to think about it. "No, I don't believe I ever have."

"You have never wondered if a man asked you to dance because you are an acclaimed Beauty," he persisted, "or because of the size of your dowry?"

"No, I haven't." A moment later, curiosity overcame good manners and she ventured a question of her own. "Why do you ask? Do you consider such factors before you ask a lady to dance?"

"No, of course not!"

The vehemence of the duke's reply, as well as the shocked expression he wore, evidenced his sincerity. Wondering why he had raised the subject, she lifted a brow, inviting him to answer her first question.

He glanced away before confessing, "I often wonder if I am accepted because I am a wealthy duke or because a lady likes me, plain Michael Winslow."

"Oh, Fairfax!" She placed a hand on his arm, to draw his attention as well as to offer comfort. "I suppose every high-ranking peer must contend with a certain amount of toadying," she said pensively. "There probably are ladies who enjoy being seen with you as much as they enjoy your company, but others—many others—delight in your company without ever giving a thought to your rank."

He smiled. Faintly to be sure, but a smile nonetheless. "You obviously fall into the latter category."

"Yes, I do. You are an admirable man, Michael Winslow, duke or not."

"Thank you, Lady Sarah." He took her hand and, raising it to his lips, brushed a kiss against her knuckles. Then he stood and assisted her to rise. "I'd best escort you back to your mother before the next set begins."

As they strolled back to the ballroom, Sarah was rather alarmed to realize that neither he nor his unexpected salute had produced the slightest shiver. *Why, oh why did Viscount Dunnley affect her so?*

The Earl of Blackburn raised nary a quiver, either, despite the fact that Sarah did not know him as well as she knew Lord Dunnley and Fairfax. Slightly above average height, with gray-rimmed hazel eyes and an off-center silver streak in his mahogany hair, the earl was very active in politics. If gossip were to be believed, he had seldom attended social events until last year, when his mother's protégée, Karolina Lane, made her come-out. Karla was now very happily married to the Marquess of Elston, but in the early weeks of last spring's Season, Blackburn had escorted her often, and many people thought he would offer for her. He may well have done so, but Karla, who was one of Sarah's dear friends, as well as a member of "The Six," had never mentioned receiving a proposal from the earl.

Is he nursing a broken heart? Sarah wondered. The patterns of the country dance did not permit more than a word or two of snatched conversation, so she held her peace until its conclusion. As they circled the ballroom on their way back to her mother, Sarah probed delicately. "Have you seen Lord and Lady Elston recently?"

"I saw them both yesterday."

Her surprise—or skepticism—must have been writ large on her countenance, for he explained, "I ran into Elston at White's yesterday afternoon, and he told me their good news. He was also kind enough to offer me a ride home—they live just down the street, you know—so I stepped in for a moment to offer Karla my felicitations."

"I called on her yesterday and ended up staying for most of the afternoon," Sarah said. "A number of our friends did, too."

"So I understand." Blackburn smiled. "She regaled us—Elston and me—with the tale of the reunion of the young ladies of 'The Six.' She was very happy to see you all."

"And we were just as delighted to see her. Letters are fine for exchanging news, but not nearly so nice as seeing each other and hearing it firsthand."

"Quite true." He cocked a brow and did a bit of probing of his own. "I had the impression that you—the six of you, I mean—are not planning to perform this Season. Elston and I were both disappointed to learn that."

"Well . . ." Flustered, Sarah was even more tongue-tied than usual. "We cannot. That is, Karla and Beth—Lady Weymouth—cannot because . . ."

"Lady Weymouth is also, um, in a delicate condition?"

"She is," Sarah confirmed with a smile, grateful for his tactful assistance. "And since neither she nor Karla will be going about in Society, we cannot perform."

"There is nothing to prevent you, Lady Deborah, Lady Christina, and Miss Broughton from singing as a quartet, is there?"

The unexpected suggestion halted Sarah in mid-step, earning her and her escort a censorious glare from the matron walking behind them. The earl smiled and, tucking her hand more firmly into the crook of his elbow, urged Sarah into motion. "I can see from your expression that the idea never occurred to you. For the sake of the *ton*'s music lovers, I hope you and your friends will consider it."

When they reached her mother, Lord Blackburn bowed over Sarah's hand and thanked her for the dance. "Speaking of Miss Broughton, I have not seen her tonight. Since the ladies of 'The Six' are usually inseparable, I assume she and her mother are not here this evening?"

"No, they aren't. They are in Kent, visiting Mrs. Broughton's mother, who is ill."

"I am sorry to hear that. If you write to Miss Broughton, pass along my best wishes for her grandmother's speedy recovery."

Sarah smiled up at him. "I will be happy to do so, my lord."

Bowing to the inevitable, Theo partnered Lady Christina Fairchild for the Sir Roger de Coverley. She'd had a schoolgirl crush on him for years, which had persisted after her release from the schoolroom and all through last Season, when she had made her come-out. Much to his dismay, he discovered that it still held her in thrall.

She was a charming girl. A bit of a hoyden still, and as much a chatterbox as ever, but a pretty and vivacious girl. But she was not, nor would she ever be, a candidate for his viscountess. Unfortunately, a gentleman could not state his intentions, or the lack thereof, so bluntly. He could, however, hint.

"Are you enjoying the ball this evening, Tina?"

She smiled. "Yes, very much so."

When the patterns of the dance brought them together again, he asked, "Are you looking forward to another Season full of social events?"

"Indeed I am."

"Have any of the young men in your court of admirers caught your eye? Or is that too personal a question from a mere third cousin?"

She looked askance at him, but the figures of the dance parted them before she could answer. When next they joined hands and circled, she informed him, "The man who has caught my eye is not a member of my court."

"Is he someone with whom you are acquainted? If not, perhaps I can introduce you."

Annoyance figured strongly in the glare she aimed at him. The patterns of the dance separated them again, but the time apart did not ameliorate her irritation. "I am acquainted with him. Very well, in fact."

Theo arched a brow. "Are you going to tell me who it is?"

"No, you dolt, I am not!" With that parting shot, she circled with him one last time, released his hand, and returned to the ladies' line.

They were at the bottom of the set now and would remain apart for the rest of the dance, unless the musicians played the tune again. With nothing else to do, Theo pondered what he could say to convince her that his feelings for her would never be anything but platonic. And how he could do so without hurting her.

As he escorted Tina back to her mother, Theo tried another tack. "A dolt, am I?"

"Sometimes, yes."

"I don't mean to be, so I shall try to make amends for tonight's doltishness. If you don't wish to tell me the gentleman's name, tell me something about him." Several beats of silence later, he tried a question. "How old is he? About my age, nearer to Stephen's, or closer to your own?"

"About your age" was her rather tight-lipped response.

"Well, I can't speak for this unknown man, but I cannot imagine marrying a young lady a decade younger than I. It—"

"Men your age marry girls making their come-outs every Season!"

"Some do," he conceded. "I didn't say it doesn't happen, Tina. I said I could not imagine marrying someone so much younger than I am."

"Why not?" she demanded.

Lord, she was as tenacious as a terrier! "Because I think it would feel more like acquiring a little sister, or a ward, than taking a wife."

"Really?" Judging from her astonished expression, it was something she had not heretofore considered.

Theo decided to quit while he was ahead. "Have you spoken with Stephen tonight?"

"Stephen who?" she asked absently. Then, on a gasp, "Your brother is here?"

"He is indeed." There were too many people between them and his brother's chair to see him, but if he had not moved, they would walk past him.

"Did he carry back dispatches? How long is his leave?"

"I don't believe he carried dispatches. He is home to recover from an injury."

"He was wounded? Where? How badly?" Tina's worried questions, and her obvious concern, made Theo wonder if she nurtured a *tendre* for his brother, too.

"He is recovering from a leg wound. He still has a limp and has to use a cane, but the doctor says the injury is healing well."

"And he is here tonight?"

"Yes, he is. He wanted to get out of the house for a while."

"Take me to him," she commanded. "Immediately."

"He can't dance, Tina."

"I don't imagine he can, if he has to walk with a cane." Every inch the duke's daughter, she ordered, "Take me to him. Now."

Although he ought to escort her back to her mother first, Theo was all too well acquainted with Tina's stubbornness, so he yielded to her demand. The duchess would deem his delayed return of her daughter less of a social infraction than the scene Tina was likely to enact if he did not take her to see Stephen. But when they reached his brother's chair, Stephen was no longer sitting there. Nor was he standing nearby.

Stopping a footman carrying a tray full of brimming champagne flutes, Theo asked, "Do you know Captain Middleford?"

"Is he the Hussar that was sitting here earlier, my lord?"

"Yes."

"Walks with a cane, right, my lord?"

"Yes."

"I can't say I know him, but I think I would recognize him if I see him again."

It was the answer Theo was hoping for. "If you see him, please tell him that the Duchess of Greenwich and her daughter wish to speak with him. The duchess is sitting about halfway down the east wall"—he pointed to the approximate location—"with Lady Kesteven and Lady Tregaron." He gave the servant a half-crown to ensure he would remember the message.

The footman smiled and bobbed his head—the closest he could come to a bow while carrying the heavily laden tray. "I will look for Captain Middleford, my lord, and I will give him your message if I see him."

"Thank you." Glancing down at Tina's frowning face, Theo led her back to her mother and friends. "Stephen will seek out your mother as soon as he receives the message."

"I hope so." Shortly before they reached their destination, Tina asked, "Where could he have gone?"

There were a number of possible answers, most of which she knew as well as he did, so Theo did not voice the one she would find most distressing: that Stephen had left and gone home. "To the card room, perhaps, or outside to smoke a cigar." Anticipating her next request, he added, "I will check the card room after I dance with Lady Deborah."

She was not happy about the delay, but neither did she want him to slight her friend. "Thank you, Dunnley. And thank you for asking us to dance."

He arched a brow. "What makes you think I had anything to do with it?"

"Who else?" she riposted, rolling her eyes. "I don't believe all three of you suddenly had the urge to dance, so one of you must have suggested it. Surely you don't expect me to believe that Fairfax, the shyest man I have ever met, proposed dancing with us? Or that Lord Blackburn did? He would much rather talk politics than dance. Therefore, it had to be your idea."

"I did suggest that we should ask you and your friends to dance, but Fairfax and Blackburn readily agreed."

"Did they really?"

Unable to decide if she was fishing for a compliment— something he was unwilling to offer lest she misconstrue it—or if she was reassessing the other two men, Theo steered the conversation into less treacherous waters. "Well, Fairfax did ask which ladies I had in mind—he didn't want his toes trod upon so early in the evening—but once Blackburn saw the three of you and assured him there was no danger of that, the duke was quite willing."

"How very kind of Lord Blackburn!" After a moment she added, "I have never danced with him before." Her last statement sounded almost shy—and might well have been if spoken by any other young lady—but shy was not a word ever used to describe Tina Fairchild.

"Best take care to avoid his toes then," he teased. "You wouldn't want to disillusion the man."

"Dunnley!" she protested, indignant. Or it might have been hurt that colored her tone. Then, with a dignity and poise he would never have expected from her—at least, not for another decade or so—she informed him, "Although you may not believe it, and perhaps you never will, I am no longer a hoyden. At least, I am no longer the mud-splattered, pigtailed hoyden you remember from visits to Greenwich Park years ago."

The latter statement was indisputably true, but Theo was not yet willing to believe that she was completely reformed. She had, however, acquired some manners. And a bit of Town Bronze. "I beg your pardon if I offended you with my teasing, Tina. It is an older cousin's privilege, you know. Some might even say it is a duty. But if you dislike it, I shall do my best to break the habit."

"Oh! I am sorry, Dunnley. I did not realize you were twitting me." She hesitated before adding, "I don't dislike it. Not if I know you are teasing."

"Then I shall try to make it more obvious in the future."

As they neared the duchess and the mothers of Tina's

friends, he saw one of the Woodhurst twins being escorted back to the marchioness's side. Thinking back over the sequence of dances thus far this evening, Theo realized that if Lady Oglethorpe followed her usual pattern, the next set would be a country dance, followed by a minuet or another waltz. Since he would much prefer to have Lady Deborah as his partner for the latter, more intimate dance, he asked Tina, "Can you tell the Woodhurst twins apart?"

"At first glance, do you mean?" Before he could answer, she lowered her gaze to the floor and confessed, "Usually not. Almost never, in fact. But I know who is who tonight because Deborah is wearing a blue sash, and Diana, a primrose one."

Excellent! When they reached the duchess, he bowed and thanked Tina for the dance, then eased both of them into the conversation of the Woodhurst twin, her partner, and her mother. The twin was Diana; her partner, Blackburn.

The group soon expanded to include Fairfax and Lady Sarah, and Lady Deborah and her partner, Sir Edward Smithson. Or, to give him the nickname he'd earned at Eton, and which his years as a Bond Street beau had confirmed was still quite fitting, "Nasty Ned."

Inclining his head toward Lady Diana, Theo requested the honor, dubious though it was, of her company for the next set. She was known to have a sharp and often malicious tongue, especially when conversing with or about other young ladies. She accepted his invitation, but with an arrogant disdain that set his teeth on edge.

He then turned to Lady Deborah and, with a smile, asked if he might partner her for the following set. She, too, accepted, but sweetly and graciously.

As the other gentlemen followed his lead, the group reformed. Lady Sarah would dance the next set with Blackburn, Lady Deborah with Fairfax, and Tina with Nasty Ned. For both her sake and his own, Theo prayed the next set would be a country dance.

And, thank God, it was. Even better, it was a dance whose patterns permitted only the briefest snatches of conversation with one's partner. Suppressing a sigh of relief, Theo led Lady Diana onto the dance floor.

Although the movements of the dance limited their conversation, it did not curb Diana Woodhurst's tongue. Theo

had the distinct impression that she believed herself too
good to dance with a mere viscount, but that she'd conde-
scended to do so out of politeness. Fortunately for her mas-
sive conceit, he was too much the gentleman to tell her
that politeness had been the sole reason he'd asked her to
dance. He had no intention of ever doing so again, unless
it was unavoidable.

Someone ought to take the viper-tongued chit down a
peg or two. She had nothing good to say about any female
except herself. Her spiteful comments were undoubtedly
motivated by jealousy, but she seemed completely unaware
that such remarks did her more harm than good. It was
quite clear that she was on the catch for a husband of high
rank and a large fortune, but unless she mended her ways,
her chances of succeeding were almost nonexistent.

The set seemed interminable, but it did, eventually, come
to an end. Eager to rid himself of Lady Diana's company,
Theo rather perfunctorily thanked her for the dance and
escorted her back to her mother by the most direct route.
He felt a great kinship to the explorers of old, who were
said to have kissed the ground when they made landfall
after a long and arduous voyage, but he forbore from following their example.

The next dance was, indeed, a minuet. Many hostesses
deemed it too old-fashioned and no longer included it in
their balls, but Theo liked its stately, graceful movements.
Liked, too, that it required almost constant eye contact with
one's partner, thus providing a wonderful, and perfectly
permissible, opportunity for flirtation—and seduction.

Not that he had any intention of seducing Lady Deborah.
Seducing innocents was against his principles. 'Twas only
the willing widows that he . . .

No! He had reformed. He would not be seducing anyone
this Season. Nor any other Season for that matter. Except,
perhaps, his wife.

But first he had to find the perfect bride.

To that end, he intended to start a flirtation with Lady
Sarah Mallory in the very near future. Perhaps as soon as
the supper dance.

Theo was intrigued by Lady Sarah. If her reserved demeanor hid a passionate nature, he was just the man to
melt her icy façade and spark the banked fires beneath.

Chapter Three

*S*arah prayed that the next set would be a country dance. Society ought to provide a way for a lady to refuse an invitation to dance from a man she did not like—without having to sit out the rest of the ball's sets, and without making herself the center of a maelstrom of gossip if she did dance again after refusing one gentleman. But the rules of polite behavior allowed only those two options, and since Sarah had promised dances later in the evening, she'd had no choice but to accept Sir Edward Smithson's hand for the next set.

Viscount Dunnley's presence disconcerted her, and made her feel quivery inside. Sir Edward repulsed her.

Whenever she found herself in company with the baronet—a situation she diligently endeavored to avoid—he leered at her and ogled her bosom. He also invariably told her, in terms she was certain were both coarse and quite explicit, although she did not understand half of them, what he thought of her and what he'd like to do to her. She might—might!—be able to manage a country dance as his partner, but Sarah doubted that she could endure any other dance with him and maintain her composure.

Nor was she at all inclined to put herself to the test. When he'd bowed over her hand to request the dance, his eyes on her bosom instead of her face, she had all but snatched her hand from his grasp, its clamminess seeming to penetrate both his glove and hers. *Please, God, let the next set be a country dance!*

Having gained what he wanted, the odious man had departed. Probably not very far, nor for long, but Sarah was grateful for the respite. It gave her time to steel herself for the coming ordeal. Her friends' presence had prevented Sir Edward from making crude remarks, but that reprieve would be as short-lived as his absence.

"I want you, Sarah—"

She started badly, his unexpected appearance behind her

as unwelcome as his low-voiced comment and the brush of his breath against her ear and cheek.

"—and I intend to have you, soon. I dream of you in my bed, your body bared for my pleasure . . ."

Tensing every muscle to keep from shuddering, she tried to ignore him, to block the sound of his words.

". . . with my hands and mouth—"

The opening notes of the next set interrupted his description. Sarah blanched, and her trembling increased as she recognized the music. *Dear God! The Bach Minuet.*

She could not dance a minuet with Sir Edward.

She *would not* dance it with him.

His smile smug, he stepped in front of her and offered his hand to lead her to the dance floor. Sarah bent her knees slightly, extended her hand, and stepped forward, deliberately treading on the hem of her gown and pretending to stumble.

The tearing sound as several inches of her skirt ripped from her bodice seemed to echo throughout the ballroom. Fearing herself the focus of far too much attention—her plan having succeeded far better than she imagined—she jerked her hand back to cover the torn seam, dropped her gaze, and mumbled, "Please excuse me, Sir Edward. I must find a maid to repair my gown. I cannot imagine how I came to be so clumsy."

Without giving him, or anyone else, time to respond, she turned and quickly made her escape. From the leering baronet and from the ballroom.

Theo watched Lady Sarah's flight from the ballroom. And he was quite certain that she was fleeing, although, if pressed, he could not have given a reason why he thought so. Did it not sound foolish, he would go so far as to say that she had tripped deliberately. But that did sound foolish, so he kept the thought to himself. Perhaps he would ask her during supper, if his curiosity overcame his manners. It would ensure a lively conversation.

Sir Edward swore viciously and stalked off without so much as a by-your-leave. Lady Tregaron and the Duchess of Greenwich, who were standing close enough to hear, stared after him. The baronet was not a happy man, and his temper was uncertain at the best of times. This clearly was not one of the better times.

Someone needed to drop a word of warning in Lady Sarah's ear. Theo thought he might as well do that during supper. It would, perhaps, give him the opportunity to ask his impertinent question.

Lady Deborah shifted restlessly beside him. Smiling an apology for his woolgathering, Theo offered his arm to lead her onto the dance floor.

He found a space between Blackburn, who was dancing with Tina, and Fairfax, whose stiff features were a sure sign of displeasure with his partner, Lady Diana. Or with something she'd said. It amounted to much the same thing, Theo supposed.

He bowed to Lady Deborah. "Are you enjoying the ball this evening?"

Smiling, she rose from her curtsy. "Yes, I am. Lady Oglethorpe has outdone herself with the decorations. I wouldn't have thought there were so many flowers in all of London this early in the spring. Especially after the long, cold winter we had."

"Ah, but flowers grown in succession houses wouldn't have been affected by the cold winter, and Oglethorpe's estate is only about three hours from London."

"Such extraordinary effort for one evening!" Deborah shook her head, her expression rueful. "I daresay I will never be a great hostess."

"I beg to differ, Lady Deborah. 'Tis not decorations that make a hostess great, but her ability to choose an amiable group of guests and entertain them well. If she succeeds at that, her guests will be pleased, regardless of the room's ornamentation."

"So a well-chosen group of guests will be as happy at a picnic as at a three- or four-course meal with many removes and side dishes?" Skepticism rang in her voice as clear as the tones of a bell.

"Yes, indeed." Theo wondered if Deborah's thoughts were always writ so clearly on her countenance. "If you don't believe me, ask your lady mother. She is one of the premier hostesses of the *ton*, and she can explain not only what she does to make her entertainments so popular, but also why."

Deborah nodded decisively. "I will ask, my lord." Then, after they circled each other, "Which other ladies do you consider excellent hostesses, Lord Dunnley?"

He ought to have expected the question, but he hadn't. To give himself time to consider his answer, he said, "Please, call me Dunnley. We have known each other long enough to forgo such formality."

"Thank you, Lord—er, Dunnley." Her expressive features formed a moue of dismay. "It may take time for me to become accustomed to the less formal address."

"Perhaps so. I promise not to be offended if you forget occasionally."

"Thank you, my lord." Deborah's smile was sweet, and also expressed her gratitude for his forbearance. "You are very kind."

Theo would not have described himself so, but since he was rarely *unkind*—at least, not without a good reason—perhaps she was right. He ought to answer her question before their conversation took off on another tangent. "You asked my opinion about other excellent hostesses. In addition to your mother, the Duchess of St. Ives, Lady Julia Castleton, Lady Blackburn, Lady Throckmorton, and Lady Sherworth are the best hostesses, I think."

Before she could ask why, or some other equally impossible-to-answer question, he added, "I feel quite certain you will one day join their ranks."

Her blue eyes widened, and she smiled in delight. "Do you really think so?"

"I do. Consider all the friends you made last Season. In fact, the formation of 'The Six' is an excellent example of a very good hostess's skill—"

"That was Beth's doing, not mine."

He shook his head. "No. Beth may have made the initial introductions, but all six of you deserve credit for developing the friendships that forged the group." In an attempt to steer the conversation toward more personal matters so that he could learn more about her, Theo asked, "Tell me, please, is there a secret to telling you and your sister apart?" It was demmed disconcerting to even consider taking a bride who was identical in appearance to another man's. Especially when her twin was Lady Diana Woodhurst.

Lady Deborah shook her head, her expression more wistful than amused. "I am the wrong person to ask. Beth or Elston might be able to answer your question. As far as I know, they are the only people outside of the family who can tell us apart."

"Really?" Theo was astounded. "None of your court of admirers can do so?"

"If so, they haven't let on that they can." Deborah shrugged, but he felt certain that her nonchalance was feigned. After a moment she added, "I do not know how Beth tells us apart, but Elston does it—at least, he did initially—by the pitch of our voices. Shortly after we met, he was able to identify us, and when I asked him how he knew who I was, he said that my voice was slightly higher pitched than Diana's."

"The difference must be very slight." They sounded the same to him.

"A quarter step, he said."

"Ah," Theo exclaimed, sighing with regret. "Being a violist, he is able to detect such subtle nuances, but I fear my ear is not as acute."

"I doubt many people can detect such slight differences."

"We spoke of your admirers earlier. I know there are some men in your court who are not in your sister's, and vice versa, but—" He broke off, appalled at what he'd almost said. Had he lost his wits and his manners earlier this evening?

"But you wonder if the men in our courts can tell us apart?"

Chagrined that she'd guessed what he'd been thinking, he smiled ruefully. "Yes, I do—ungentlemanly as such a thought is."

"It is a perfectly logical question. One that troubles me a great deal. It is my opinion that they cannot. They court us merely because we are popular, and because other members of their set do. The fact that we are twins accounts for most of our popularity—"

"No, Lady Deborah, it does not."

"Yes, Dunnley, it does. 'The beautiful Woodhurst twins,'" she quoted with a grimace of distaste, "are the rage because we are twins."

"For some callow fellows that may be true," he conceded, "but not for most."

Peering up at him, she studied his face with a bit more intensity than was comfortable. "I did not mean to imply that all men are so shallow. Certainly you are not, or you would not have asked how to distinguish between us."

Realization hit Theo with the force of Gentleman Jackson's left hook. "You dislike it, don't you? You want to be admired and courted for yourself, not because you are a twin."

"Yes, I do. And it is often quite difficult to determine if a man is interested in me, or if he merely wants to be seen with one of the Woodhurst twins on his arm."

"I daresay that presents quite a conundrum." As they circled each other, he considered her dilemma, but found no solution. "I wish I could solve your problem, but I cannot. However, it may comfort you to know that all the eligible peers on the Marriage Mart find themselves in the same quandary—wondering if they are admired for themselves or for their titles and wealth."

"Really?" Her blue eyes widened in surprise. "I had no idea gentlemen worried about such things."

"That is undoubtedly because you are too smart, and too sensible, to marry a man merely because he has a title and a fortune. I imagine you are hoping to make a love match. Or, at the very least, to marry a man you like and respect."

"Of course I am. Preferably a love match." One blond eyebrow arched inquiringly as she asked, in a tone of curiosity mingled with astonishment, "Is that not what you—and every other gentleman—hope for?"

"I cannot speak for any other man, but I certainly hope that, when the time comes for me to choose a bride, I will find a lady who loves and respects me." He chose his words carefully, not wanting the world to know that he was seeking a wife.

She smiled, clearly pleased by his answer. As much as he enjoyed being the recipient of her smiling regard, honesty compelled him to add, "But you must know that some women—and some men, too—marry for gain. For a fortune, or property, or connections and social position, or a title."

"I know that it happens sometimes, but surely not often in this day and age." Her voice ascended in pitch with each word of the last phrase, turning her response into a question.

"Probably more often than either of us realizes."

Hearing the final bars of the music, Theo bowed, and Deborah dropped into a deep curtsy. As he assisted her to rise, he thanked her for the dance and for her company, both of which he'd enjoyed.

They strolled around the perimeter of the ballroom, stopping occasionally to speak with friends and acquaintances. When they reached the marchioness, Theo again thanked Deborah for dancing with him, then spent a few moments chatting with her and her mother. And doing his best to avoid Lady Diana.

When the musicians began a country dance, Theo took his leave. But not before bespeaking another dance with Deborah after supper.

Lady Deborah Woodhurst was a lovely girl, her heart and character as beautiful as her face and form. Some gentleman of the *ton* would be very fortunate to claim her as his bride, but Theo doubted that he would be that man. He liked her, and admired and respected her, but she did not intrigue him like Lady Sarah Mallory did. Deborah's musical performances often hinted at fiery emotions, but apparently he did not spark them, as he did Lady Sarah's.

Thus, he would concentrate his attention on Sarah Mallory. He hoped a slow, subtle, ingenious courtship would reveal her deepest emotions. And a hidden fire he might fan to a burning flame.

Sarah stayed in the ladies' retiring room after Lady Oglethorpe's maid finished repairing her gown. Her hastily conceived plan to avoid dancing with Sir Edward had succeeded even better than expected, and Sarah was determined not to return to the ballroom until the minuet had ended. She would give the lecherous baronet no opportunity to claim even a portion of the dance he'd requested. And which she'd gone to such trouble to avoid.

As she stepped into the corridor, Sarah wondered if her luck had entirely deserted her this evening, for the very first person she saw was Viscount Dunnley. She could not avoid him: he stepped out of the card room directly into her path.

It was impossible to say who was the more startled by the encounter, since they both jumped back a pace. Lord Dunnley grasped her arms, as if fearing she'd fall tip over tail, but although her legs felt wobbly, Sarah could not have said if her rubbery knees were a result of the narrowly avoided collision, or if they were due to the viscount's presence.

She suspected, however, that the near mishap was not the cause. Especially since her stomach felt as if a meadowful of butterflies had taken up residence there.

"I beg your pardon, Lady Sarah. Apparently, I was not watching where I was going."

"I am sorry, Lord Dunnley. I did not see you until too late."

Their apologies were almost simultaneous, but the smiles such coincidental remarks usually drew were noticeably absent.

The viscount released her arms. "I did not hurt you, did I?"

"No. I am fine."

"After two such incidents tonight, you must think me the clumsiest man in the realm."

The viscount's comment was so far from the truth that Sarah almost smiled. He was one of the most graceful and elegant men in the *beau monde*. One of the most eloquent, too, but both his grace and eloquence seemed to have deserted him tonight—at least in her presence.

The notion that she disconcerted him was far-fetched, but also rather appealing, since he had the same effect on her. But it was discomfiting, too, in a way she could not define.

"May I escort you back to the ballroom?"

"Are you returning so soon?" she asked, surprised. "You could not have played cards for very long. Well, not unless the minuet was a very short one."

He smiled and offered his arm. "The minuet was its usual length, and ended about five minutes ago. I didn't go into the card room to play, but in search of my brother. Tina expressed a wish to speak with him."

Accepting his escort, Sarah traversed the corridor at his side. "I am not acquainted with your brother. 'Twas my understanding that he is a soldier fighting on the Peninsula. Or"—she flushed with embarrassment—"perhaps you have more than one brother?"

She ought to know how many brothers he had. She could quote chapter and verse from *Debrett's Peerage* for any Welsh title, but for English and Scottish and Irish titles, she knew only the names of the men who held the titles, and the more socially prominent members of their families. It was a shocking admission for a young lady on the Marriage Mart to make, but Sarah had never expected to have a Season in London, since her mother rarely ventured to the Metropolis. And neither her mother nor her governess, who also was Welsh, had deemed such knowledge an important part of Sarah's education.

Fortunately, Lord Dunnley did not seem offended by her ignorance. "I have only one brother, my lady. He is a captain in the Seventh Hussars and a member of Wellington's staff, but he was wounded and sent home on leave to recover."

"Oh dear! I hope his injury is not serious." *Stupid! If it was not serious, he would not have been sent home.*

"Serious enough, but he is making a good recovery, albeit a much slower one than either of us would like." After a moment, perhaps belatedly realizing how his remark could be misconstrued, he added, "Not that I am eager to see the back of him. I am not. In fact, I dread his return to the fighting. But I do wish Stephen's hip—er, that his wounds were healing more quickly."

"Of course you do. Any brother or sister would."

"Is Lan—I am sorry, I don't exactly remember your brother's title."

"Llanfyllin."

"Hlan-*vu*-hlin." He sounded the syllables carefully, aspirating both occurrences of the double *l*. "Er, did I pronounce it correctly?"

"Yes, my lord, you did," she reassured, pleased that he was concerned enough to ask. So many Englishmen did not care if, or how badly, they mangled Welsh names.

"Is he your only brother? Or do you have other brothers and sisters?"

"I also have a younger brother, Dafydd, who is eleven. But no sisters."

"Is there a tradition in your family that the boys are given Welsh names and the girls English ones?"

"No. But Mama named the boys, and Papa named me,

which may account for the difference. I am named after his grandmother, who was English. My middle names are Welsh, though.''

He smiled down at her, his gray eyes atwinkle. "Dare I ask? Welsh names can be devilishly difficult for an Englishman to pronounce. And even harder to determine the correct pronunciation from the spelling.''

"Sarah Iola Rhiannon.''

"Your name is almost as lovely and musical as you are.''

"Th-thank you, my lord.'' Sarah was unaccountably flustered by the compliment, although she'd received far more effusive ones in the past.

Lord Dunnley stopped short of the ballroom entrance, but since the receiving line had dispersed, there was no one to notice the impropriety of their being alone together. "A word of warning before we go back inside. Smithson seemed quite angry about not being able to dance with you. His temper is volatile, and sometimes violent, so . . .'' He paused as if seeking the right words, but instead of finishing the sentence, he suggested, "If he requests another set, you might want to sit it out, or stroll with him instead of taking the floor. You are less likely to be the target of his ire if there are other people nearby.''

"Oh dear. That sounds even worse than—'' Sarah averted her gaze, aghast at what she'd almost revealed.

"Even worse than what?'' The viscount's tone was conversational, but there was a hint of steel underlying the words.

Knowing that, impolite as it might be, he would demand an answer, if only out of a gentlemanly sense of concern for and protectiveness toward a lady, Sarah stifled a sigh and capitulated instead of trying to fob him off. "Even worse than his leering and improper remarks.''

Lord Dunnley's tawny brows rose in shocked disbelief. "He dares to subject you to such . . . such rudeness and coarse behavior?''

"Yes.'' Demeaning as it felt to admit such a thing, Sarah was comforted by the viscount's anger on her behalf.

"It is not my place to offer you advice, but I strongly recommend that you make your parents aware of Smithson's behavior. Your mother would not have granted his request to dance with you had she known.''

He was right, of course. Her mother would not have deemed the baronet an acceptable partner for Sarah—or any other young lady—if she had known. "It is not an easy thing for a young lady to admit. To her parents, or to anyone else."

"I don't imagine it will be, but I think it is not only necessary, but essential." After a moment's hesitation, he asked, "Would you like me to speak to your father?"

Astounded by the viscount's willingness to help her, Sarah could not help but stare at him. "It is very kind of you to offer, but I think it would be best if I tell my parents. I do, however, greatly appreciate your generosity. And your concern."

"If you change your mind and wish for my assistance, you need only ask."

"Thank you, Lord Dunnley."

"Do you think you could bring yourself to call me Dunnley? I would be honored to count you, and to be counted by you, as a friend."

He wants to be my friend? Sarah was not at all certain if her stomach and her knees could endure a more intimate acquaintance with the viscount, but courtesy dictated her answer. "I would be honored to do so. Thank you, Dunnley." Unfortunately, the rules of Polite Behavior would not rid her stomach of butterflies or strengthen the bones in her legs.

"It is I who am honored." He glanced around as if to ensure no one was nearby, then asked, "Does the appreciation you mentioned a few moments ago extend to allowing me a rather impertinent question?"

Taken aback by his request, she stammered, "I-I suppose so." Then, recovering her wits, she amended, "That is, you may ask, but I do not promise to answer."

"Fair enough," he agreed, a smile quirking the corners of his mouth and brightening his gray eyes almost to silver. Lowering his voice almost to a whisper, he asked, "Did you deliberately trip on your hem so that you wouldn't have to dance with Smithson?"

Sarah felt the fiery color heating her cheeks—and her entire face. That was undoubtedly answer enough, but she managed to choke out, "Y-yes, I did." Mortified both by his deduction and her reaction to his question, she wished a trapdoor would open beneath her feet and whisk her away to some obscure place far from Dunnley's intent, and much too perceptive, regard. But, alas, her luck was entirely out this evening, for no such fortuitous opening gaped.

Placing his hand over hers where it rested on his coat sleeve, the viscount voiced a softly spoken but clearly heartfelt apology. "I beg your pardon, Sarah. It was not my intent to distress you."

Although she was comforted by both the gesture and his words, Sarah still could not meet his gaze. "I know that, Dunnley. You are always a perfect gentleman, and you would never deliberately upset a lady." Several seconds passed in silence before she mustered the courage to ask, "How did you know? Was it so obvious?"

"No," he hastened to reassure her, "it was not at all obvious. And I didn't know for certain until you blushed. I only guessed because you are always so graceful. I have never seen you stumble, or even misstep in a dance."

There was some comfort in that. Not much, but enough to convince Sarah that her cheeks and face might regain their normal hue before next Tuesday. "I can only hope everyone who was standing nearby is not as astute as you are."

Then the rest of his words penetrated the fog in her brain—that he had watched her dance often enough to say she never misstepped, as well as his assertion that she never stumbled—and suddenly she was, once again, disconcerted. *Why has he observed me so closely?*

"Do you know what Smithson's nickname was at Eton? A soubriquet, I might add, that seems as fitting today as it did then."

"I have no idea." Bemused, she shook her head. "How could I possibly know?"

"I thought someone might have told you. Or that you might have overheard it. It was Nasty Ned. Apt, isn't it?" Dunnley's arched brow, as well as the look of inquiry he bent upon her, invited her to express her opinion.

"Very," she agreed wryly. "Although it ill-becomes me, as a lady, to say so."

"Who better? After all, you have experienced his nastiness firsthand. You are not passing along unfounded gossip, but commenting based upon your knowledge of his character.

"And," he added, with perhaps a slight emphasis, "you are making your comments to a friend—a friend who will respect your confidence."

"Thank you, Dunnley." How many times had she said that, or some variation of it, to him tonight? Quite a few, she was certain; it was beginning to sound a bit repetitive.

"Would you like a glass of lemonade or punch before we return to the ballroom?"

Sarah smiled at her handsome, elegant, well-mannered escort. He truly was a nonpareil among gentlemen. Or he would be, if he did not discompose her so. "No, thank you. I had best return before my mother begins to wonder if my gown is beyond repair."

"Fortunately, that does not appear to be the case." He assessed her with a glance that swept from her coiffure to the toes of her dancing slippers—one that did not linger anywhere it should not.

"I am glad of it, too." Removing the hand covering hers, he resumed their walk toward the ballroom entrance. "I have been looking forward to the supper dance."

Why did he have to say that? Sarah's stomach and knees, which had returned almost to normal during their conversation, were again beset by flutters and tremors. "I cannot imagine why, my lord. You have danced with me on any number of occasions."

"Indeed I have, and enjoyed them all. Perhaps my memory is faulty, but I cannot recall anticipating one with quite as much eagerness as I am the supper dance."

Good Lord! It was tantamount to a declaration—of his interest, if not his intentions. *Why me?* she wondered. *Why is he suddenly so interested in me?* But she could not ask him those questions, so she settled for saying, "Dunnley, I hope you will not be disappointed when I tell you that my ploy to avoid dancing with Sir Edward was a bit too successful. Lady Oglethorpe's maid was able to partially repair my gown, but not completely. Unfortunately, I am going to have to leave, and I—"

"You won't be here for the supper dance." He said it levelly, but the tightening of his features betrayed some strong emotion. Sarah was not sure if it was anger or disappointment. Or, perhaps, a bit of both.

"Regrettably, I will not. I do apologize. It is shockingly

ill-mannered of me, I know, but there is little I can do now, save beg your pardon." A moment later, she blurted, "It is so unfair to you! I could not refuse Sir Edward's request because I'd promised you the supper dance. I was praying it would be a country dance. I could have managed a set of country dances with him and maintained my composure, I think, but not the minuet."

Halting again, he turned to face her. "I understand, Sarah. Truly I do. Because of his past behavior, you would have been very uncomfortable partnering him in such an intimate dance, so you took drastic measures to avoid it."

"Yes, I did, but now my missishness—"

"Not missishness." He covered her tightly clasped hands with his. "More like self-preservation."

"I am sorry, Dunnley." Surprisingly, given her earlier dismay and the unsettling feelings he evoked in her, she did regret that she would not be able to dance and have supper with him.

Tucking her hand back in the crook of his arm, he led her toward the ballroom. "You may assuage my disappointment by promising me two dances at Almack's tomorrow, and a waltz and the supper dance at the Enderbys' ball on Thursday."

Dunnley *never* bespoke dances in advance. That was an accepted fact among the *ton*, as well known as his elegant manners and famed address. Sarah had no idea why he was changing his habits now, nor could she ask. Instead she said lightly, in the tone with which she teased her brothers, "Four dances in lieu of one, my lord? That seems a bit excessive, but you may have them if you wish."

"I do."

"In that case, have you a preference for any particular dances at Almack's?"

"Let us say the first minuet and the third waltz." He smiled down at her. "I will save you from Ordeal By Minuet with Smithson."

"I appreciate that, Dunnley. The first minuet and the third waltz it shall be."

The stairs loomed before them, beckoning like a chasm and distracting her. She must have clutched Dunnley's arm more tightly, for he paused and looked intently at her. "Is something wrong?"

Too disconcerted—by the stairs, the evening's events, and his startling declaration and request—to guard her tongue, she answered frankly. "I do not like this staircase. It is so wide. Ladies are not supposed to mind their steps until they reach the dance floor, but . . ." Her attempt at a shrug fell short of the mark, feeling more like a shudder than a show of nonchalance. "I fear I put creases in Rhys's coat sleeve when we arrived."

"I daresay my sleeve can withstand a wrinkle or two." His smile was as kind as his words.

Glancing at his creaseless coat, she muttered, "I did warn you, my lord," then gripped his arm more tightly and nodded for him to proceed.

She didn't draw breath again until they reached the bottom. Without mishap, thank God. Dunnley kept up a spate of inconsequential chatter as they strolled toward her mother's chair. Once there, he bowed over her hand. "Good evening, Lady Sarah." Then, with a smile for the three older ladies, he departed.

Leaving Sarah to explain how she had come to be in his company.

And causing her to wonder yet again why he, and he alone, had such a strange effect upon her.

Theo meandered around the ballroom, but his promenade was not as desultory as it appeared. He was searching for his brother. And, if truth be told, for Smithson. The baronet had much to answer for, and Theo was not inclined to let him off lightly.

He could not say anything, of course. Not tonight.

But if the dastard upset Sarah again there would be hell to pay. And Theo would gladly tote up the reckoning and present the bill.

Chapter Four

The morning after Lady Oglethorpe's ball, Sarah awoke more tired than she'd been when she went to bed. The fact that she'd spent most of the night tossing and turning—wondering why Dunnley affected her so strangely, and so strongly—instead of sleeping, was largely to blame. The rest was due to her excitement after the ball, and, strangely enough, her disappointment at having to leave early, which had led her to read for an hour or more before she even sought her bed. Although it was difficult to compare last Season with this one, Sarah did not think she had felt so exhilarated after her first ball. Or after her first appearance at Almack's.

Until the minuet she'd gone to such lengths to avoid last night, she had danced every set. But that was not unusual. She did not have a court of admirers clamoring for her attention like some of the more popular girls did, but it was rare for her to be without a partner. What was unusual was that she had so thoroughly enjoyed herself, even when conversing with people she did not know very well. Although she had resolved to try to overcome her shyness, Sarah knew that much of her success in that regard last night was not the result of her own efforts, but those of her friends—Deborah, Tina, and Dunnley.

Dunnley. How strange it was to think of him as a friend! But strange or not, he had been very helpful, and his skill as a raconteur had eased her way several times last night, allowing her to act on her fledging resolution. Even though dancing with him, or just standing beside him, set her nerves aquiver.

Why he had such a strange effect on her, she did not know. It was not fear—after last night, she was as certain of that as she was of her own name—but she could not identify the cause. At least, not yet. But she would, she vowed, figure out why her stomach fluttered and her legs turned to jelly whenever he was near.

Even if doing so required her to spend a considerable amount of time in his company.

When Theo awoke, instead of immediately ringing for Carter, his valet, he lay in bed for several minutes thinking about last night's ball and pondering how best to further his acquaintance with Sarah Mallory—without seeming to court her. He did not want to create expectations, in her mind or the *ton*'s. At least, not until he was certain that she was the perfect bride for him.

He could and should call on her today, since he'd danced with her last night. He would send flowers, too—to Sarah and to several other young ladies he'd partnered, including Deborah Woodhurst. And, though it went against the grain, to her sister. Sending a posy to Deborah only, when he'd danced with both twins, would demonstrate a marked partiality for her company. While it was quite true that he favored her over her sister, Theo did not want to flaunt his preference. Nor did he particularly want anyone to know that he enjoyed one twin's company more than the other's.

He should also call on Lady Oglethorpe. And, he supposed, on Tina Fairchild. The duke's daughter was *not* a candidate for his viscountess, but calling on her, as well as on two other members of "The Six," would help to obscure the object of his interest.

Last night, Sarah Mallory had most definitely piqued his interest. Not only by her reaction to him while they waltzed, but also with her frankness during their discussion outside the ballroom. He had been surprised, but quite pleased, when she'd confided in him. Especially once he realized that she had not told anyone else about Smithson's appalling behavior. The honor Theo had felt at being the recipient of her confidences had lessened his disappointment at not being her supper partner. And the dances she'd promised him later this week had mitigated his frustration over her early departure.

Then, his afternoon planned, Theo reached for the bell-pull. Once he was dressed, a brisk ride in the park would be just the thing to help clear his head of the visions of Sarah that had haunted his dreams.

It was a demmed good thing that his vow to reform placed no restrictions on his nighttime fantasies.

*   *   *

Morning calls, despite the fact that they occurred in the afternoon, were one of Sarah's least favorite parts of the Season. Making such calls was not so bad, but receiving them was a far different story. If you were paying calls, you knew who you would see—at least, the principal people; guessing who else might be in their drawing room was not possible. But when you were at home to callers, as Sarah and her mother were this afternoon, it was impossible to deduce who might stop by. Generally, the day after a ball, a young lady might expect a visit from any or all of the gentlemen she had danced with the night before. That rule of Polite Behavior was the source of Sarah's present concern.

She was almost sick with fear that Sir Edward Smithson would call.

And she was, by turns, anticipating and dreading a visit from Viscount Dunnley. Anticipating it because he had been very kind to her last night, offering his friendship, as well as his assistance with the problem of Nasty Ned. Dreading a call from Dunnley because she was always so flustered in his presence. Or so discomposed by it.

Sir Edward's rude behavior and lewd remarks discomfited her, too, but not in at all the same way. The baronet outraged and infuriated her, and sometimes frightened her. Dunnley, on the other hand, caused butterflies to take up wing-beating residence in her stomach and, quite often, weakened the bones in her legs. In his presence, she was even more reserved than usual, lest her wits had gone a-begging along with control over her body. With the baronet, however, her manners were all that kept her from raging at him like a Billingsgate fishwife.

'Twas a shame that she could not summon half as many words when Dunnley spoke to her.

Being the compleat gentleman that he was, the viscount was certain to call today. Especially since he had sent her the loveliest bouquet of flowers this morning. Because she had not been able to honor her promise to partner him for the supper dance last night, Sarah hoped that her words and her wits would not desert her when he appeared. At least, not until after she apologized again. And preferably not until after she thanked him for his kindness, and for the flowers. No matter how ineloquent and inadequate her words might be.

She had done everything she could to bolster her confidence. She was wearing her favorite new afternoon gown, a lovely deep pink muslin that, according to her maid, put roses in her cheeks and flattered, but did not flaunt, her figure. Her hair was perfectly, if not elaborately, styled. And she was wearing her favorite jewelry. The pearl earrings her parents had given her for her seventeenth birthday adorned her lobes, and her grandmother's cameo brooch, which Sarah had loved since she was a little girl, was pinned to a ribbon that circled her throat.

But as she descended the stairs to the drawing room, it became quite clear that not only were the dratted butterflies already in residence and stretching their wings, but they had invited all their friends to visit this afternoon. And every single invitation they'd extended had been eagerly, perhaps even gleefully, accepted.

How did one get rid of such pesky creatures?

The moment she stepped into the drawing room, Dunnley rose to his feet. Handsomer than ever in a bottle green coat and biscuit pantaloons, he finished his comment to her mother, then crossed to Sarah and greeted her.

How did he know I was here? He was looking at Mama, not toward the doors. "Good afternoon, Dunnley. Thank you for the lovely flowers."

Cupping his hand around her elbow, he escorted her to a chair next to his. "You are very welcome. I am glad they found favor with you. And I am relieved to see that you do not appear to be suffering any ill effects from last night's stumble."

Grateful that he had not let on that he knew she'd tripped deliberately—and even though she had confessed her deception—and the reasons for it—to her mother last night, Sarah smiled. "No ill effects at all, my lord, though I was sorry to miss the supper dance. Will you tell us about the rest of the ball?"

She thought—or fancied—that his eyes smiled when she mentioned the supper dance, although the rest of his features did not change. He shrugged slightly, then said, "It was a ball like many others. Quite unexceptional, really."

"I daresay you didn't tell Lady Oglethorpe that," Sarah's

mother commented wryly. "Was there nothing that distinguished it from other balls?"

He shrugged again. "It was an enjoyable entertainment, but the things that stand out most in my mind are the profusion of floral decorations, you and your daughter leaving early, and Lady Diana Woodhurst's attempt to steal one of her sister's partners by pretending to be Lady Deborah."

"Who?" asked Lady Tregaron at the same moment that Sarah exclaimed, "Oh, how awful for Deb that her sister treats her so shabbily!"

Dunnley looked from the countess to Sarah, then answered both comments. "It *was* very poorly done of Lady Diana. Lady Kesteven was mortified that her youngest daughter would behave so. Especially because, when the gentleman—it was Fairfax—said Lady Diana wasn't his partner for the dance, she taunted him that he could not tell them apart."

"Which he obviously can," said the countess, clearly pleased by the duke's perspicacity.

"Perhaps he cannot," Sarah suggested, "but he remembered what color sashes they were wearing last night."

"I hadn't considered that, but you may be right, Lady Sarah." The viscount sipped his tea, his expression thoughtful. "During my first dance with Lady Deborah last night, I asked if there was a trick to telling her and her sister apart. She suggested that I ask Beth Castleton—Beth Weymouth, now—or Elston, since they are the only people she is aware of, other than her family, who can distinguish them."

"I suppose it is possible there are more, but you would think—I would think—that the twins would know everyone who can tell them apart. If only because one must know them very well to do so. At least," she amended, "it seems so to me. I have known them for a little over a year, and I cannot."

"I would have said the same, but from what Lady Deborah told me, both Beth and Elston were able to tell them apart almost immediately."

"Really?" The countess's eyes widened in surprise. "I wonder how they do it?"

"I intend to ask, my lady." Dunnley grinned, but Sarah had the sense that there was a reason, other than gentlemanly courtesy, behind his desire to be able to differentiate between the twins.

Had he developed a *tendre* for Deborah? They would suit very well, Sarah thought. And they would be an extraordinarily attractive couple.

The thought was accompanied by a pang. Or perhaps the stupid butterflies were again stretching their wings. Ignoring the strange sensation, she returned her attention to the conversation.

". . . promises to be a very interesting Season," her mother was saying.

"Undoubtedly so, my lady. They nearly always are, in one way or another." Turning toward Sarah, Dunnley set his cup and saucer on the table between their chairs. "I hope you haven't forgotten the dances you promised me at Almack's tonight, Lady Sarah."

"No, my lord, I have not forgotten." *As if I could!*

"Excellent!" He rose and bowed over her mother's hand, thanking her for her hospitality. When he turned to her, Sarah mutely extended her own hand. Bowing over it, he proclaimed, "I am looking forward to dancing with you this evening."

With that, he strolled from the room, leaving Sarah's heart thumping at an alarming rate.

And causing her to wonder, yet again, why he had chosen her to be the recipient of his marked—and entirely unprecedented—attentions.

Theo was well pleased with the results of his morning calls, even though the Duchess of Greenwich and Tina had not been at home. But he'd had a surfeit of female conversation, so he directed his curricle toward St. James's Street, knowing that at White's he could counter all the feminine chatter with talk of parliamentary matters and sports. Entering the main room, he glanced at the gentlemen gathered there, hoping to see one of his particular friends. Surprisingly, none were present—a most unusual circumstance for this time of day, especially early in the Season. Since he had no desire to join a rather loud argument between two young dandies about how to tie a proper neckcloth—nor to settle the matter for them—and was not in the mood to gossip with Alvanley and his set or to play cards, Theo asked a waiter to bring him a brandy and headed for a chair in the far corner. And, he hoped, a few minutes of quiet reflection.

Much to his delight, he found Fairfax ensconced there. They had known each other since they'd entered Eton, where they had become fast friends, even though the duke was more studious and less interested in sporting pursuits than Theo was. Their schoolmates, seeing only the contrasts between the quiet, gentle, rather plain duke and the talkative, often boisterous, handsome viscount, had dubbed them "The Opposites," and the two of them had derived great amusement from the inaccurate epithet. Although not Theo's oldest friend—his cousin George held that distinction—Fairfax was Theo's closest friend, as Theo was his. They could discuss anything with each other, and over the past nineteen years, they probably had.

"Well met, Fairfax!"

"If you are looking for intelligent conversation, you won't get it from me. I just spent two hours paying calls with my grandmother."

Settling into a chair beside the duke, Theo inquired, "Since when do you dislike making morning calls? Or is the fact that you did so with your grandmother the reason for your complaint?"

"I don't mind making them, generally—at least, I haven't until this year. But Grandmère has decided that it is time for me to marry and set up my nursery, so she is constantly singing the praises of some chit or other. Even that wouldn't be so bad were each one not more featherheaded than the last." The duke groaned. "I swear, Dunnley, I heard enough talk about bonnets and ribbons and plumes and other such falderal today to open a millinery shop!"

Theo could not help but laugh, although he'd heard quite a bit of the same kind of chatter. "You should do it. You'd be the biggest prize on the Marriage Mart—a duke with a millinery shop." A moment later, he shook his head. "What am I saying? You already are the Catch of the Season."

"Yes," the duke said glumly, "and that's at least half the problem."

"Problem? What problem?"

"How am I supposed to know if a young lady is interested in me, or if she merely wants to snare my title and fortune?"

"Well—" Theo broke off as the waiter approached with his brandy. He took a sip, nodded his satisfaction with the vintage, then waited until the servant was out of earshot before answering. "I can't deny that many marriages are made for gain, and have been for hundreds of years, but I can think of a number of young ladies who are not likely to choose a husband because of his rank and fortune. Any number of people like you, Michael—and the fact that you are a duke has nothing to do with it."

"You sound like Sarah Mallory."

"Do I?" Theo was pleased by the comparison. Puzzled, but undeniably pleased.

Fairfax nodded. "She said much the same thing to me last night."

"She is an intelligent young woman. She doesn't say a lot—I think she is a bit shy—but when she does speak, her conversation is worth listening to."

"I agree, although I'd say she is more than just a bit shy. Why, she makes me seem almost gregarious, and God knows I am not." Extending one finger, the duke opined, "She is one who won't choose a husband by his rank and the size of his purse. Who are the other young ladies you mentioned?"

"Deborah Woodhurst." After a moment's hesitation, Theo added, "But I am not certain the same can be said of her twin."

"I don't think so, either." When he did not immediately add to the list, Fairfax prompted, "Who else? Besides Harriett Broughton and Tina Fairchild. They are the only others I can think of."

"I don't know Miss Broughton well enough to say."

"Take my word for it. She is as shy as I am, so no matter how high a man's title or how deep his pockets, she won't marry him unless she genuinely likes him."

Theo was rapidly running out of names. Because of his friendship with Beth Castleton—Beth Weymouth now that she was married to his cousin—he knew the young ladies of "The Six" better than any of the others who had made their come-outs in the last few years. Hoping to forestall another "who else?" from Fairfax, Theo said, "Speaking of the Woodhurst twins, what was that business with Lady Diana trying to claim her sister's dance with you last night?"

The question elicited another groan from the duke. "I

haven't got the slightest idea. But then, Lady Diana ain't the most rational female in the *ton*. Maybe she was just jealous that her sister had a partner when she herself did not, so she tried to steal Deborah's partner—me."

"That is possible, I suppose, but it seems unlikely. I don't think either of the twins has sat out a dance since they got the nod to waltz last year." Theo suspected that Diana's reason, whatever it was, was far more complex—and far less benign—than mere envy. "Besides, I had the impression that young Martin was Lady Diana's partner. If not, why was he standing there?"

"Martin minor, d'you mean?" the duke asked, referring to the young man by the name he'd been known by at school. "He was there, wasn't he?" It was apparent from his tone that he had not, until that moment, considered the reason for Mr. Martin's presence.

Theo nodded, then asked, "Can you really tell the twins apart, Fairfax, or were you bluffing last night?"

"I can't bluff worth a damn, as you well know. I think I have lost every game of brag I ever played. Of course I can tell the twins apart. Not from across the room, though. I have to be within a few feet of them to know which is which."

Fairfax made it sound as if everyone could identify the twins at a glance, which Theo knew was not the case. "Can you tell them apart if only one is present? Or do they have to be side by side so you can compare them?"

"They don't have to be together. I don't think Lady Deborah was there at the beginning of last night's contretemps." After several moments' thought, the duke amended, without a trace of uncertainty in his voice, "I *know* she was not there at first."

Theo had not arrived on the scene until the "contretemps," as Fairfax styled it, was nearly full-blown. "No, she wasn't," he agreed. "She was my partner for the set of country dances that had just ended, and we stopped to speak with several people as we strolled around the room. When we walked up, Lady Kesteven was sputtering in outrage at her younger daughter's audacious lies and shocking want of conduct."

"How did Lady Deborah react when she realized her twin was trying to steal her partner?"

Something in the duke's voice made Theo wonder if Fairfax had a *tendre* for Lady Deborah. Perhaps it had not progressed that far yet, but Theo knew his friend well enough to be certain that Fairfax greatly admired her. Might his respect and admiration lead to more? Would he fall in love with her? She would be a good match for the shy, scholarly duke—if she returned his regard.

"She was . . . stunned." It was the best description Theo could contrive, but it seemed woefully inadequate. "She hid her distress well, but I believe she felt betrayed—either by Diana's lies or by Diana herself."

"And rightly so. What did Lady Deborah say when she realized what was happening?"

"Did you not hear her call her sister's bluff?"

"Yes, I heard that, but I wondered . . ." Fairfax huffed out a breath. "I wondered if Lady Deborah commented on her sister's behavior."

"Not in my hearing. But I imagine she—and Lady Kesteven, too—had a great deal to say about it later, after they left the ball."

"I don't understand why Lady Diana did it—I don't think she likes me above half—but I don't want to talk about her anymore."

Nodding in understanding, Theo deftly turned the subject. "How do you tell Lady Deborah and Lady Diana apart?"

The duke thought about it for a moment or two, then shrugged. "I don't know how I know which twin is which. I just do."

"Would you be able to tell them apart if you were in a dark room and couldn't see them clearly?"

"You've got more questions than a grumpy headmaster this afternoon, don't you?" Fairfax grumbled. "I don't know if I could or not."

"Are there any young ladies you would know in a dark room—or a dark garden?"

Although obviously perplexed by the question, as well as Theo's reason for asking it, Fairfax gamely attempted to answer. "In this hypothetical dark room or garden, how close am I standing to these young ladies?"

"Two or three feet. An arm's length away."

"Hmmm . . . The Woodhurst twins, probably. Maybe

Miss Castleton—Lady Weymouth. Possibly Miss Broughton and Lady Sarah Mallory."

"Why those four—er, those five? And how would you know them?"

"I don't know that I would, Theo," the duke said, clearly exasperated. "I have a different feeling around Lady Diana than when I am with her sister. Lady Weymouth because . . . I don't know why. Or how. I just think maybe I could recognize her and the others in a dark room."

Fairfax's tone made it clear that he would brook no more strange questions. But his last answer had given Theo *his* answer. He could probably detect Tina Fairchild, his youthful nemesis, in a dark room; he would surely feel the urge to run. And Jani Brooks, his mistress for the past six years, because she was as comfortable as an old pair of boots. He might also be able to recognize his friend Beth Weymouth. But Theo knew, with absolute surety, that he would be able to identify Lady Sarah Mallory anywhere, and at any time.

Because of the feelings she roused in him. And the urge he felt to protect her from all harm.

No other woman had ever incited such extremes of emotion in him. He was beginning to think no other lady ever would.

Chapter Five

*A*lmack's. Sarah was certain that no other place figured so prominently in the lives of young ladies who came to Town to make their bows to Society. And in gentlemen's lives, too, although to a lesser extent. No one, male or female, could receive a voucher to attend the subscription balls there unless their application was approved by all the lady patronesses. Admittance to the assemblies conferred the highest status, allowing a young lady to move in the first circles of Society; refusal blasted her prospects for an advantageous marriage. According to the tabbies, quite a number of matches had been made within Almack's hallowed halls. And many a courtship pursued or advanced there.

As she, her mother, and her brother drove through Mayfair, Sarah felt the same tingle of alarm and anticipation that had presaged her attendance at Almack's last year. Dread that she would commit a solecism or some *faux pas* that would put her irrevocably beyond the pale. Anticipation that this would be the night when she was introduced to her future husband. But the excitement of such an enticing possibility was tempered with terror that she would become impossibly tongue-tied when faced with the necessity of conversing with a stranger. She looked forward to dancing with a dazzling array of eligible men, but at the same time, she feared that she would forget the steps of a dance when all eyes were upon her.

Dunnley had already bespoken two of her dances—the first minuet and the third waltz. And if, by some strange quirk of fate, no other gentlemen requested a set with her, the patronesses would do their best to provide her with suitable partners. After all, they had the institution's reputation as "the Marriage Mart" to uphold.

Yet the prospect of dancing a minuet and a waltz with Dunnley held its own terrors. Would her stomach and legs betray her as they had last night whenever he was near? If she spent more time in his company, would she eventually become accustomed to the tremors he evoked? Or might the problem grow worse?

Either way, she would find out soon enough.

When they turned onto King Street, the coach halted almost immediately, then began inching forward.

"There must be quite a line of carriages tonight," Lady Tregaron said. "I don't believe we ever stopped quite this far down the street last year."

"Oh, I hope we are not late," Sarah exclaimed, twisting the cords of her reticule.

"Of course we aren't late, goose," her brother retorted. "It is nowhere near eleven o'clock."

She shot him a reproachful glare. "I know we aren't too late to attend. I meant late for the first set."

With an exaggerated, long-suffering sigh, Rhys reached into his waistcoat pocket and pulled out his watch. Flicking open the cover, he held the timepiece under a carriage lamp. "We should arrive in time for the first set." As he tucked the watch away, he inquired, "Who have you promised it to?"

"That will depend on what kind of dance it is. Lord Dunnley requested the first minuet. Lord Howe, the first country dance. And the Duke of Fairfax asked me to reserve the first waltz for him. If it is a quadrille or a cotillion or . . . some other dance, then I don't yet have a partner."

"Howe and Dunnley bespoke dances in advance?" The incredulous tone of Rhys's voice confirmed how unusual such requests were.

"Indeed they did."

"Never known Howe to do that before. Mayhap you have made a conquest," he teased. Then, more thoughtfully, "Nice to have one of my best friends as my brother-in-law."

"Rhys! He only requested a dance, not permission to pay his addresses."

"Children." Though the countess spoke only one word, and that in a conversational tone, there was a note in her voice reminiscent of their days in the schoolroom that silenced them both.

Smoothing nonexistent wrinkles from her long, cream-colored silk gloves, Sarah sought her rapidly fleeing composure. Before she felt quite ready, the coach stopped, and a footman opened the door and lowered the steps. Rhys clambered out, then offered his hand to assist his mother and his sister to alight.

Almack's!

His cravat finally tied to his satisfaction, Theo picked up his *chapeau bras* and his walking stick, then thanked his valet and left his dressing room. When he reached the first-floor landing, he hesitated for a moment, then crossed to the library. Stephen was sprawled in a wing chair in front of the fire, with his bootheels propped on the fender, a glass of brandy on the Sheraton table beside him . . . and a book open on his lap.

The sight was so astonishing, Theo almost stumbled over the threshold. The ungraceful movement caught his brother's eye. After a head-to-toe perusal, Stephen pronounced,

"Complete to a shade, aren't you? No wonder you are one of the fashion leaders of the *ton*."

"Have you changed your mind about attending Almack's this evening?"

Marking his page before closing the tome, Stephen spread his arms wide. "Do I look like I have reconsidered?"

Since he was wearing pantaloons and Hessians, not knee breeches and dancing pumps, the question was clearly rhetorical, but Theo answered anyway. "No, but I would be happy to wait while you change."

Stephen closed his eyes for a moment, then repeated the argument he had used at the breakfast table and again at dinner. "There is no point in a man who cannot dance attending Almack's."

The note of strained patience in his brother's voice prevented Theo from reiterating his previous responses to that statement. Instead he teased. "My dear boy, how will you while away the evening if you don't intend to darken the door of Willis's Rooms? Which hostess will you gratify by gracing her entertainment with your presence?"

"Cut line, Theo." Despite the emphatic tone, a smile tugged one corner of Stephen's mouth. "You are the one who delights the *ton*'s hostesses by attending their events. I am not going anywhere. I intend to sit here in comfort and read this book."

Quirking a brow at his brother's uncharacteristic—and possibly unprecedented—choice of entertainment, Theo drawled, "A book? What is this masterpiece that holds you in such thrall?"

Stephen waved a hand dismissively, but his rather sheepish expression caught his brother's gaze. "Just a novel that Beth recommended."

"Beth?" It was the best response Theo could muster—and much better than goggling at the idea of his stalwart soldier brother reading a novel. Or pestering him with questions about his health.

"Yes, Beth. Our cousin George's wife." After a long beat of silence, Stephen added, as if prompting an old man's flagging memory, "You know, the tall, slender, lovely brunette with the American accent who plays the violin like an angel?"

"I know who Beth is," Theo retorted dryly. "I just wasn't aware that she guided your reading choices."

"Well, she never has before. But she recommended this book because she thought I might like it, and George and Uncle Andrew agreed, so I decided to try it."

"Were they right? Do you like it?"

"So far, it is rather entertaining."

"Since you appear to be about halfway through the first volume, it must be diverting indeed." Again Theo asked, "What is the title of this masterpiece?"

"Pride and Prejudice."

"Ah. I enjoyed that myself. The lady has written another book, *Sense and Sensibility*, that you might like even better. One of the heroes is a military man."

"Perhaps I will read that one next."

Amazed, and more than a bit concerned that Stephen had chosen to spend the evening reading instead of out on the town with his cronies, Theo said only, "I will leave you to it then, and take myself off to Almack's. Good night, Stephen."

"G'night, Theo."

Shaking his head in bemusement, he quietly closed the library door and suited action to words.

Half an hour later, although his carriage had not quite reached the assembly rooms, Theo opened the door and jumped out. He was eager for the evening to begin and, thus, less patient than usual with the slow progress of the line of vehicles waiting to disgorge their passengers.

As he strolled toward the entrance, he saw Sarah's brother standing at the open door of a carriage, his arm extended to hand someone down. Since that "someone" was undoubtedly his mother or his sister, Theo halted, awaiting his first glimpse this evening of the lady who had occupied his thoughts for much of the day.

Lady Tregaron emerged first and delicately shook the wrinkles out of her skirts. A long moment later, Sarah appeared in the portal—and Theo's breath caught in his throat.

God, she is beautiful.

Wearing a rosy pink gown with a spangled, cream-colored shawl draped over her arms and her hair in its usual smooth knot, à la Psyche, with no wisps or curls around her face, she looked like a vision from a man's—any man's—dreams. When she, too, shook out her skirts, he noticed that her slippers and long gloves matched the creamy color of her shawl, but it was not until he recovered his composure enough to step forward that he saw the pearl earrings adorning her lobes and the pearl necklace encircling her throat.

Sapphires. She should wear sapphires to match her eyes. The thought speared across his brain like a flash of lightning, stunning in its intensity. As powerful and blinding as the celestial bolt, it was also, at the moment, as distractingly unwelcome.

Gathering his scattered wits, Theo bowed and greeted the trio, then said, "I would be honored to escort one of you ladies inside."

"Thank you, Dunnley. It is very kind of you to offer." The countess stepped forward and took his arm. She was not the partner he had hoped for, but the smile Sarah gave him over her shoulder helped to alleviate his disappointment.

Startled to find himself at the top of the stairs with no memory of climbing them save for a recollection of the gentle sway of Sarah's hips beneath the rose silk gown, Theo flushed, hoping his companion had not noticed the direction of his gaze. "I beg your pardon, my lady. What a rude escort you must think me, woolgathering instead of conversing."

Lady Tregaron smiled and patted his arm. "I don't think anything of the sort, Dunnley. And I am quite accustomed to an escort who falls into a brown study. My husband and son frequently do so."

Grateful that she had not realized the subject of his musings, he offered, "Shall I take them to task for you, my lady?"

The countess's musical laughter bubbled forth. "I can't imagine it would make a whit of difference—at least, not with Tregaron—but I thank you for offering. Llanfyllin is, perhaps, not beyond hope. If ever you see him staring into space when he ought to be paying attention to a lady, you might drop a word in his ear."

"Gladly, ma'am."

They greeted the patronesses; then, while Sarah promenaded on her brother's arm, Theo guided his partner to a chair against the wall. Lady Kesteven sat nearby, her three youngest children gathered around her, and Lady Tregaron smiled her pleasure at his choice. After greetings were exchanged, he seated her, then to pass the time until her children returned, he inquired, "Are your daughter and younger son also inclined to brown studies?"

"Dafydd is not, but he is only eleven, so perhaps he is too young. Sarah is . . ." A slight frown creased the countess's brow. "I don't know that 'brown study' is the proper description. Sarah is a dreamer, but—"

The arrival of the young lady under discussion prevented Theo from learning more. Promising Sarah that he would return for the first minuet, he excused himself, then spoke briefly with Lady Kesteven and her daughters, requesting dances with both girls. Lady Deborah granted him the first waltz; her sister, the second country dance. Or, more accurately, the twin with the amaranth sash—the one he thought was Deborah—was his partner for the waltz.

Lord help him if he'd confused the names and colors since greeting the twins.

As he strolled around the ballroom, in between greeting acquaintances and speaking with his friends, Theo pondered what he had learnt about the Mallory family.

So Sarah is a dreamer, is she? How delightfully unexpected.

And how fortunate the man who was the object of her dreams.

Theo could not help but wonder if he ever figured in her reveries. And how he might ensure himself a leading role in her dreams of the future.

As much as Viscount Dunnley's mere presence disconcerted her, Sarah could not ignore the feeling of disappointment that enveloped her like a dark cloak when he took his leave. Nor could she deny experiencing pangs of something remarkably akin to jealousy as she watched him laughing and chatting with the Woodhurst twins. She did not know if she was envious of the ease with which Deborah conversed with him, or of her friend's ability to draw his smile and laughter, but Sarah would have welcomed the talent to do either. Or both.

Wishing would not make it so. But if she kept her resolution to overcome her shyness and make more effort at conversation, perhaps someday she, too, would draw smiles or a laugh from Dunnley.

How astonishing—and how very, very strange—that such a goal could persuade her to redouble her efforts. But unlikely as it seemed, it had done just that.

Bemused, Sarah shook her head, her eyes following Dunnley's tall, graceful, elegantly clad form on his perambulation around the room. If someone had told her two days ago that she would someday yearn to bring a smile to the handsome viscount's face, Sarah would have laughingly denied such a claim. After all, doing so would require her to spend time in his company—something she did not want to do.

Or did she?

Lord, help me! If I continue like this, I will be a bedlamite before the end of the Season.

Dunnley suddenly appeared before her, and Sarah started guiltily. Although he did not know the direction of her thoughts, she was blushingly aware of them.

He quirked an eyebrow. "Did you think I would forget our dance, Lady Sarah? I assure you, I have been looking forward to it."

Why does he say things like that? Clenching her teeth against a moan of frustration, she shook her head in answer to his query. A fresh wave of color heated her cheeks, the crimson hue no doubt an unattractive contrast to the color of her gown.

Where are your wits? a little voice in her head chided. *Remember your resolution.*

Dragging in a breath, Sarah attempted to comply. "I did not think you would forget, my lord. But I was . . . um, woolgathering and didn't see you approach, so you startled me."

"I beg your pardon." When the musicians played the opening measure, Dunnley reached for her hand and led her toward the dance floor.

"How did you know the first dance would be a minuet and not a waltz promenade?"

His gray eyes twinkling with amusement, he bent his head and whispered, "I asked Sally Jersey."

As she dropped into the deep curtsy that was the opening figure of the dance, Sarah glanced around the room. "It would appear, my lord, that you sacrificed yourself for naught. Sir Edward isn't present this evening."

"It was not—and is not—a sacrifice, Lady Sarah. I enjoy dancing with you."

Color rose to her cheeks again, although not as hotly as before. Gathering her courage, she met his gaze and asked, "Why do you say things like that, my lord?"

"Like what?"

Sarah would have bet her quarterly allowance that he honestly did not know what she meant. "Things that put me to the blush."

Both tawny brows rose. "An honest compliment puts you to the blush?"

"Yours do," she retorted without thinking, then had to stifle a gasp of dismay at such an artless and inadvertent confession. *Lud, what is wrong with me tonight?*

But he did not laugh at her foolish admission. Indeed, he seemed rather disconcerted by it. "I . . . um, I . . ." He glanced away for a moment, as if attempting to recover his composure, then asked, "Why is that, do you suppose?"

"I don't know."

"It is worth considering, is it not?"

She frowned in confusion. "What is?"

"Why my compliments put you to the blush. Do no other gentlemen's have that effect?"

Circling him, she pondered the question. "Sometimes the flowery, blatantly false ones do."

"What do you consider a 'blatantly false' compliment?"

"Dunnley!"

"Yes, my lady?"

"You cannot expect me to repeat such things!"

"Why not? I am trying to understand why my sincere accolades disconcert you."

"Please, may we change the subject?" Sarah begged, dropping her gaze to the top button of his white brocade waistcoat and wishing, as she'd done last night, that a hole would open in the floor and swallow her.

She felt his eyes on her face, scrutinizing her features, before he conceded, with obvious reluctance, "Yes. For now."

"Thank you." She sighed in relief and drew a full breath for the first time since the music had begun.

"Sarah."

"Hmmm?" She prayed, without much hope of success, that he would launch a new, entirely unrelated topic of conversation.

"Look at me, Sarah." It was more command than request, a steely note edging his usual melodious tenor.

Slowly, reluctantly, she dragged her gaze up the pristine folds of his starched cravat—a waterfall—over his chiseled chin and lips, up the blade-straight nose, and met his eyes. There was no twinkle in their gray depths now, no hint of a smile, but there was something. Some softer emotion.

"We will discuss this again, my lady, but not in such a public setting."

Not if I can avoid it in public or in private . "Why?"

Some men might have pretended to misunderstand her, but, to his credit, Dunnley did not. "Because pursuing this conversation may prove beneficial to us both."

Sarah could not imagine why he thought so, nor could she think of any advantage he might gain from such a discussion. But she did not argue, choosing instead to say nothing at all.

Now it was the viscount's turn to sigh. "I am sorry if this conversation has upset you. That certainly was not my intent. But I assure you that any compliments I have given you in the past—and any future ones—are sincere."

"Thank you, my lord."

As they reached the end of the room and turned, he suggested, "Shall we begin anew?"

She nodded, appreciating his thoughtfulness. "I would like that, I think."

"Very well." His lips turned up in a smile that did not reach his eyes. "Good evening, Lady Sarah. You look lovely tonight. That particular shade of pink suits you very well."

She was flattered, of course. What woman would not be? Especially since he just vowed never to offer her Spanish coin. "Thank you, Dunnley."

But, she decided, two could play at this game. "You look quite handsome, too. Black and white evening dress suits you well. Particularly in contrast with the gold of your hair."

His eyes widened in astonishment. Or, perhaps, shock. "Gold, my lady? My hair is brown. Light brown, but brown nonetheless."

"I would describe it as tawny, but it looks almost gold in this light."

"While yours is the blue-black of a raven's wing."

"Oh dear," she muttered, knowing she had ventured into waters far above her head.

He smiled fully then, gray eyes alight. "You have made your point, my dear." Several moments passed before he asked, "Will you be performing at the Duchess of Greenwich's musicale?"

"Yes, I will."

"Would you sing a duet with me?"

"Wh-what?" she stammered, certain she had misunderstood.

"I do not have a particular song in mind. I thought it would be best if we chose together."

"Are you seriously asking me to sing a duet with you?" The incredulity in her voice was not very flattering—to either of them—but Sarah could not prevent it. She required all of her concentration to keep her feet moving in the stately patterns of the minuet, instead of stopping dead and gaping at him.

"Indeed I am." He made no attempt to hide his amusement at her astonishment.

"But you usually sing madrigals in an octet!"

"I will do that, too, but that does not preclude another performance. I would also like to sing a duet with you."

"Why?"

His expression puzzled, he, perhaps unconsciously, turned her previous question back on her. "Are you seriously asking me why I want to sing a duet with you?"

"Yes, I am."

Apparently that was not the answer he expected; he seemed even more bemused. "Did I not know you better, I would think you were fishing for compliments. Since I am certain that is not the case, I cannot help but wonder why such a commonplace request surprises you."

Sarah had no intention of telling him that his request was

not only uncommon, but unprecedented. She was, however, pleased that he knew she was not the kind of girl who sought praise, whether it was deserved or not. Before she could come up with a response, however, he said, slowly, as if speaking his thoughts aloud, "But perhaps I am mistaken. Upon further consideration, I wonder if perchance the other young ladies are too much in awe of your voice and talent to sing with you. Maybe only someone with a strong voice and a great deal of confidence in his or her abilities would risk singing with you, for fear of showing poorly in comparison."

"Balderdash!"

Dunnley's eyes widened at her vehemence. "Is it?" he asked mildly. "And here I thought it quite a reasonable explanation."

Mortified by her unguarded response, Sarah felt the color heating her cheeks and feared her face was the same shocking shade of crimson as Lady Mortimer's gown. "Your explanation may well be correct. I meant that it is foolish for anyone to think of a duet as a . . . a competition."

"Perhaps so, but people can be remarkably foolish sometimes."

"As I have been tonight," Sarah muttered under her breath.

"What was that, my lady?" Dunnley bent his head closer to hers.

"Naught but more of that foolishness you just mentioned." Suddenly changing her mind, she confessed, "Your request did surprise me. No one has ever asked to sing a duet with me before." She glanced away before asking, half fearfully, half hopefully, "Do you truly wish to?"

"Yes, Sarah, I do."

"But you usually sing a cappella madrigals, while I always sing Welsh songs and accompany myself on the harp."

"True, but neither fact prevents us from singing a duet— either a cappella or with your harp. Or accompanied by any other instrument, for that matter."

Since he had not suggested a particular song, she decided to speak her mind on the subject of their proposed duet. "If we are going to sing together, I would prefer not to play the harp."

"And not to sing a cappella, either, I suppose."

It was not really a question, but she answered anyway. "I would rather not."

"If we are going to do something different, it should be quite, quite different?" he suggested, voicing the very thought in Sarah's mind.

"Yes." She smiled up at him. "Surely we can find a pianist to accompany us."

"I am sure that we can. But first, we must decide what to sing." A frown creased his forehead for a moment, then eased. "I am not sure how much, if any, duet music I have here in Town. May I call on you tomorrow or Friday so that we can look over whatever I have, as well as what you have?"

"I am not certain what my mother has planned. Could you come tomorrow morning or Friday morning?"

"Of course," he agreed readily, as if young ladies suggested such early morning visits all the time. "Perhaps before our next dance you can ask your mother which day, and what time, would be best?"

"I will." As the musicians played the last measure of the minuet, she sank into the final curtsy, looking up at him through her lashes. "The third waltz, isn't it?"

"The third waltz," he concurred, the depth of his bow a tribute to her dancing skills.

After escorting her back to her mother, Dunnley bowed over Sarah's hand again, thanked her for the dance, then left to find his next partner. Sarah stared after him, wondering if her wits had gone abegging. Dancing with him was one thing; agreeing to sing a duet with him something altogether different.

I must be all about in the head!

Bats might have taken residence—temporarily—in her belfry, but they were gone now. Sarah vowed to find a simple duet, one that would require only one or two practices with the devilishly disconcerting viscount. Anything more, and those pesky, wing-fluttering butterflies would set up housekeeping—permanently—in her stomach.

Theo was pleased—very pleased—by the success of his impromptu plan to ask Sarah to sing a duet with him at the Duchess of Greenwich's musicale. For the next several hours, he divided his attention between his partners and trying to remember the most difficult duets he had ever heard. Or heard of. He wanted a song that would require at least twice-weekly practices for the next four weeks, but one that was not beyond his abilities. He was a good singer, and his voice would match well with Sarah's, but her talent was far greater than his.

Finding songs that met both criteria would not be easy. Finding one by tomorrow morning might prove impossible. But the difficulty of his self-imposed task would not deter him. Music was one of her passions, and Theo very much wanted to see the passionate side of Lady Sarah Mallory's nature. He hoped their rehearsals would reveal it to him, as well as give him the opportunity to get to know her better.

But rack his brain though he did, he could not think of a single duet that would suit. He solicited Lady Tina's opinion during the first country dance and Lady Deborah's during the first waltz, but Tina did not know any duets, and all of Deborah's suggestions, although lovely songs, were too simple to require as many hours of practice as he desired.

Finally, it was time for the third waltz. As he strode around the perimeter of the ballroom toward Lady Tregaron, he spotted Sarah, who had been cornered by Sir Edward Smithson. Even if Theo had not known of the baronet's reprehensible behavior and Sarah's aversion to the man, her rigid posture and pale, tense face clearly broadcast her distress. Almost before those facts registered in Theo's mind, he changed direction, intent on rescuing her from Nasty Ned.

". . . cannot wait to bury my face between your luscious breasts, and my—"

"Ah, here you are, Lady Sarah," Theo exclaimed from several feet away, hoping his words would drown Smithson's. "I believe this is my dance." Extending a hand to her, he used the other to lift his quizzing glass to his eye, then subjected the baronet to a pointed, and rather protracted, head-to-toe scrutiny.

Her beautiful blue eyes conveyed her gratitude more eloquently than any words she might have spoken. As did the speed and fervor with which she grasped his hand. "Indeed it is, my lord."

Giving Sarah's hand a reassuring squeeze, he led her away from the odious baronet. Without taking leave of

Smithson. Without, in fact, having acknowledged him in any way. It was not the cut direct—he had surveyed "Nasty Ned" at length—but it was unquestionably a cut. The gasps and titters that followed in their wake made it clear that everyone in the vicinity had understood Theo's actions, as well as his intent.

Once they had moved out of earshot, Sarah drew in a shuddering breath and, in a soft voice that wobbled rather alarmingly, said, "Thank you, Dunnley."

He smiled, hoping to cheer her. "You looked like a damsel . . ." *In distress.* "In need of rescuing."

"A damsel in distress is what you are no doubt thinking, but are too much the gentleman to say. And I was. But your rescue was as gallant and chivalrous as any performed by the knights of yore."

"My armor may be a bit rusty, but I will gladly assist you, my lady. Always."

"Thank you, kind sir." Her face still pale, she smiled up at him.

Slowing their pace, lest they reach the dance floor before she could answer, Theo asked, "Shall we dance? Or would you prefer to sit out this set?"

"Have you changed your mind? You need not dance with me if you would prefer another partner, my lord."

Chagrined that she had so misinterpreted his intentions, he flushed. *Lord, when was the last time that had happened?* "Nothing would please me more than to waltz with you, Lady Sarah. My question, maladroit as it was, was intended to allow you to change *your* mind if the encounter with Smithson upset you."

"Oh." She ducked her head as if embarrassed. "I beg your pardon, Dunnley. It did upset me, but not in the way you mean. I was not distraught—well, I was, but mostly I was angry."

"And rightly so." As the musicians played the first chords of the waltz, he quipped, "Has the urge to slap someone passed?"

She choked on a giggle. "Yes, it has."

"Then waltz with me, my lady."

Circling the floor with Sarah in his arms, Theo was buffeted by the strangest mix of feelings. Admiration. Euphoria. A fierce, unprecedented protectiveness. The urge to take Sarah

somewhere private and kiss her breathless, so he could discover if she was as passionate as he suspected, warred with
an equally powerful impulse to pummel Smithson bloody.

He wanted to hear her laugh with delight. He wanted to
carry her off to his bed and introduce her to the joys of
passion. He wanted to make her happy, not just for a few
hours tonight, but always. To care for her, now and forever.
In essence, he wanted to convince her that he was the perfect husband for her.

Beating his head against a wall might be easier and less
painful. Sarah was not ready to hear any of that. And convincing her of his worthiness might take some time. Theo
hoped his resolve would not falter before he did.

Chapter Six

*T*he suddenness of it was almost Sarah's undoing. One
minute she was so furiously angry at Sir Edward that
she wanted to kick him in the shins, grind her heel down
on his instep, then on his toes, and punch him in the nose.
The next moment she wanted to throw her arms around
Dunnley and thank him for rescuing her. Or, perhaps, just
to throw herself into Dunnley's arms.

The turbulent shift of emotions was disorienting. For a
moment Sarah forgot where she was. Indeed, she would
have been hard-pressed to say *who* she was.

Somehow, though, she must have thanked Dunnley for
rescuing her, and responded appropriately to his questions
and comments. If she hadn't, he would not be smiling at
her as he was now. Nor saying, in a way that made her
toes curl inside her dancing slippers, "Then waltz with me,
my lady."

As she moved within the circle of his arm, Sarah wondered if she had imagined the intimate tone of his voice.
Or the slight emphasis on the words "my lady." It had
sounded almost like an endearment.

A thrill shivered through her. She fought the urge to press herself against him, to climb inside his jacket and . . .

"Sarah."

The sharp note underlying the whisper-soft word brought her to her senses. Given the wayward direction of her thoughts, she could not—dared not—meet his gaze, but she did manage to nod.

She felt the tension ease from the muscles in his hands and arms. Felt, too, the movement of his fingers against the small of her back, and was comforted by the caress. "Don't fall apart on me now. You are doing wonderfully well. Just hold on until the end of the dance, and I will take you outside."

Praying that she could hold on, that she would not react in her usual goosish way, Sarah nodded. A breath of fresh air sounded wonderful, but she knew he only meant out of the ballroom. They would not be private there, but neither would there be quite so many watchful eyes. "Thank you, Dunnley."

"You are as brave as you are beautiful."

Her gaze slewed upward, locking with his. The gray eyes met hers levelly, his sincerity—and his admiration—apparent. Disconcerted again, although for different reasons, she begged, "Talk to me, please." Then, because she needed distraction, not conversation, she amended, "Tell me about yourself."

She felt his start of surprise at the naked pleading in her voice, heard and felt the sharply indrawn breath that followed. His concern for her almost palpable, he ordered, "Take a deep breath, Sarah. And keep your eyes on mine."

Her first breath sounded almost like a gasp, so she took another.

"Good girl," he commended, a smile of approval curving his lips and brightening his eyes. "Just listen to the music and don't think about Smithson—or anyone else."

As if any young lady could think of another man while waltzing with the handsome, charming, oh so gentlemanly viscount! Especially when she was the sole object of his attention. Sarah could not say that, of course. She was not altogether certain she could say anything at all—nothing, rather, that wouldn't make her sound even more piteous than her last unguarded utterance—so she nodded to indicate her compliance.

"I am nine-and-twenty, and I have held the title since I was twelve . . ."

Sarah let the words wash over her, feeling strengthened by his calm tone and steady gaze. Strange as it sounded, she felt . . . sheltered by his assurance, his air of command, his competent handling of what could have been a very unpleasant situation. He had rescued her after Sir Edward cornered her, taken control from the leering baronet and into his own hands. Taken her in hand, too. A very good thing, indeed, since her emotions had been running amok since Nasty Ned approached. And, in its own way, another heroic rescue. If left to her own devices, she might well have besmirched her reputation by bolting from the ballroom at the first opportunity.

Not only had Dunnley saved her, he had also turned the tables on the loathsome baronet, routing the rotter. It was, Sarah suspected, a new—or, at least, quite an uncommon—experience for Sir Edward, since, from what she had seen and heard, he preyed on those younger, smaller, and weaker than himself. Particularly young ladies, who could do little to defend themselves without courting social ruin.

Fear of ruination had been her main concern tonight when Nasty Ned confronted her. Five of the patronesses were present this evening! They were known for spotting every *faux pas* young ladies made within these hallowed halls, but apparently they were blind to men's more heinous transgressions.

"Dunnley, why do the patronesses allow Sir Edward to attend? One would think his reputation and behavior more than enough reason to refuse him entrance."

"An excellent question, my dear. Unfortunately, it isn't one that I can answer. You would have to ask one of the patronesses."

"I can hardly do that!"

"I suppose not. But I can ask them. And I will," he promised.

"Thank you."

As the waltz wound to a close, Sarah began to tremble. Neither clenching her teeth nor tensing her muscles had the slightest effect; the tremors became more violent with each measure.

Dunnley looked sharply at her, then drew her closer. "Sarah, what is wrong?"

Lud! I am about to make a complete cake of myself in the middle of Almack's, and he asks what is wrong? "Get me out of here. Quickly."

Though the words were forced out between gritted teeth, he understood the urgency of her plea and whirled them nearer to the entrance. He looked over her shoulder, his eyes scanning the room. Apparently espying the person he sought, he gestured with his head, twice.

Praying for the dance to end before her legs would no longer support her, Sarah had little thought to spare for his actions. "Please get me out of here," she begged.

"I will. The moment the dance ends."

He was as good as his word. The instant the final chord died, he tucked her hand in the crook of his arm and led her from the ballroom, nodding at Lady Sefton, who stood in the doorway, as they passed.

Once they were in the corridor, he turned toward the card room. Sarah, her eyes closed in an effort to hold onto a semblance of composure, had no idea where he was leading her. Nor did she care, as long as their destination was far from the scandalmongers' eyes.

Theo kept his eyes on Sarah's pale face as he led her toward a small room just past the card room. As he hoped, it was empty, so he led her inside and, after a moment's hesitation, closed the door.

It was a risk—a thoroughly compromising situation if anyone other than Sarah's brother followed them, and possibly even then—but her reputation would suffer as much or more, albeit in a different way, if anyone saw her now.

She stood with her head bent and her arms wrapped tightly around her waist, trembling even more violently than before. Stepping close behind her, he put his hands on her shoulders. *Lord, she is cold!*

"Sarah, what is wrong?" He rubbed her arms from shoulder to elbow, hoping the brisk strokes would warm her.

"I don't know." She sounded miserable. And frightened.

"Is it a belated reaction to your encounter with Smithson?"

"Yes."

His hands on her shoulders, he turned her to face him. Then, hoping to both warm her and comfort her, he wrapped his arms around her and drew her close. "Shhh. Everything is fine, Sarah."

Somewhat to his surprise, she was not crying. But she was still trembling, and still far from her usual calm, composed self.

Theo had never felt so damned helpless in his life.

Nor, after guiding her head to rest on his shoulder, quite so content.

Stroking his hand along her spine, he felt the tension cording the muscles of her back. "Relax, Sarah. You are safe from Smithson now."

He thought he heard the door open and close behind him. But no cries of shock and outrage followed the soft *snick-snick*, and when he glanced over his shoulder, no one was there. Hoping they were still undiscovered, he tightened his embrace slightly and continued his efforts to comfort and reassure Sarah. Having just realized that his purpose in life was to take care of her and make her happy, Theo intended to devote himself to the pleasurable task with every resource at his command. And all the love brimming in his heart.

It took the better part of a set of country dances for her to regain her composure. When she did, she gave a shuddering breath, then stepped back and turned away, her face downcast and her cheeks flushed with embarrassment. "Thank you, Dunnley. I am more grateful than I can say, and so very sorry I subjected you to that . . . that . . ."

"Don't distress yourself, my dear. You have done nothing that requires an apology. I am glad I was able to help you, although, in truth, I did very little."

Her head came up at that, her eyes locking on his. "That is not true—"

Smiling slightly, he shook his head. "Let's not argue about it. Instead, if you feel up to it, I would like to ask you a few questions."

"What—" She sighed and studied the toes of her dancing slippers, then rather reluctantly agreed. "Ask your questions. I will try to answer them."

"Was Smithson nastier than usual tonight?"

She darted a look at him, as if surprised by the question.

Judging by her hesitation, it was not one she wanted to answer. Or, perhaps, one she didn't know how to answer.

"I know it is an impertinent question, as well as none of my business, but I—"

"Since you rescued me, you have the right to ask. I just . . ." Frowning, she bit her lower lip. "I . . . It . . . What he said was much the same as always. At least, I think it was—I never understand above half of what he says."

And thank God for that! "Go on."

"I don't think he said anything very different, but it bothers me that he said it here, where any number of people might have walked by and overheard."

That bothered Theo, too. Greatly. "Is he usually not so bold?"

"He has spoken so in ballrooms—they are generally the only places I encounter him. But until tonight, it has always been during a dance, or while escorting me to or from the dance floor, when there was less chance of being overheard."

"So his manner was bolder tonight, even though his words were not?"

"Yes, that's it exactly!" She flashed a thankful but fleeting smile. "I could not have phrased it half so well, but that was the most disturbing difference tonight."

"You give yourself too little credit, and me too much. I only summarized what you already said. Remember, I have the advantage, if such it can be called, of having known Nasty Ned since Eton."

"I would not consider long acquaintance with Sir Edward any kind of advantage."

"A double-edged one at best."

Frowning again, she hesitantly, almost reluctantly asked, "Do you think that this new boldness will continue?"

"Much as I would like to say otherwise, I think it is quite likely."

She huffed out a breath that was half sigh, half exclamation of dismay. "I feared that would be your answer."

"I am sorry, Sarah. Instead of worrying about that, let's consider how best to thwart him."

"An excellent idea, Dunnley, but this is not the time or place for such a discussion."

Theo started—badly—at the sound of Lady Tregaron's

voice. Flushing like a schoolboy caught in mid-prank, he spun around to find her and Llanfyllin standing no more than two feet behind him. "My lady, I—"

Her eyes steady on his face and her voice firm, the countess said, "You escorted Sarah from the ballroom when she was feeling unwell, and stayed with her until she recovered. Laudable deeds both, and I thank you most sincerely."

It was quite obvious that she was telling them the formal explanation for their departure and absence from the assembly room. Theo nodded to indicate he understood. "I am glad that I was able to help."

Llanfyllin moved past and slipped an arm around his sister's waist. "Come, *bach*. It is time to go home."

Sarah stumbled, and Theo feared she would fall, but her brother said something short—and sharp—in Welsh that straightened her spine. It also garnered a glare, which the young man ignored. Worried, Theo asked the countess, "Is Sarah ill?"

She sighed. "Not ill, exactly. Sarah hates conflict of any kind. When she is frightened, she hides her fear and keeps her head until the crisis has passed, but afterward . . . It is like watching a tightly wound clock spring come uncoiled. All the terror she held at bay overwhelms her, and she trembles—violently, sometimes—and often faints."

"Sarah did tremble violently tonight, but not until near the end of the waltz. She didn't faint, though. But she begged me to take her out of the ballroom quickly, so she may have feared that she would."

"Undoubtedly so."

"Will she soon recover?"

"She will be fine after a good night's sleep."

Greatly relieved, he offered his arm to Lady Tregaron. "May I escort you downstairs, my lady?"

"Thank you, Dunnley. And thank you again for helping Sarah tonight. Not only for escorting her from the ballroom, but also for rescuing her from Sir Edward."

"I was happy to do both."

"Sarah mentioned earlier that you wanted to call tomorrow or Friday to look at some duet music. Although I said Friday, under the circumstances, I think tomorrow would be best."

"Sooner is probably better." Sooner was most definitely

better, but Theo did not want to worry Lady Tregaron any more than she already was.

"Is ten o'clock too early? I want my husband and son to hear your ideas for thwarting Sir Edward."

"Ten o'clock is fine." Having Tregaron and Llanfyllin there was both an advantage and a disadvantage. Theo would only have to explain his as yet nonexistent plans once, but he would have to word his explanation very carefully in order to convey his concerns to the men without alarming Sarah and her mother.

They reached the street just as the Tregaron town coach pulled to a stop. Theo bid Sarah good night, brushing a kiss against her gloved hand as he bowed over it. Turning back to assist the countess into the vehicle, he saw a smile teasing the corner of her mouth. "Was my bow not *comme il faut*, my lady? Or is it I that amuse you?"

"Your manners are faultless, Dunnley. You are a gentleman to the core."

As he watched the carriage drive away, Theo could not help but wonder if there was some deeper meaning in Lady Tregaron's last statement. And to wonder just how long she and Llanfyllin had been in that little room upstairs.

Chapter Seven

*P*ropped up in bed against a pile of pillows as she drank her morning chocolate, Sarah's memories of the assembly seemed disjointed, like pieces of a puzzle that would not quite fit together. She recalled portions of the evening clearly, others not at all. The early events—from the opening minuet with Dunnley to dances with Howe, Fairfax, and a succession of other gentlemen—were as sharply etched in her mind as the facets of her mother's Waterford goblets. The middle of the evening was blurry; the end, blank as a freshly washed slate.

Rhys had once described the effects—and aftereffects—

of a night of drinking, and the resulting gaps in his memory. She seemed to be experiencing much the same phenomenon this morning, despite having drunk nothing stronger than lemonade!

Vowing to unravel the mystery, she replayed the evening in her mind, beginning from the moment she'd stepped out of the carriage. The unexpected meeting with Dunnley on the pavement, then Rhys escorting her up the stairs while the viscount gallanted her mother. Sarah remembered talking with Deborah Woodhurst and Tina Fairchild, and giggling over the latter's most recent escapade. Remembered, too, wishing she had the other girls' ability to converse with gentlemen, and resolving anew to overcome her shyness— a resolution she now, perhaps incorrectly, attributed to a desire to draw Dunnley's smile and laughter. His request that she sing a duet with him at the Greenwiches' musicale was vividly clear, as was her determination to choose a simple song that would require only one or two practices.

She knew she had danced every set. Every set, that is, until the confrontation with Sir Edward Smithson. After that, her recollections were decidedly murky, save for the utter certainty that she'd avoided dancing with the leering baronet.

Throwing back the blankets, she rose and reached for her dressing gown. But although she paced the length and breadth of her bedchamber, an activity that usually helped her think, her memory was no clearer than before. Frustrated, she abandoned the effort for the nonce and crossed to her dressing room to make her morning ablutions. Then, wearing a new morning gown of muslin sprigged with deep blue forget-me-nots, with long sleeves that buttoned at the wrist, Sarah draped a kasimir shawl around her shoulders and wandered downstairs, humming *Llwyn On*. Or, as the English called it, *The Ash Grove*.

When she entered the dining room, her mother was seated in her usual place at the foot of the table, drinking a cup of tea and reading the newspaper. The countess's portion of the morning mail—a dozen or more letters, most probably invitations—was piled on a salver to her left, awaiting her attention.

"Good morning, *bach*. Did you sleep well?"

Amused as always that her mother, who was several

inches shorter, still called her "little one," Sarah bent to kiss her mother's cheek. "Good morning, *Mam*."

Once the butler had seated Sarah in her usual place to the countess's right and served her, she turned her attention to her breakfast, wondering how best to question her mother about the latter portion of the previous evening.

There was no good way, she decided, stifling a sigh. "Mama, what happened at Almack's last night?"

Her mother's dark eyebrows arched in surprise. "What happened?" she queried, clearly puzzled. Or, perhaps, confused by the question.

"It is very strange. I remember everything that happened before Sir Edward waylaid me to request a dance, but after that, I can recall almost nothing."

"Hmmm . . . What do you recall after that odious man confronted you?"

"I vaguely recall Dunnley rescuing me from Smithson, although I cannot say how he came to do so, nor how he accomplished the feat."

The countess nodded but said nothing. Feeling foolish, Sarah continued, "I *think* I danced another set with Dunnley later in the evening, but I am not altogether certain. I have tried to remember the particulars of that dance, if indeed there was one, but it is like . . . like trying to grab a wisp of morning fog."

She clenched her fists as if trying to catch the elusive fog, although she did not realize that she had until her mother's hands covered hers.

"You did, indeed, dance again with Dunnley. He partnered you in the waltz immediately after he rescued you from Sir Edward."

"But why can't I remember it?" Sarah all but wailed. "Or anything else?"

"Because, dearling, you began to feel unwell during the waltz. So poorly, in fact, that Dunnley took you out of the ballroom as soon as the dance was over. We left shortly afterward."

"But I feel fine now."

"I am glad to hear it." The countess lifted a hand to cup Sarah's cheek. "Dunnley will be here in"—she glanced at the enameled watch pinned to her bodice—"about an hour. You can ask him then how he rescued you from Smithson."

"An hour! I haven't looked through my music yet." Sarah pushed back from the table, but her mother gripped her hand to halt the motion.

"Dunnley isn't coming to peruse duet music. Well, he may do that, too, but it is not the main reason for his visit."

"Then why is he coming?"

"To discuss with us his ideas for stopping, or at least thwarting, Sir Edward."

"Wonderful! I hope Dunnley has a lot of ideas. . . . Oh dear!" Sarah sat down again with a decidedly unladylike thump.

"What is wrong?"

"Papa doesn't know—"

"I told your father about Sir Edward last night."

"Was Papa very angry?"

"He was furious." Quickly, her mother added, "Not at you, *bach*. At Sir Edward."

"Oh." Weak with relief—she adored her father and hated being at odds with him—it was the best response Sarah could contrive.

"If you have finished eating, why don't you look through your music until Dunnley arrives?"

"Perhaps I will."

As she climbed the stairs, Sarah felt strangely unsettled about seeing Dunnley. So much so that when she reached the drawing room, she did not even glance at the cabinet that held the family's music. Instead, she seated herself at her harp, hoping the familiar notes and rhythms of her favorite songs would restore her composure. And her memory.

Given that Dunnley had rescued her from Nasty Ned last night, she ought to be pleased that she would have the chance to thank him in such a timely—and relatively private—manner. And, indeed, she was, since she could not remember if she had thanked him last night. Even so, the thought of seeing him was even more disconcerting than usual. She had the lowering feeling that she might have disgraced herself in some way last evening, and forfeited all or part of his esteem. Why that troubled her so, she was not certain. But it did.

Lud, what a muddle!

* * *

Arriving at Tregaron House a few minutes before ten o'clock, Theo was immediately ushered into a charming, sunlit morning room, where he was warmly welcomed by the earl, Lady Tregaron, and Llanfyllin. Sarah was not present. Theo did not know if she was still feeling unwell, or if there was a more ominous reason for her absence. Suspecting the latter, since no servant was sent in search of her, nor was any explanation given for her absence, Theo squared his shoulders and faced the earl.

"Lord Tregaron, I am aware that my actions last night may have compromised your daughter's reputation—"

"Dunnley!" The countess stared at him as if he'd lost his wits. "You did no such thing. Quite the opposite, in fact."

The earl's smile was wry. "Prepared to sacrifice yourself on honor's altar, are you?"

"I don't see it as a sacrifice, sir," Theo said rather stiffly, "but I am prepared to make your daughter an offer if you—or she—believe it is necessary."

"I do not. Nor does my wife. It is my understanding that you escorted Sarah from the ballroom because she was not feeling well."

"Yes, sir, that is true. But anyone who saw us would not know—"

"Anyone who saw you would have seen Rhys leave, too," Lady Tregaron countered.

Theo was a bit surprised by the countess's staunch defense. Many mothers would take advantage of the situation to marry their daughter to a wealthy, eligible peer. Although he was glad the countess was not of that ilk, honor compelled him to add, "You should be aware that Lady Sarah and I may have been seen alone together. Shortly after we entered the room, someone opened the door. I did not see who—"

"That was me," Llanfyllin said. "Unless the door was opened more than once?"

"I only heard it open once."

"Mystery solved." The younger man grinned. "I followed you, saw that Sarah was upset, and went to get Mother."

"I fear you mistake my meaning. I only heard the door open once," Theo repeated. "I did not hear you and Lady Tregaron enter, so if anyone else opened the door, I may not have heard them, either."

"So it is possible that you and Sarah were seen alone together," the earl summarized. "You don't know if you were, but you cannot say for certain that you weren't."

"Exactly, sir."

"In that case, perhaps we should wait and see if there is any gossip."

"Perhaps," Theo countered, "we should allow Lady Sarah to make the decision. She may believe that being alone with me compromised her reputation."

"Oh dear." For the first time, Lady Tregaron sounded truly distressed.

"Is something wrong, my lady?" Theo asked, just as the earl inquired, "What is it, Bronwen?"

The countess looked from one man to the other, then sighed. "Sarah remembers almost nothing after Dunnley rescued her from Smithson."

"What?" All three men spoke simultaneously.

Judging from Tregaron's and Llanfyllin's reactions, loss of memory was not Sarah's usual reaction to a terrifying incident. *What the hell had Smithson said to her last night?*

After recounting the conversation with her daughter, the countess said, "I think leaving the decision to Sarah will only confuse her more."

Theo glanced from Lady Tregaron's distraught countenance to the earl's bewildered but very concerned one, then back. "You know your daughter far better than I do, but given what you have just told us, ma'am, I think it essential that Lady Sarah decide."

Both Sarah's parents, as well as her brother, frowned as they attempted to follow his logic. The countess was the first to abandon the effort and ask, "Why so, Dunnley?"

Although he strongly believed that the choice should be Sarah's, Theo was not at all certain that he could explain the reasons for his conviction. "Aside from the fact that Sarah is the person whose life will be most affected by the decision, by allowing her to make the choice, we give her control over what must seem a frightening situation."

"You would sacrifice your bachelorhood just to make Sarah feel better?" Llanfyllin blurted, incredulous.

"But how can she decide if she doesn't remember what happened?" the countess expostulated.

Tregaron steepled his fingers and peered at Theo over

the top of his spectacles. "Your concern for my daughter is admirable, Dunnley, and your arguments solid . . ."

"But?" Having heard a number of the earl's speeches in Lords begin in much the same manner, Theo was certain that Tregaron had a counterargument.

"But my wife and son have raised valid points, too. It will be difficult, if not impossible, for Sarah to make a decision if she doesn't remember what happened last night. And you might well be sacrificing your bachelorhood just to give her some command over these quite exceptional circumstances. It is my understanding that you escorted Sarah from the ballroom at her request."

It was not really a question, but Theo chose to treat it as one. "Yes, sir. Toward the end of the waltz, she began to tremble—visibly and uncontrollably—and she begged me to take her from the ballroom as quickly as possible. Which I did, as soon as the dance ended. Fortunately, I was able to catch your son's eye"—he did not attempt to pronounce the younger man's title, fearing that, nervous as he was, he would mangle it—"and signal him to follow."

"Did my daughter give a reason for her behavior or her extraordinary request?"

Thinking back, Theo could not remember if she had. "I don't believe so, sir. But neither did I ask. I assumed she was having some sort of belated reaction to her encounter with Smithson. I also assumed that she wanted to leave the room so that no one would see her . . . er, her loss of composure."

"Hmmm . . ." The earl pulled off his spectacles and, holding them by an earpiece, began twirling them in a perfect circle. It was obviously a habit of long standing. Judging from the expressions on the countess's and Llanfyllin's faces, it was also one that amused Tregaron's family. Looking from one member to the other, Theo was struck by the realization that the children combined the best features of both parents. Sarah and her older brother had the countess's midnight black hair, vivid blue eyes with long, curly lashes, and porcelain skin, though Llanfyllin's complexion was a bit darker due to his fondness for sporting pursuits; they also had their father's height, lean frame, and facial features. In addition, Sarah had inherited her mother's curvaceous form. Given the marked resemblance between

Llanfyllin and Sarah, Theo suspected that the youngest Mallory had the same distinctive features.

Lady Tregaron grasped her husband's wrist, stilling the spectacles' motion and recalling his attention to the room's other occupants. "It is quite a facer," he admitted.

Uncertain which of the several problems confronting them had exercised the earl's mind, Theo hoped the rest of the man's conversation would not be as cryptic. When Tregaron said nothing more, his wife prompted, "What is, dear?"

"Whether or not Sarah should decide—or even can decide—if her reputation was compromised by spending a few minutes alone with Dunnley."

His emotions fluctuating between delight and dismay, Theo offered what he hoped would be a compelling argument. "Would your decision be easier, sir, if I tell you that if my offer is not accepted today, I intend to court your daughter?"

The earl's brows lowered. "To court her?"

Hoping the frown was one of confusion and not appalled shock, Theo explained, "To dance with her as often as possible, call frequently, take her driving in the park. And to offer to escort Sarah and Lady Tregaron to social events any time you or your son are unable to do so."

Tregaron's brow unfurrowed, but he said nothing. The countess, however, was smiling and quite voluble. "Thank you, Dunnley. I know Sarah would enjoy dancing and driving with you. We would be pleased to accept your escort, too. In fact, if you are not otherwise engaged, you may begin this evening, since Tregaron cannot attend the Enderby ball."

"I would be honored to, ma'am—if Lord Tregaron does not object to my courtship of Sarah."

The earl gestured as if brushing away any objections, then apparently changed his mind. "Perhaps you and I should talk privately for a few minutes, Dunnley."

Since he'd come to his feet on the words, Theo knew it was more command than suggestion. "Of course, sir." He rose and followed the earl from the room.

Waved to a seat in front of the earl's desk in his study, and feeling rather like a schoolboy called before the headmaster, Theo resisted the urge to squirm. Tregaron subjected him to a piercing scrutiny before leaning back in his chair. "Now, if I understood you correctly, you are not asking for permission to pay your addresses to Sarah. You merely stated your intention of courting her."

"Yes, sir, that is correct." After a beat of silence, Theo amended, "Or, to put it more precisely, if you choose not to let Sarah decide whether or not her reputation was compromised by being alone with me last evening, then I am not *at this time* asking permission to pay my addresses to her. If, however, you intend to allow Sarah to make that decision, then I am, indeed, asking permission to offer for her."

"How can she make that judgment if she doesn't remember what happened?"

"With all due respect, sir, once I have described the events she does not recall, she will be better able to make that decision than you are now."

A smile twitched one corner of the earl's mouth, then disappeared. "This explanation, will it be private or public?"

Although he hoped to make it in private, Theo had no choice but to say, "I daresay it would be easier for Sarah if it were private, but I will offer it in whatever setting you and Lady Tregaron deem best."

"Why do you think Sarah would prefer a private explanation? Did you commit some impropriety of which my wife is unaware?"

"No, sir, I did not," Theo snapped, seething at the insult. *How dare he impugn my honor!* The earl raised a placating hand, indicating that no insult was intended.

Struggling to find a civil tone, Theo silently counted to ten and took a deep breath. "If I woke up and couldn't remember some of the previous night's events, I would question my sanity. Perhaps even wonder if I were a candidate for Bedlam. Sarah probably feels foolish at the least, maybe even a bit freakish. The fewer people watching her trying to remember, the easier it will be for her."

The earl nodded. "I hadn't considered that, but you are right. Sarah does not like to be the focus of attention."

"If you are concerned about the proprieties, sir . . . Sarah probably would not object to her mother's presence, since she told Lady Tregaron about her memory loss."

"Perhaps we should leave that choice to Sarah as well," Tregaron said, his tone abstracted. But there was nothing vague about the steely glare that accompanied his next statement. "My wife said that when she and Rhys entered the room, Sarah was crying on your shoulder."

His cravat suddenly too tight, Theo clasped his hands so that he would not tug on it. "She wasn't crying, sir. Although obviously distraught, she never shed a tear. She did, however, have her head on my shoulder. And I was holding her in a loose embrace and rubbing her back, trying to comfort her."

Surprisingly, the earl did not comment on that impropriety. "Why did you close the door?"

"Because I knew Sarah would be even more upset if anyone witnessed her distress."

"Hmmm . . ."

Watching Tregaron deliberate his choices, Theo could not predict which outcome was more likely. Nor could he have stated with any surety which result he hoped for. He loved Sarah, and he believed that they would suit, and suit well. But how could he be certain when he did not know her feelings? How could he know how well matched they were when he had never kissed her, never held her except to comfort her?

Ah, but there had been hints, tantalizing glimpses of the fire beneath her reserve and regal, composed façade . . .

"Hmmm . . ." the earl said again. "Explain to me what exactly you intend to do if I allow Sarah to decide whether or not her reputation was compromised last night."

"First, I will tell her what happened after I rescued her from Smithson. Then, I will explain that we were alone together for a time—I don't know how long myself—"

"According to my wife, the four of you left Almack's almost half an hour after you escorted Sarah from the ballroom. You and Sarah were not alone together all that time, of course."

"Does Lady Tregaron know how long we were alone?" Anticipating the earl's next question, Theo added, "Sarah may well ask me that."

"About ten minutes. Rhys had to escort his partner to her chaperone before he could follow you, and once he found you and informed my wife that Sarah was unwell,

Lady Tregaron had to make their good-byes before she could leave."

Frowning, Theo thought back to the previous night. *Sarah felt so good, so right, in my arms, but surely I can remember more than just how wonderful—and wonderfully right—it felt to hold her.* A sudden feeling of alarm skittered down his spine. "Much as I hate to say it, sir, I do not think it could have been your son I heard opening the door. Well, not unless he is much more efficient at dispatching his dance partners than I am."

Tension—or worry—strangled Tregaron's laugh; it emerged as more of a snort. "I don't suppose Rhys raced her back to her chaperone and ran from the room, but he does not have your address, Dunnley."

Although pleased by the compliment, especially offered by this man at this particular time, Theo was more concerned about Sarah's reputation. "I *think* the door opened before your son could have found us."

"Lord!" Tregaron rubbed his hands over his face, then dragged his fingers through his gray-flecked, dark brown hair. "Let's ignore that problem until I resolve this one. You intend to tell Sarah what happened after you rescued her from Smithson. . . . Do you think—" He shook his head. "Forget that for now, too, but remind me later that I have a question about Smithson."

Theo nodded, then resumed his much-interrupted explanation. "I will tell her about my rescue and our waltz, explain that we were alone together for a time, and that it is possible—quite likely, in fact—that we were seen together, either entering the room or inside it. Finally, I will ask her to do me the honor of becoming my wife."

"She will know that honor prompted your offer."

"Undoubtedly so, sir, but . . ." Theo shrugged. That was not, to his mind, such a disadvantage. Or it hadn't been until he realized that someone had seen him and Sarah together. He'd been hoping that she would refuse him today, so she could choose him freely later. Now he was not at all certain that she could have such freedom of choice.

In a mild voice that belied his gimlet gaze, Tregaron inquired, "Do you feel any affection for my daughter? Are you even the least bit smitten?"

Theo almost laughed. "I have the greatest admiration

and respect for your daughter. I value her friendship. I am
in awe of her talent—her musical talent, though I don't
doubt that she has others of which I am unaware. But I
am not smitten. Fascinated, yes. Intrigued, yes. Even a bit
in love with her." He was fathoms deep in love, but unwilling to confess to Sarah's father at this time. "But smitten,
no. That is far too weak a description of my feelings."

"Ah." The earl leaned back in his seat, looking happier,
as well as a bit relieved. With his elbows braced on the
chair arms, he tapped his steepled forefingers against his
lips. "You are able to support a wife in the style to which
my daughter is accustomed?"

Although he resented the question, Theo could not deny
Tregaron's right to ask it. "I believe so, sir. I have five
estates, of which Dunnley Park is the largest and most pros-
perous, a townhouse on Upper Grosvenor Street, a hunting
box near Melton, and an annual income of forty to fifty
thousand pounds, depending on crop prices and the success
of various investments."

The earl's eyes, which had widened when he heard the
size of Theo's income, narrowed a bit. "How much of your
income results from investments?"

"About twenty percent. Perhaps a bit less."

"How large is Dunnley Park?"

"Nearly fifty thousand acres."

"How close to fifty thousand?"

"Forty-seven thousand nine hundred eight-six acres."
Keeping a neutral tone was increasingly difficult, but Theo
managed it.

Tregaron's smile was wry—and a bit chagrined. "I
thought that was a diplomatic way to determine how ac-
tively involved you are in the estate's management, but
obviously I was mistaken."

Theo chuckled, his annoyance forgotten. "Not diplomatic
perhaps, but I daresay the result is more revealing than
asking outright."

"Dunnley Park is reasonably close to London, isn't it?
In Hampshire or Buckinghamshire?"

"Closer than Wales, certainly. It is in Hampshire."

"Anything south of the North Riding is closer," the earl
said dryly. "Where are your other estates? I don't suppose
you have one in Wales . . . ?"

"Not in Wales, no. The others are in Kent, Shropshire—western Shropshire, in fact—Norfolk, and Northumberland."

"I shall endeavor to convince my lady wife that western Shropshire only *borders* the back of beyond."

Theo laughed, then promised, "And if Sarah accepts my offer, either today or later this Season, I shall endeavor to spend more time at that estate."

"Debts, encumbrances, mortgages?" The earl's tone was brisk, as if he felt he had to ask for duty's sake.

"No mortgages or debts. The only money I owe is to tradesmen for purchases made this month." Theo knew some people thought him odd to pay bills promptly, but tradesmen had to feed and clothe their families, too. "As for encumbrances, my brother, great-uncle, and great-aunt receive allowances from the estate's coffers."

"Your brother is in the army?"

"Yes, the Seventh Hussars, although he has been here for about a month, recovering from a hip wound."

"He is making a good recovery, I hope?"

"Yes"—Theo nodded—"he seems to be, although not as quickly as he would like."

"Are your relatives in Town for the Season?"

"Stephen—my brother—is. So is Uncle Michael. He is the Bishop of Lymington, and he can be found in Lords most days."

"Good God! I have known him for years, but never realized . . ." The earl shook his head as if astounded by his obtuseness. "Is your aunt in Town, too?"

"My great-aunt is not. She dislikes traveling and rarely ventures far from Dunnley Park. But my Aunt Caroline—Lady Richard Winterbrook—is here."

"One more question, then we will return to the problem of what to do."

"You may ask as many questions as you feel are necessary, sir." Politeness decreed that response. Theo had not expected that the obligatory parental interrogation would feel quite so intrusive. It was rather like baring his soul.

"Just one." Tregaron's tapping fingers did not hide his wry smile. "I well remember having this interview with Caradoc—my father-in-law."

"I didn't know the late duke well, but I suspect he was a skilled inquisitor."

"Yes, he was."

After a moment of reminiscence, the earl's gaze sharpened into one of his hawkish stares. "If you marry my daughter, either because of this incident or later in the Season, do you intend to honor your marriage vows? *All* your marriage vows?"

Theo felt the rush of hot color to his face and had to avert his gaze. *This was soul-baring indeed!*

Almost apologetically, Tregaron added, "I ask because you are reputed to be a bit of a rake." •

"Am I?" Gritting his teeth, Theo fought to maintain a neutral tone. "I have kept a mistress for several years and, on occasion, have enjoyed the favors of willing widows."

He forced himself to meet the earl's eyes. "I believe in the sanctity of the marriage vows, and I will honor all of them. Just as I will honor the promises I make to you today."

"Thank you for answering. It was a demmed impertinent question, but I love my daughter—"

"I understand, sir." And, surprisingly, he did.

As he waited, wondering if his responses would give rise to additional questions, an alternate solution occurred to Theo. Before he suggested it, though, there was another matter to resolve. "Your earlier question about Smithson, sir. Were you wondering if he might have followed Sarah from the ballroom and seen us together?"

"I was, yes."

"Unless he had a partner for the waltz, I suppose he is as likely as anyone else present, save Lady Sefton."

The earl's frown returned. "Is Lady Sefton exempt or more likely to have followed you?"

"More likely. She was standing in the doorway when we left the ballroom."

Tregaron muttered something that Theo couldn't quite hear.

"There is another choice—a possible solution—we have not yet considered. And under the circumstances, sir, I think we should."

"I am willing to hear, and to discuss, all potential resolutions."

"Assuming that you choose to allow Sarah to decide whether or not her reputation was compromised last night—or, at least, to let me explain what occurred after I rescued her—"

"Yes to the latter. We will discuss the other after you tell me about this as yet unconsidered solution."

His heart beating wildly in his chest, Theo dragged in a breath. "If even one person saw Sarah and me together unchaperoned, gossip is inevitable. We couldn't prevent it even if we knew who saw us together, which we don't. The only way to preserve Sarah's reputation and stop the *ton*'s scandalmongers from spreading grossly exaggerated versions of the tale all over Town before sunset is to give them something better, something even more surprising, to discuss—a wedding or betrothal."

The earl jerked upright, eyes wide, but Theo barreled on. "I doubt that Sarah will agree to a quick wedding, but she might consent to an engagement. A very public announcement today—and you and I can do that by drinking a celebratory toast at White's—will salvage her reputation. She can always cry off at the end of the Season if she believes we will not suit."

Tregaron raked his fingers through his hair, then began to pace between the desk and the fireplace. After several minutes, he detoured to a table in the corner and poured two glasses of brandy. Returning, he offered one to his guest, then perched on the edge of his desk, one leg swinging idly. "We have traveled so far afield from where we started, I am not sure how we landed here." He raised his glass and drank deeply.

For politeness' sake, Theo took a small sip, then set his glass aside. He did not want Sarah to think he was foxed when he offered for her. "Do you disagree with my assessment, sir? Or with my conclusions?"

"No, I don't. I almost wish I could."

"Because," Theo asked as evenly as possible, "you don't want me as a son-in-law—"

"Good God, Dunnley! Of course not."

Theo flinched. Time—and his heart—stopped.

Both resumed their usual pace a moment later when Tregaron rubbed a hand over his face and muttered, "God, I am making *such* a mull of this."

Draining his glass, he slammed it down on the desk, then grasped Theo's shoulders. "What I meant is," the earl said, his expression anguished, "of course that isn't the reason. Any man would be proud to have you as a son-in-law."

Straightening, he offered Theo his hand. "Now, go tell

my daughter what happened last night and offer for her. If she is as smart as I have always believed, she will realize how fortunate she is to have won your regard, and will accept. For both your sakes, I hope she does."

Theo might have wondered if Sarah's father truly was in favor of the match had Tregaron not stopped with his hand on the doorknob and, with a twinkle in his eye, added, "A kiss or two can be very persuasive."

As he followed the earl from the room, Theo hoped Sarah was as susceptible to his kisses as her mother had been to Tregaron's.

Chapter Eight

*C*limbing Tregaron House's wide, carved staircase to the drawing room, Theo felt like he was tumbling tip over tail toward an unknown future. And he was not at all certain whether he would land on his head or his heels. It was difficult to credit that his aspirations had undergone such a profound change in the hour since his arrival. Whereas earlier he had hoped that Sarah would refuse his offer, now he prayed that she would accept it, since a betrothal announcement was the only way to halt the spread of harmful gossip. Last Season he had watched, powerless to help, as malicious rumors savaged a young lady's character and threatened to crush her spirit. This year he was determined to thwart the scandalmongers before they could spew their poison.

Unfortunately, he had not the slightest idea what to say to convince Sarah to betroth herself to him. Having just realized the utter necessity of their engagement, he'd had no time to think of compelling arguments to persuade her. Nor, with the butler standing in the entry hall below and a footman stationed in the corridor a few feet past the drawing room, did he have an opportunity to ponder the matter.

The delicate notes of a harp, its strings plucked by a master hand, greeted Theo as he approached the first floor.

For a respite, as well as for his own pleasure, he stopped short of the drawing room doors and let the hauntingly elegant song Sarah was playing wash over him.

But after a few moments, just listening wasn't enough. He wanted to see her, to watch her slender, graceful hands moving over the instrument's strings, so he stepped closer, leaned a shoulder against the portal, and drank in the sight and sound, letting them soak into his skin and down to his very bones.

And, for the first time since he'd held her last night, he felt content, his soul and mind at peace.

As the echoes of the final chord of her own arrangement of *Llwyn On* began to fade, Sarah placed her palms against the strings. Setting the harp upright, she closed her eyes and leaned her head against its curved back, exhausted from the concentration required to play the piece yet somehow invigorated by the effort. The sound of quiet applause jerked her erect. Twisting abruptly toward the doorway, she almost fell off her stool. The sight that met her eyes was so unexpected that she gaped for several seconds before finding her voice. "Dunnley! What are you doing here?"

"I have been listening—with great pleasure—to your marvelous playing. I had no idea a harp could be used to perform such . . . intricate"—he gestured with one hand, as if apologizing for an inadequate description—"music. I daresay very few harpists have the skill to play that particular piece."

He strode toward her. Sarah tried to stand, only to find that her legs did not want to support her. In an instant, he recognized her plight and was at her side, one hand under her elbow to steady her. "Are you unwell? Should I ring for your maid? Or run downstairs and get your mother?"

"No, thank you. I will be fine in a moment."

He studied her face, then said, in a tone that made it clear he was not as convinced of a quick recovery as she was, "At least let me help you to a chair."

"Thank you." Her legs were a bit steadier now—enough that she need not fear falling on her face.

Instead of offering his arm, he scooped her off her feet.

"Dunnley!" she squeaked, alarmed. At five feet and seven inches, she was no pocket Venus, and although he was five or six inches taller, he was not a large man. But as he carried her across the room, she discovered that his well-cut blue superfine coat concealed hard, corded muscles. Whether by instinct or by chance, she'd looped her arm around his neck, and as he bent to seat her on the sofa, she could feel the muscles in his shoulder and upper back moving under her hand and arm. *What would he look like without his coat?* she wondered, then blushed at such an improper thought.

"I could have walked, but thank you."

"It was my pleasure." He sat beside her. "In this day and age, there aren't many dashing deeds a gentleman can perform to impress a lady. The knights of yore had an easier time of it," he quipped. "There were dragons to slay, damsels to rescue—"

Was he trying to impress me? She could not ask him that. Nor was she altogether certain she wanted to know the answer. "Speaking of damsels in distress, I want to thank you for rescuing me from Sir Edward last night."

"Again, it was my pleasure." He shifted position, turning to better see her. "Your mother said you don't remember everything that occurred after your encounter with Smithson last night. Would you like me to describe the events you don't recall?"

His matter-of-fact offer put paid to any lingering embarrassment about her memory loss. "Yes, please."

"What is the last thing you remember clearly?"

"Sir Edward's insistence that I dance the waltz with him." She shuddered at the memory. "I know you rescued me, although I don't know how."

"Nothing after that?" There was no hint of censure or condescension in his voice.

"I thought I might have danced with you later, and Mama said that I did." A bit nervous—she had never been alone with a gentleman before—but not at all frightened, she glanced at the doorway, wondering why her mother had not yet appeared.

Catching the motion, he explained, "Your parents and I thought it might be easier for you to remember without an audience."

Sarah did not think that the presence of her family would have any effect on her brain's ability to recall the previous night's events, although she would be more comfortable without their concerned, loving eyes watching for signs that her memory was returning. But even so, it was *very* unusual for a young lady and a gentleman to be unchaperoned. Unless, of course, the gentleman had been granted permission to pay his addresses—something Dunnley surely had no intention of doing this morning! Nor any other morning, for that matter.

"Sarah? Would you prefer to have your family here?"

"Oh dear, I was woolgathering, wasn't I?" Feeling a flush of embarrassment heat her cheeks, she dipped her head, hoping he would not notice. "I am sorry, Dunnley. And no, it isn't necessary for my family to be here."

He brushed the back of one finger against her cheek. Light and quick as the brush of a feather, the gentle gesture felt both tender and protective, as absurdly contradictory as that seemed. "Do I frighten you?"

Shocked, her eyes slewed to his, and she almost choked on the breath she'd been dragging into her suddenly air-starved lungs. "No, of course not!"

"Are you uncomfortable here, alone with me?"

"No. I have never been alone with a gentleman before, except for my father and my brothers. I feel a bit . . . awkward, but it is the situation, not you."

"Are you certain?"

Despite his obvious concern, she wanted to shake him. Since she could not literally do so, she had to achieve a similar effect with words and return the conversation to its intended purpose. "Yes, I am quite certain. Sometimes I find your presence disconcerting, but this morning isn't one of those occasions. Now, are you going to continue quizzing me, or are you going to tell me what happened last night?"

"Why do I sometimes disconcert you?"

Lud, he was tenacious! "Perhaps we can discuss that later"—*much, much later*, she amended silently—"after you tell me about last night."

"That is another conversation we should definitely pursue, since it is likely to benefit both of us." He shifted position again, turning toward her even more, his back now against the arm of the sofa. "Last night, then. It was my waltz Smithson was trying to steal, although I would have come to your aid even if it had not been. I could see that he had angered and upset you."

"You could? Oh dear."

Smiling gently, he shook his head. "Don't distress yourself. It was not so obvious that anyone would notice."

If that was true, how had Dunnley known the state of my emotions? And why had he noticed?

He described the rescue, how he'd cut Smithson and led her away from the odious baronet, then onto the dance floor for the waltz. Dunnley even recounted their conversation as best he could recall it, and as he explained, she remembered everything . . . everything until the end of the waltz when she began trembling and begged him to take her out of the ballroom.

That she did not remember at all.

"I must have been upset, indeed, to do something so . . . so shockingly forward! How strange that I remember everything but that." She bit her lip, mystified by the whimsical nature of her faulty memory. "You would think that I would recall such unnatural behavior, even if I forgot all else."

"I would say, rather, that you were overset. That being the case, perhaps it isn't so surprising that you don't remember."

Pondering the distinction, Sarah said nothing.

"Shall I continue?"

"There is more?" she gasped. If the rest was anything like the last, she was not at all certain she wanted to hear it.

"A bit, yes."

There was nothing in his calm tone but kindness and concern, nothing in his expression to indicate whether the remainder was better or worse than the events heretofore recounted. Deciding it was better to know, she requested, "Please tell me the rest."

"After signaling to your brother to follow us, I escorted you from the ballroom to a small chamber near the card room. You were still overset—trembling violently and cold as ice. I did what I could to calm you, then—"

"What did you do?" Curiosity sparked the question, not only about the extent of her foolishness, but also his reaction to it.

"I held you and said the kind of reassuring things one does at such a time."

He held me? Good Lord, I cannot believe I don't remember that! But perhaps that explained why she was not experiencing that butterflies-in-the-stomach feeling this morning. They had undoubtedly all died of shock last night!

"I am very sorry to have caused you such trouble, Dunnley. For your sake, I hope I regained my composure quickly."

"You need not apologize. It is not your fault that Smithson is such a bas—er, such a reprobate."

"No, of course not. But I certainly must take the blame for acting like a ninny."

Shaking his head again, he offered her another gentle smile. "You did not." Before she could protest that foolish gallantry, he repeated, "Truly, you did not. Once you recovered your composure, we talked about why the encounter with Smithson distressed you more than usual.

"Not," he added darkly, "that there is anything usual about such reprehensible behavior."

"I don't remember any of this. Why did it upset me so?"

"You said it was because his manner was bolder, even though his words—what you understood of them—were much the same."

Comparing what she remembered of the baronet's behavior last night with previous occasions, she shivered. "He has never been so . . . obvious before. So blatant. Usually he says such things when no one is likely to overhear."

"That is what you told me last night."

Dunnley shifted position—and seemed to move closer. "Sarah, there is one more thing."

Dread coiled in her stomach like a viper about to strike, rendering her mute.

"Will you do me the very great honor of becoming my wife?"

"*What?*"

Chapter Nine

*T*he look in Sarah's eyes drove Theo to his feet, which did not stop moving until he had traveled some six or seven feet, with Sarah's shocked exclamation still ringing in his ears. Hoping a trick of the light had given her eyes and face that half-disbelieving, half-horrified expression, he turned, but her expression was unchanged. It was, perhaps, wariness, not fear or horror, but even so, she appeared no more pleased—and no more likely to accept his proposal—than she had been a few moments before.

"I believe you heard me well enough." It required a steadying breath and a conscious effort to keep his tone calm and gentle, and to give no indication of the pain inflicted by her appalled reaction. "I asked if you would do me the honor of marrying me."

"Why?" she demanded baldly. "I do not believe that you have suddenly fallen in love with me."

"Whether you believe it or not, it is true, although it was not particularly sudden." Sarah deserved an honest answer, so he sought words to explain his confused, rather tumultuous feelings, as well as the reason for his precipitous offer. "I had not, however, intended to offer for you until later in the Season. I wanted to court you as you deserve, and to give us more time to get to know one another. Unfortunately, we were seen together last night. Shortly after we entered the room, someone—and I don't know who it was—opened the door, looked inside, then closed it again."

"It was probably Rhys. You said you signaled for him to follow us."

"I did, yes. But I don't think it was your brother. He had a partner for the waltz.

"Sarah." Crossing to her, he knelt at her feet and grasped her hands. "I know you were not expecting a proposal this morning. I realize that you might not feel you know me well enough to commit your life, and your self and your happiness, into my keeping. But you also need to realize that whoever opened that door saw you standing with your head on my shoulder and my arms around you."

She closed her eyes and bowed her head.

"Gossip is inevitable. You know that as well as I do. You saw what happened to Beth last year, so you know that rumors, even false ones, can destroy a young lady's reputation."

Involuntarily, his grip tightened. "I couldn't bear to see you suffer as she did. I admire you and respect you too much—and, though you don't believe it, love you too much—for that. Please, for both our sakes, accept my proposal.''

When she lifted her head, her beautiful blue eyes were awash in tears. "I—"

Unwilling to accept an answer until he was certain she understood her choices, and all the possible repercussions, he barreled on. "If the idea of marrying me is abhorrent to you, you can cry off at the end of the Season. By then the scandalmongers should have forgotten us and turned to newer, more scintillating fodder.''

Rising, he drew her to her feet, then raised her hands to his lips and brushed a kiss against the back of each one. "Please, Sarah, will you do me the honor—the very great honor—of agreeing to become my wife?"

Her eyes met his for an instant, then dropped to his cravat for several heartbeats—six, to be precise, though his pulse was thundering as if he'd just completed a footrace— before returning to his face. "I-I don't know what to say."

"Say yes," he suggested, smiling over their clasped hands. "Say, 'Yes, Theo, I would be very happy to marry you.' ''

She shook her head. "I cannot. I am well aware of the honor you do me—"

Ruthlessly cutting her off before she could refuse flat out, he offered another choice. "Then say, 'Theo, I cannot marry you now, but I will agree to an engagement until the end of the Season and make my decision then.' ''

Another shake of the head. "I cannot do that, either. It wouldn't be fair to you.''

"Then say, 'Theo, I don't know what to do. Sit down, please, so that we can discuss this further.' ''

That suggestion garnered a small smile. "Dunnley, please sit down. We need to discuss this more.''

He seated her, then sat beside her, still holding one of her hands in his, and waited to hear what she would say.

And while he waited, he prayed.

The arrival of the butler with a tea tray offered Sarah a welcome reprieve, not only from the conversation about Dunnley's staggering and entirely unexpected proposal, but also from the emotions battling within her. Pouring the tea presented a different challenge, since her hands, like her emotions, were far from steady. The interlude did, however, give her an opportunity to think.

And given everything that had happened this morning, she desperately needed an interval of quiet reflection.

As they sat side by side drinking tea, Sarah realized that her feelings about Dunnley—or, perhaps, just her perceptions of him—had undergone a rather significant change in the past two days. Little more than thirty-six hours ago, she had feared him—rather, she'd been frightened by the strange, and strangely disturbing, feelings she experienced whenever he was near. Yet last night he had been her savior and her port in a storm, sheltering and comforting her while she recovered from the tempestuous emotions wrought by her encounter with Nasty Ned.

Now Dunnley wanted to be her husband—or, at least, her fiancé—so that he could protect her again. And even more.

She did not doubt his desire to protect her. He had demonstrated the protective side of his character last night by rescuing her from Sir Edward, then removing her from the ballroom—thus saving her from the *ton*'s inevitable censure had they witnessed her loss of composure. What she found difficult—perhaps even impossible—to credit was that he loved her. Not just the fondness of friendship; he had fallen in love with her.

It was much easier to believe that a strong sense of honor compelled his proposal. Or maybe she wanted to cling to that belief because it was simpler. Not to mention a great deal safer.

But wishes, no matter how fervent, could not change the world, or even a tiny corner of it. Sarah had to deal with circumstances as they were, not as she wished them to be, which meant she needed to find a solution to her current dilemma. And that handsome dilemma was sitting beside her, elegantly clad in Weston's finest tailoring, sipping tea and patiently awaiting her response to his proposal. Proposals in the plural, for he'd asked her at least three times to marry him, and he had given her several choices—an immediate marriage, a wedding announcement now with the ceremony to take place in the next few months, or an engagement throughout the Season with the opportunity to decide at its end whether to cry off or to marry.

If she did not have an answer, preferably a rational, sensible one—and she did not—then she needed to think of some questions that might help her reach a decision.

Setting her cup and saucer aside, she turned to the viscount. "Dunnley, you have been remarkably forbearing and patient with me this morning, for which I thank you most sincerely. And you have demonstrated an unexpected perceptiveness—" Blushing furiously, she covered her face with her hands. "Oh, that did not come out well at all."

Surprisingly, he chuckled. "I am glad to know I am not the only person who is tongue-tied this morning." Gently grasping her wrists, he pulled her hands away from her face, then captured one and held it. "Forget what you said and how it might have sounded. Instead, tell me what you intended to say."

"I meant, I was surprised that you understand my concerns so well."

One tawny brow arched as his eyes widened. "I am not sure why that surprises you. Did I not dance at least once with you at every ball we both attended last Season? And call on you with some frequency, and take you for several drives in the park?"

"You did all of those things. But several other men could say the same, and I daresay none of them understands me half so well."

"Perhaps I am just an exceptionally perceptive fellow," he suggested, a smile twitching the corners of his mouth.

"I would say, rather, that you are an exceptional man." Today she was discovering his heretofore hidden depths and realizing just how extraordinary he was. "As well as an exceptionally perceptive one."

"Thank you, my lady." He raised her hand to his lips and brushed a kiss against her knuckles. A fiery tingle flashed up Sarah's arm and throughout her body, all the way down to her toes, stealing her breath as it shot through her lungs.

"Did my demonstration of perceptiveness and understanding help you reach a decision, Sarah? Or has it only raised more questions?"

"It is reassuring to know that you possess those qualities in such abundance, but since I still haven't reached a decision, I can't say the knowledge was especially helpful."

"Tell me what troubles you the most. Or, if it is easier,

ask me questions about the things that bother you. I will answer as honestly as I can, but"—a wry smile accompanied his caveat—"that same honesty compels me to confess that I have never been particularly adept at describing feelings and emotions."

"I don't think many people are. It is difficult to describe anything one doesn't understand well, and feelings and emotions quite often seem to fall in that category."

"Indeed they do."

"But," she mustered a rather wobbly smile, "I will try."

"As will I."

"It bothers me that I did not realize that you held me in such high regard—high enough to consider offering for me. And it troubles me even more that you were forced to change your plans because of Sir Edward and my . . . my missishness."

"First of all, your behavior was not the least bit missish. You stood up to him, endured his insults and innuendo with your head held high, even if you were quaking inside. That, my dear, is bravery, not missishness.

"Second, and even more important, I was not forced to change my plans. I *chose* to change them, for both your sake and mine. I care about you, Sarah, and I want the right to care for you, too. As your husband or fiancé, I can protect you from Nasty Ned and others of his ilk. As your friend, there is little I can do."

"Caring about someone isn't the same as loving them."

"It is to me. I care—and care deeply—about the people I love. I am concerned about my friends and acquaintances, but I don't worry overmuch about them. Nor do I lose sleep, tossing and turning 'til dawn while seeking solutions to their problems."

Sarah's breath caught at the image of Dunnley tossing and turning in his bed as he worried about her. "Have you lost sleep because of my problems?" The boldness of her question was countered by modesty, which necessitated ducking her head to ask it.

He curled his fingers under her chin, raising her face and turning it to his. "Two nights' worth. But it was you, more than your problems, that kept me awake."

"I don't understand," she confessed, feeling unaccountably foolish.

Dunnley smiled and rubbed the back of his fingers along her jaw. "I know you don't, sweet Sarah, but perhaps someday soon you will."

Before she could think of another question, Dunnley said, "We have strayed a bit from the point. I do love you, although I am not certain I realized it myself until the other night. I knew I was in love with you before then, but I didn't realize how much until I saw you at the Oglethorpe ball."

Something in her expression must have revealed her surprise. In a wry tone that matched his expression, he added, "I promised you honest answers. They may not be particularly flattering—to either of us—but they are truthful."

"What makes you think that answer was unflattering?"

"Well," he drawled, "I doubt that I am aiding my cause by demonstrating that I am a bit of a slowtop in matters of the heart."

"Isn't the fact that you did realize it more important than when it happened?"

"I would like to think so, but perhaps that is just an excuse—"

"No," she shook her head to emphasize the word, "I don't think it is."

"Thank you for that." Several seconds passed in silence, then he prodded, "What else troubles you?"

"That events forced you to change your plans. That I am not certain how I feel—about any of this. I wonder who saw us together. I wonder if—"

"Whoa! Let's concentrate on one problem at a time. They generally seem less overwhelming that way." Twining his fingers with hers, he repeated with quiet yet pointed emphasis, "Events didn't force me to do anything. I chose to offer for you today—not so much because of what happened, but because what happened made me realize how important it is to me to have the right to protect you."

Sarah wondered what had made Dunnley realize that he loved her, or how much he loved her. But since she did not love him, it seemed unfair to ask. Instead she queried, "What do you expect from marriage and a wife?"

"Like most people, I *hope* for a love match and a wife who will be friend, companion, confidante, and lover. I *hope* my wife and I will have common interests, as well as mutual friends. Not all of them, of course—that isn't realistic—but it would be nice to have several pursuits that interested us both. Ideally, I would like my wife to listen to my speeches for Lords and plans for my estates, and to be interested enough, and knowledgeable enough, to suggest improvements. And I hope that she will seek my opinion on matters that interest her."

Sarah nodded. Her hopes for marriage were quite similar to his.

"What I *expect*," he continued, "at the very least, is a marriage based on mutual respect and a degree of affection. I *expect* loyalty and faithfulness, in every regard—"

"And can your wife *expect*," she mimicked his emphasis, "loyalty, fidelity, respect, and affection from you?"

"Yes."

Sarah's eyes widened at the unflinching assurance in his voice, but she said nothing. He, however, had quite a bit more to say. "I will honor my marriage vows—each and every one of them—and demand that my wife do the same."

Shoving a tawny lock that had fallen onto his forehead back into place, he raked his hand through his hair. "I want a wife who likes me at least as much as she likes my title and the size of my purse. A companion, not just a . . ."

"Not just a woman who lives in your house and serves as hostess for your parties, but one who shares your life? Or, at least, shares parts of it?"

"Yes! That is exactly what I want." His gaze was both appreciative and assessing, and it felt as if it bored through her skin and down to her very soul. "Were you able to provide such an excellent description because you hope for the same things?"

"Perhaps." She shrugged. "I do hope for some of the same things, but I . . ."

"What do you hope for from a husband and marriage, Sarah?"

Dunnley's earnest expression and obvious sincerity made it easier to answer such an exceedingly personal question. "I hope for a love match, of course. I hope for a husband who finds my mind as attractive as my face and form. I would like to be my husband's friend and confidante, and for him to share my interests in music and literature. I want to be more than just a hostess, the woman he escorts to social events, and a . . . a broodmare." Her face flamed at such plain speaking.

"Those are all perfectly reasonable requests. What else do you want?"

"I want respect and affection. And I will expect my husband to honor all his marriage vows, since I will honor mine."

"I can promise you—I do promise you—all of that and more. Will you marry me, sweet Sarah, and make me the happiest of men?"

"But I cannot promise you the love match you hope for!" She jumped to her feet and began to pace, no longer able to sit quietly through his gentle yet persistent interrogation. "And you deserve to love and to be loved in return."

Her head down as she tried to blink back the tears that suddenly and inexplicably pooled in her eyes, Sarah was not aware that Dunnley had risen and crossed the room to intercept her until she bumped into him.

The resulting embarrassment was more than her tenuous composure could withstand. As she stammered out an apology, the tears spilled over. She turned away to hide them, but gentle hands on her shoulders pivoted her around, into his embrace.

"Shhh. . . . Everything will be fine, my dear. There is no reason for such distress."

For some reason, his comforting words made her cry even harder. Burying her face against his coat, she tried to muffle her sobs.

Her brother would have cut and run long since, but Dunnley was made of sterner stuff. He nestled her against his chest and, still murmuring words of comfort, began rubbing her back.

When her sobs dwindled to an occasional watery sniffle— a process that took far longer than Sarah would have liked, although anything more than two seconds would have been excessive in her opinion—Dunnley, without loosening his embrace and without a word of reproach, handed her his handkerchief.

"Here, my dear. Mop up your tears."

"Thank you." She managed to grasp the pristine white

linen, ironed and folded into a perfect square, without exposing her ravaged countenance to his gaze. She would not be able to hide it much longer, unfortunately, and would have to face him soon, despite her mortification. But strangely enough, the real reason she wished to postpone the inevitable was neither her reddened eyes and nose nor her embarrassment, but the fact that she was loath to leave the comfort of his embrace.

"I beg your pardon, Dunnley," she muttered into his lapel as she employed the handkerchief. "I am generally not a watering pot."

"I don't imagine you are. Given the emotional turmoil you have experienced in the past twelve hours, a few tears are not unexpected. Nor do they require an apology. Most women would have been in strong hysterics, or had a fit of the vapors. I thank you—"

She glanced up in surprise, her red-rimmed eyes forgotten. A hint of a smile curved the viscount's mouth as he continued, "—for not indulging in either."

Sarah believed in giving credit where it was due, and Dunnley certainly deserved praise for generously dismissing her weeping as "a few tears." A few bucketsful was far more accurate a description. "And I thank you, sir, for not departing posthaste at the sight of the first teardrops. Especially after I drenched your coat last night—"

"You never shed a tear last night, you just trembled uncontrollably. That was more terrifying than tears."

"It was? Why?"

"Because I didn't know what to do, except hold you and try to calm you."

Laying her aching head on his shoulder again, she asked, "Is this how we were seen last night?"

He moved a bit closer and began rubbing her back again. "Yes, just like this. But you were trembling instead of crying."

"I am sorry that you had to deal with my emotional excesses, but I do thank you for your stalwart assistance. Rhys would have fled in terror and consternation at the sight of the third teardrop—three being enough to convince him that many more are in store—and although my father would have stood his ground, he undoubtedly would have wanted to escape, too."

"My aunts have been known to indulge in bouts of weeping from time to time, so perhaps I have more experience with lachrymose females than your father and brother do."

Fascinated by this unexpected glimpse at his life, she glanced up at him. "How many aunts do you have? Or should I ask how many of them have drenched your coats with their tears?"

"I have three—well, two aunts and a great-aunt. One lives in India, and I haven't seen her since I was a boy, but both Aunt Caro and Aunt Meg have dampened my shoulder a time or two. Caro more often than Meg." He grinned like a mischievous schoolboy. "You are wondering who they are and if you know them, aren't you?"

"I am," she confessed, offering a sheepish smile of apology for her curiosity.

"I don't believe you have ever met my great-aunt, Miss Margaret Middleford. She rarely comes to Town. But you are acquainted with Aunt Caro. She is Caroline, Lady Richard Winterbrook."

"But she is Lord Weymouth's aunt!"

"She is indeed, his aunt by marriage. But she is also my late mother's sister."

"Then how . . ." Sarah frowned, trying to puzzle out the relationship between the Winterbrooks and the Middlefords. The younger members of the families were cousins, but their connection to Lady Richard did not account for their kinship. "Was Lord Bellingham's wife another of your mother's sisters? That is, did he and Lord Richard marry sisters?"

"No. Bellingham's wife was my father's only sister."

"Ah!" Resolving to resume her study of *Debrett's Peerage*—every English girl making her bows to Society undoubtedly knew who Dunnley's aunts were, as well as the connection between his family and the Winterbrooks—Sarah barely noticed when Dunnley tucked her arm in his and guided her back to the sofa, then seated himself beside her again. But his next statement jolted her back to the present, and returned them to their previous discussion.

"I am sorry my questions upset you."

"It was not your questions. It was . . . everything."

"The past twelve or so hours have been eventful ones for you, haven't they? And, I suspect, quite a strain."

"Yes."

Reaching over, he caught her writhing hands in one of his and separated them, enveloping her icy fingers within his warm clasp. "Much as I regret being the cause of even the slightest part of your distress, we need to return to the subject at hand."

She could not dispute that, but neither was she eager to further discuss his startling proposal.

"It seems that we hope for many of the same things from marriage. You said earlier that you could not promise me a love match, but you didn't rule out the possibility, either. Do you find the prospect of marriage to me abhorrent?"

"Of course not!" she blurted, shocked that he could even think such a thing.

"Do you think it is possible that, given time, you might come to love me? Or, at least, to feel some affection for me?"

Never having even imagined such a frank discussion with a gentleman, much less participated in one, Sarah fought the urge to squirm. "Yes, I think so."

"Do you think that, if we were to marry, you could be my companion and partner?"

It was a more difficult—and far more complex—question. "I don't think I would have any difficulty filling either role, but being a wife encompasses far more."

"Yes, it does, but I am quite certain you will be an exceptional hostess and, when the time comes, an excellent mother. If you can be my friend, companion, and partner, and if you believe that in time you will love me, or feel affection for me, then the success of our marriage is assured."

His description did not fit the love match of her dreams—or his—but Sarah could not fault his logic. Even so, she was far from convinced. But since she most definitely did not want to discuss the wifely role that most concerned her, she didn't dispute his conclusion. A moment later, when he proposed again, she almost wished she had.

"Dunnley, I am sorry, but I cannot agree to an immediate marriage. It is too soon . . . and too much."

"An engagement, then. Will you consent to that, at least?"

Sensing his frustration, his feeling that he was failing in his self-appointed role as her protector, she did not reiterate her argument that an engagement wasn't fair to him. Instead she tried a different tack. "I will—on one condition."

"What is your condition?"

"You must promise that you will tell me if anything—*anything*—happens during the Season to make you question the wisdom of your decision. Or to doubt, even the slightest degree, the success of a marriage between us."

"I—" A frown creasing his brow, he sputtered to a halt. Time—and Sarah's nerves—seemed to stretch interminably before he explained. "Having been taught since boyhood that an honorable man never withdraws from an engagement, I am loath to make that promise, because I honestly don't know if I could cry off. I will, however, freely agree to discuss any concerns with you."

His response did little to allay Sarah's misgivings. But before she could decide whether or not to accept his compromise, he suggested, "Perhaps we could mutually promise to discuss any doubts and concerns with each other, preferably as they arise, and to decide together at the end of the Season whether or not we will suit."

Greatly relieved, she nodded. "Thank you, Dunnley. That seems quite fair."

"Then you agree?"

Hiding a smile at his eagerness, and his earnestness, she gave him the answer he sought. "Yes, I agree." For clarification, she added, "I agree to promise myself to you."

Dunnley rose, drawing her upright and securing both her hands. "Thank you, sweet Sarah. You have made me a very happy man." He brushed a soft kiss against her lips.

Brief though it was, his gentle salute made her knees buckle—and heralded the return of the butterflies, all of whom were frantically flapping their wings.

His proposal and their protracted discussion might not have been the stuff of a maiden's reveries, but his response to her acceptance had been all that a young lady could ask for.

Sarah felt quite certain that his kiss would inspire many a dream.

What a nightmare! Theo had been anticipating Sarah's acceptance ever since he'd entered the drawing room, knowing that he would feel as if he were in heaven when she said yes. Now that she had finally agreed, he knew the coming weeks were going to be hell.

Even worse, it was a hell of his own making.

One he had, in fact, eagerly embraced. But that was before he realized the effect a single chaste kiss would have upon him.

Oh yes, Lady Sarah Mallory was the perfect bride for him. Whether he would survive the coming months and live to make her his wife was an entirely different question. He could foresee a Season of cold baths. Daily, at least; perhaps even more frequently than that.

When he returned home, he would have to remember to warn his valet.

Chapter Ten

Willing his body to calm, Theo returned his attention to his fiancée. He could only hope that her dazed expression was a sign that she, too, had been strongly affected by their kiss. Hopefully, pleasantly surprised. Given her habitual reserve, Sarah's bemused reaction suggested that it was her first kiss. He shook his head in amazement, wondering how she had reached the age of one- or two-and-twenty and remained so innocent. So unaware. Were the men of Wales blind to her inner and outer beauty? Or were they so bedazzled by it, and by her, that they feared rejection and never approached her?

A second, more comprehensive look at Sarah revealed a slightly disheveled coiffure and red-rimmed eyes. The former was a result of his attempts to comfort her while she was crying; the blame for the latter could probably be laid at his door, too. How to tactfully inform her of both, preferably before her parents spotted either, was his current dilemma. Well, one of them.

"Sarah, I fear I disarranged your hair a bit when I was

holding you. Do you wish to tidy it before we go downstairs and tell your parents our good news?"

She crossed to the pier glass, hanging between the windows and framed by their blue velvet draperies, then froze and covered her face with her hands. "Good heavens! How could you bring yourself to offer for such a fright?"

Turning away, she headed for the door, but he intercepted her. "You are beautiful, tears notwithstanding. And you will still be beautiful when we are old, with wrinkles and snow white hair, because your beauty is bone—and soul—deep."

"What a lovely compliment. Thank you, Dunnley. You always know exactly what to say to restore my spirits." She touched his hand fleetingly. "Please excuse me for a few minutes so that I can repair my appearance."

After escorting her to the stairs, he resumed his seat on the sofa and wondered, not for the first time, how such a lovely, intelligent, and talented lady could be so unaware of the appeal those traits held for the gentlemen of the *ton*.

Wondered, too, how best to show her the power they—and she—exerted over him.

When Sarah returned to the drawing room, she felt—and looked—more like herself. Rather, she felt as close to normal as was possible given the strange morning she'd had. And it had certainly held more than its share of surprises, both pleasant and unpleasant. Even when Dunnley rose, bowed over her hand, and smiled that special smile he'd bestowed on her several times this morning, she still found it difficult to believe that he had proposed to her.

Perhaps even harder to credit that she'd accepted.

But he had and she did and now they needed to break the news to her parents. Sarah could not help but wonder if they would be as astonished as she had been. Or—she darted a glance at Dunnley—had he made his intentions known by asking permission to pay his addresses?

"Yes, my lady?" he inquired, a hint of amusement lacing his voice.

"I was wondering if my parents will be as surprised by your proposal as I was."

"Is that all?" His mirth was more obvious now. "You looked at me as if you weren't quite sure who I was. Or, rather, as if you weren't entirely certain that I am the same man you have known for more than a year."

Tucking her hand in the crook of his arm, he escorted her toward the stairs. "Your father knew my intentions. He grilled me for quite half an hour before giving me permission to offer for you. When he sent me upstairs to speak with you, he was on his way to inform your mother."

"You didn't mind being questioned?"

"I cannot claim to have enjoyed the experience, but as your father, it is his responsibility to ensure that your husband will respect and cherish you, as well as be able to provide for you."

He stopped several feet short of the morning room doors and leaned down to confide, "Besides, he promised to do his best to convince your mother that Shropshire isn't quite the back of beyond in exchange for my pledge to spend more time at my estate there."

Sarah smiled. "Papa set himself a difficult task."

"Fortunately, I am rather fond of that estate. I think you will like it, too."

"Dunnley . . ." It was disconcerting to hear him speak as if their marriage were a certainty, but, she supposed, to him it was.

"Yes, my dear?"

"Never mind. I daresay I am being foolish."

"I doubt that. What is troubling you?"

"Nothing. Truly," she reassured as one tawny brow arched quizzically.

"Er, you haven't . . . um, changed your mind, have you?"

Hiding a smile—she had never seen him so discomposed—she shook her head. "No, Dunnley, of course not. I am not so fickle."

"Do you think, sweet Sarah, that you could call me Theo when we are private?"

Disquieted by his request, which would remove the sense of distance inherent in a more formal mode of address, she responded with more honesty than politeness. "I don't know."

He scrutinized her features, seemingly to the bone, then with a gentle smile curving his lips and brightening his eyes, he inquired, "Are you willing to try?"

She could not resist that smile. "Of course. I just do not know how successful I will be."

"All I ask is that you try."

His gaze dropped to her lips, which immediately began to tingle. Not at all sure she wanted him to kiss her again, since she still felt a bit dazed and wobbly from the first one, but quite convinced that she dare not attempt another now, with the butler hovering nearby and her parents yet to be informed of the engagement, Sarah could do naught but whisper imploringly, "Dunn—Theo."

He offered her a tender smile, then brushed the back of one finger against her cheek. "Yes, my lady?"

"My parents are waiting to hear . . ." Only now did she wonder if they expected her to accept Dunnley's proposal.

Fortunately for the state of her nerves, he allowed her no time to speculate. Securing her hand more firmly against his arm, his free hand covering hers, he resumed their stroll toward the morning room.

When he halted again just outside the open double doors, she glanced up in surprise. His tone soft but urgent, he entreated, "Tell me again how to pronounce your brother's title. I was afraid to say it earlier, fearing I would mispronounce it."

"Llanfyllin."

Frowning in concentration, he sounded the syllables with care. "Hlan-*vu*-hlin."

"Exactly right." Smiling, she teased, "But you need not pucker your brow in order to say it."

He returned her smile—and the teasing. "*You* may not need to pucker yours, but I am just an ignorant Englishman." Then, still smiling, he repeated, "Hlan-*vu*-hlin."

"Perfect!"

"Thank you, sweet Sarah."

Her father rose when they entered, but not before exchanging a knowing look with her mother. Before either could voice a question, Dunnley asked, "Llanfyllin did not wait to hear the happy news?"

That brought Sarah's mother to her feet, too. The earl explained, "We thought it might be easier for both of you if he wasn't present when you returned." He hugged Sarah, then shook hands with Dunnley.

After a searching glance at her daughter, the countess smiled and greeted him, too, her delight apparent when she welcomed him to the family—in Welsh.

As she translated, Sarah wondered how best to inform her mother that there would not be a wedding. At least, not in the near future. With his usual aplomb, Dunnley said, "Thank you, my lady. You are very kind, if a bit premature. Sarah and I don't plan to marry immediately . . . unless scandal threatens her reputation."

Taken aback by this heretofore unstated condition, Sarah stared at her fiancé, feeling slightly alarmed. Unperturbed, he smiled at her, squeezing her hand in reassurance, then continued, "And I will do everything I can to prevent that."

"Let's sit down and discuss what we need to do." The earl crossed to the bellpull and, when the butler appeared, summoned his heir. Then, wise to the speed at which the servants' grapevine spread gossip from one house to another, he asked the man to fetch a particular bottle of champagne from the cellar.

By the time her brother sauntered into the room several minutes later, the news of her engagement had probably traveled through the house and out to the mews. Crossing to the sofa where she and Dunnley sat, Rhys glanced from one to the other, then inquired, "Am I to wish you happy, *bach*?"

He pulled her to her feet before she could answer and hugged her, then with one arm still around her, offered his hand and his congratulations to Dunnley. As they resumed their seats, her fiancé asked, quietly but with discernible bewilderment, "*Baakh*? Is that a nickname?"

"In a way, I suppose it is. It means 'little one' in Welsh."

"Unusual but fitting, even if no longer accurate. But since you are the only girl, Llanfyllin may feel more protective toward you than toward your younger brother."

As he turned his gaze and attention to her family, his demeanor transformed to the urbane, sophisticated viscount who was a leader of the *ton*, not the tender, teasing, smiling one who was her fiancé. "There are things we need to consider, and to do, to prevent—or, at least, to divert—any gossip that might arise. First, you"—he nodded to Sarah's parents, who were sitting across from them—"need to decide if you want to formally announce Sarah's engagement at your ball, or at some earlier event."

"A ball? Are we giving a ball?" Lord Tregaron looked from Dunnley to his wife.

"Tregaron!" she chided, her tone half exasperated and half amused acceptance of his foibles.

Rhys was quick to demonstrate that he had paid more attention. "Yes, Papa, we are. Next month."

"Not next month, in a fortnight." The countess enunciated each word precisely, as if to a child. "Two weeks from tonight."

When her father pulled out his pocket diary to make a note of the date, Sarah glanced at Dunnley, who grinned, then bent his head to whisper, "This, I take it, is a typical result of the brown studies to which your brother and father are prone?"

Sarah nodded, wondering how he knew of their tendency toward abstraction. A bit sheepishly, he confessed, "Your mother mentioned it last night. I, um . . . I fell into a similar state while escorting her up the stairs."

Unable to imagine this nonpareil among gentlemen behaving so atypically, she stared, wondering if she had gone mad or if everyone else had. He smiled and took her hand in his. "I will explain later."

Her father tucked his diary back in his pocket. "The ball seems an ideal time to announce your engagement, but a fortnight is too long to wait."

"We will, of course, see to it that the news is widely known before then." Dunnley twined his fingers with hers.

The countess glanced from her husband to Dunnley. "How will we do that?"

"In several different ways," he explained. "Lord Tregaron and I—and Llanfyllin, too, if he wishes—will drink a toast to Sarah's happiness this afternoon at White's after discussing the marriage settlements. Then, tonight, I will escort Sarah and you to the Enderby ball."

Surprised but not at all displeased by the arrangement, Sarah glanced from her fiancé to her mother. The countess nodded, her expression serene, and Dunnley continued enumerating plans. "Saturday, I hope you will attend a dinner—a family dinner—at my home. My younger cousin, David Winterbrook, was married last month, and he and his wife are coming to Town for a few days. The dinner is mostly to honor them, but also because Weymouth and his wife will be leaving for Dorset next week. Your presence at the dinner, then as members of my party at the Opera, will be as effective an announcement as a notice in the *Gazette* or *The Times*."

"We were planning a quiet meal at home before the Opera," the countess said, "but we would be pleased to dine with you and your family. And to attend the Opera with you."

Listening to her mother and Dunnley, Sarah had the disquieting feeling that her life was spiraling out of her control. He turned to her, raised her hand to his lips, and requested, "Will you attend the Opera with me, sweet Sarah?"

Steeling herself against the *zing* that snaked up her arm, she nodded, mutely acquiescing. By the time the fiery tingle reached her toes, she found her voice. "Surely your box is not big enough to seat everyone?"

"No, it isn't. But Elston's box is next to mine, and my uncle's is adjacent to Elston's. Between the three, we should be able to seat everyone, since your father's box is on the opposite side of the theater."

"Or," the earl suggested, "you and two or three of your relatives could sit in our box, and allow your cousins and their wives the use of yours."

"That might be even better. Thank you, sir."

"But"—Sarah looked from her fiancé to her parents, then back to Dunnley—"just being seen together will not spread the news of our engagement, will it? It seems more likely to cause gossip."

"Of course the news will spread, goose," Rhys said in the superior tone only an older brother can produce. "Especially after we confide it to our close friends tonight."

Dunnley nodded in agreement. "You wouldn't keep such a secret from Lady Deborah and Lady Tina, would you?"

"Nooooo," Sarah drew the word out as she considered, "I don't suppose so. But Deborah would not repeat a confidence."

"Possibly not, but my flibbertigibbet of a cousin will."

Sarah stifled a groan at the thought of Tina's probable reaction to the news of the betrothal. When his words finally penetrated her brain, she stared at him in astonishment. "Tina is your *cousin*?"

"My third cousin."

I must study Debrett's Peerage, *else I will make a fool*

of myself at Dunnley's dinner party. "Will Tina and her parents be attending your dinner?"

"No, my dear." Dunnley smiled as if greatly amused by the thought of inviting Tina, then sobered and explained. "David's wife is very hard of hearing due to an accident several years ago, so Stephen and I limited the guest list to our closest connections. We will sit down," he paused to consider, "about twenty to dinner."

Dismayed at the prospect of meeting so many members of Dunnley's family, Sarah stammered, "T-twenty? Your family must be a great deal larger than mine if you number twenty people amongst your closest relatives."

"Perhaps I miscounted. Stephen and I." He held up two fingers, adding others in pairs as he named the guests. "Aunt Meg and Uncle Michael—that is, my great-aunt, Miss Margaret Middleford, and my great-uncle, who is the Bishop of Lymington. Then George and Beth, Lady Julia and Lord Castleton, and Bellingham and Aunt Caro—er, Lady Richard Winterbrook." All ten fingers were now extended. He fisted his hands, then began anew as he continued, "David and Lynn, or to give them their proper form, Lord and Lady David Winterbrook. Elston, Karla, and Lady Lavinia. And the four of you." Nine fingers were now extended. "Nineteen in all."

Fortunately, Sarah had met all but five of the guests last Season. "I didn't realize Elston was related to you. I know he is your cousin's—Lord Weymouth's—best friend, but I didn't realize there was also a family connection."

"George and Elston aren't related, but he is a distant cousin—fifth cousin, I believe—of mine. My great-aunt or his can explain the connection." Waving a hand dismissively, he explained, "Stephen and I stretched the rules a bit because Elston and George are closer than most brothers, and because, like George, Elston and his lady will be leaving Town in a few weeks."

"So," Sarah's mother summarized, "this afternoon at White's, you"—she nodded at Dunnley—"Tregaron and Llanfyllin will conspicuously raise your glasses in a toast and, if questioned, tell anyone who asks about Sarah's and Dunnley's engagement. The gentlemen will then, we hope, pass the news on to their wives and daughters. Then tonight, you"—another nod at Dunnley—"will escort Sarah and me to the Enderby ball. Tregaron and Llanfyllin"— she shot a "don't dispute me" look at her husband and son—"will join us there as soon as they are able. Then on Saturday, we will dine with you and your family and attend the Opera together."

"Yes, my lady," Dunnley confirmed.

The earl consulted his pocket diary. "I should be able to join you by midnight."

Rhys tugged at his cravat, looking distinctly uncomfortable. "I will be a bit later."

The prospect of being the subject of gossip and whispered rumors, even of the pleasantest sort, was daunting in the extreme. Fighting the urge to squirm, Sarah glanced down at her lap to regain her composure and was startled to realize that Dunnley still held her hand. Peeking up at him, she was caught by the tender look he was bestowing upon her. "W-will that be enough to spread the news of our engagement? And to halt any gossip that might have arisen last night?"

"It should be more than enough to inform the *beau monde* of our betrothal. There is no way to know what effect it might have on rumors about our leaving the ballroom together last night—if there are any—but our engagement will provide fresh fodder for the gossipmongers."

Sarah was not as confident that news of their engagement would halt the spread of gossip about their absence from the ballroom last night, especially if someone had seen them alone together, but Dunnley had far more experience with the *ton* and its ways than she, so she did not dispute his conclusion. Instead she rather hesitantly voiced another of her fears. "What about Sir Edward Smithson? Do you think he will cease importuning me after he learns about our engagement?"

"That rotter? Probably not," Rhys opined.

"Much as I would like to be able to reassure you, Sarah, I cannot," Dunnley said with obvious regret. "I don't know how he will react."

"The safest course, dearling, is to assume that he will not," her father advised. "That way, you will be prepared if he continues his despicable behavior."

"We will all do everything we can to ensure that reprobate doesn't come near you." The countess's assertion was roundly seconded by all three men.

Sarah did not doubt for a minute that her family and her fiancé would do their best to keep Nasty Ned out of her orbit. And to keep her out of his. Not that she'd ever wanted to be anywhere in his vicinity, but he had a way of turning up when she least expected him. What concerned her was that Sir Edward might become even nastier. But since no one else seemed to think that was likely, she was happy to discount the possibility. It was one less thing to worry about.

And Lord knows she had plenty of those already.

"Just to be prudent, my dear, you are not to leave the house without Dunnley, your brother, or me escorting you," her father said. "Or, if none of us are available, one of the footmen—Emrys or Idris—must accompany you." The two men named were the largest of the Mallorys' servants, both several inches over six feet tall and strong as oxen.

Sarah's sense of well-being evaporated as quickly as the morning mist, replaced by a dark foreboding. *If trouble is unlikely, then why are such precautions necessary?*

By the time he returned home late that afternoon, Theo was well pleased with the day's events. Not to mention eagerly looking forward to the evening. Sarah had accepted his proposal; his reaction to their first—and, regrettably, only—kiss had been potent enough to convince him that he'd chosen the right bride; and the news of their engagement had spread through White's like a tidal wave before a storm. The only goal he had not achieved was selecting a song or two to perform with Sarah at the Greenwich musicale next month, but there would be time for that in the days ahead.

And rehearsing would, he hoped, provide plenty of opportunities to kiss his lovely fiancée and plumb the depths of her passion.

Oh, it was going to be a wonderful Season! Whistling, Theo climbed the stairs to bathe and change into evening clothes for dinner with the Mallorys and the Enderby ball.

Chapter Eleven

*I*t was going to be a horrible Season!

Not in every respect, of course. Sarah would be the first to acknowledge that in some ways the Season had already proven an enormous success. She was, for instance, already engaged—less than two full days after vowing to do her best to find a husband this Season. But she was not at all certain that she wanted the gentleman she'd caught. Or, more precisely, who had caught her.

Her concern had naught to do with ineligibility. Handsome, charming, wealthy, and titled, Dunnley was one of the most eligible bachelors of the *ton*. One of the Catches of the Season, in fact. There were unmarried gentlemen with higher titles—Fairfax and Blackburn, for example—and a few with deeper pockets, but none of them could claim the standing in Society that Dunnley had so effortlessly achieved.

Nor did she doubt that he would be a kind, attentive husband. Given what he had told her this morning, he was as determined to be a devoted, faithful, and loving husband as she was to be a loyal and supportive wife.

So, unlike some girls, she need not worry about her suitor's eligibility or his intentions. She was, however, quite concerned about the motive that had prompted his proposal. Had honor compelled it, or was it solely due to his feelings for her?

Not that she doubted his sincerity. She believed that he believed that he loved her. But while she dressed for dinner and the Enderby ball, Sarah questioned the depth of his feelings, and whether or not they would last.

As she sank onto the stool at her dressing table so that her maid, Marged, could style her hair, Sarah faced herself in the mirror and finally, and rather reluctantly, admitted that the source of her qualms was not Dunnley, but herself.

Specifically, her fluttery, weak-kneed reaction to his presence.

Surely such feelings could not be normal? Especially since he was the only man who so affected her.

Unfortunately, that was not the kind of question a reserved young lady could ask her mother. Not without the mother wondering if her daughter had lost her wits. Sarah hoped to have an opportunity at Dunnley's dinner party to ask Beth Weymouth and Karla Elston if they had ever experienced such extraordinary sensations.

Hoped, too, that her friends would not think that a large colony of bats had taken up residence in her belfry.

Returning to Tregaron House at seven o'clock, Theo was admitted by the stiffly formal yet fierce-looking butler and immediately ushered to the drawing room. Accepting a glass of sherry, he wandered around the room while Jones went to inform the Mallorys of his arrival, admiring the portraits on the walls and finally, almost inexorably, drawn to Sarah's harp.

At first glance, it appeared similar to, if less ornate than, the instrument in the music room at Dunnley Park, but a closer look revealed that it had three sets of strings, not two. Plucking the strings, trying to determine how the three ranks were tuned, he was not aware that Lady Tregaron had entered the room until she greeted him.

Starting like a schoolboy caught in mid-prank, he came within a hair's breadth of anointing his waistcoat with the sherry. Quickly setting the glass aside, he crossed the room to greet her and to thank her again for inviting him to dinner.

After seating the countess and pouring her a glass of sherry, he gestured to the instrument that had so intrigued him. "Are you also a harpist, my lady?"

"Yes, but I am not nearly as talented as my daughter."

"Having heard Sarah perform several times last Season, as well as for a few minutes this morning, I doubt that there are many people as talented as she."

"Such sentiments, though biased, do you credit." The countess smiled, revealing a charming pair of dimples. "I daresay you have never attended an *eisteddfod*."

"An eye-*stedh*-vod?" Theo attempted to mimic her pronunciation of the strange word. "No, I don't believe I have. What is it? In English, please," he requested, smiling.

"We will soon have you speaking more Welsh than Tregaron," she said as her husband entered the room, her sapphire blue eyes twinkling. "An *eisteddfod* is a grand Welsh music and poetry festival that takes place every summer."

The earl greeted Theo, poured himself a glass of sherry, then joined the conversation. "That won't be difficult, Dunnley. I don't know above a hundred words."

" 'Tis a sorry Welshman you are, Owain Mallory," his fond wife proclaimed.

"But, my dear, I am only half Welsh. Besides, that is about four words for every year we have been married."

The countess muttered a short phrase in Welsh.

Laughing, Tregaron turned to Theo. "I only know a few of those words—enough to know I am being castigated, not complimented."

"I have learnt two Welsh words today, which seems a creditable start."

"Creditable indeed," the earl nodded, "although my wife may disagree. What was the other word?"

"*Bach*. Llanfyllin called Sarah that this morning, so I asked her what it meant."

"*Cariad* is a good word." In a whisper, as if they were fellow conspirators, Tregaron added, "It means sweetheart or darling."

They did have a joint goal, Theo supposed: assuring the happiness of the Mallory ladies. Until his lady arrived, he would lend his assistance to the earl.

Theo knew Sarah was approaching two or three seconds before she entered the room. He could not say how he knew, nor define why he knew, he just did. Stranger still, there was no hint of her approach. She did not speak to someone in the corridor or on the stairs, nor did soft footfalls or the susurration of silk or satin skirts announce her presence. But even so, Theo knew, with the same certainty he knew his own name, that she was nearby.

Maybe it was an instinct, similar to whatever sent salmon swimming upstream to their spawning grounds every spring. Or whatever impulse drove a swarm of lemmings over a cliff. Maybe it was something even more elemental. Regardless of its source, the feeling or knowledge or whatever it was made him even more certain that Sarah was the right bride—the perfect wife—for him.

Not that he needed more convincing.

Rising to his feet, he turned . . . and there she was. A vision of loveliness in a celestial blue silk gown, she made his breath catch, his heart falter, and sent most of his blood rushing straight to his loins.

He would rather not have experienced that last effect, since Sarah's parents were seated not five feet away from him. With, one might say, a bird's-eye view.

When the few blood cells remaining in his head finally acted on his brain, allowing coherent thought, Theo hurried across the room to greet her. "Good evening, Sarah. You are breathtakingly beautiful tonight."

"Th-thank you."

"Surely my compliment comes as no surprise? Your mirror must have told you the same." Resisting the impulse to twine his fingers with hers, he cupped his hand around her elbow and led her to the chair beside his.

"It never tells me such things," she murmured, her voice so soft that he was not certain if she was speaking to him or to herself.

"In that case, my dear, you need a new mirror."

She smiled shyly, but before he could comment further, Llanfyllin entered the room. As Theo greeted him, Sarah's father brought her a glass of sherry, eliminating Theo's chance to serve his lovely fiancée and demonstrate his devotion.

After several minutes of general conversation in response to Lady Tregaron's question about the men's visit to White's, which had been more successful than Theo had hoped, he turned to Sarah and asked, "Will your younger brother be joining us? I have been looking forward to meeting him, too."

"No. Dafydd is at school."

"At Eton? Someone of my acquaintance has a younger brother there, although, at the moment, I can't recall who. But I do remember that he is about Dafydd's age."

"Are you an Etonian?" Sarah asked at the same moment her father said, "Dafydd has an interest in architecture, so we broke with tradition, since there are several masters at Winchester who encourage students' interest in science and mathematics."

Theo glanced from Tregaron to his son, then said, in

accents of mock horror, "Why do I suddenly have the feeling that I am the only Etonian in the room?"

Llanfyllin grinned. "Probably because Father and I are Harrovians."

"I daresay I ought to have realized that before now. You are about the same age as my brother and younger cousin, but you didn't look familiar when Sarah first pointed you out to me."

"I am not acquainted with either man, but I look forward to meeting them on Saturday." Then, almost as an afterthought, he added, "I am five-and-twenty."

Theo nodded. "So is Stephen. David is a year older."

Dinner was a convivial affair, with much teasing and bantering amongst the Mallorys. Theo was on the receiving end a few times, too, mostly from Llanfyllin, and gave as good as he got. It reminded him a great deal of his family's meals—before Stephen was wounded. Now Theo and his great-uncle, who lived with him at Dunnley House when Parliament was in session, felt like they were walking on eggshells, fearing they would say something that might upset Stephen. As the men left the table to rejoin the ladies, the earl's smile and nod of approval warmed Theo's heart. He'd received many accolades from his uncle and great-uncle in the years since his father's death, and although both were scrupulously honest men, they were relatives, either by blood or by marriage, and perhaps not entirely impartial. Tregaron, while just as sincere, was no relation, so, at least on this occasion, his praise seemed of greater moment.

Though his father had been dead for seventeen years, Theo suddenly missed him more than he had since shortly after the late viscount's death. With all his heart, Theo wished that his father were alive today, to express his approbation of the bride his heir had chosen.

As Dunnley helped her alight from his carriage at Lord and Lady Enderby's London residence, Sarah's tempestuous emotions threatened to overwhelm her. Mixed with the usual anticipation a young lady experiences before a ball was fear that her behavior last night might have made her the subject of scandalous gossip, concern about how the news of her engagement would be received by her friends and by the *ton*, and also worry about Dunnley, who had been very quiet since dinner. Studying him as he handed her mother down, Sarah was racked by anxiety and doubt. *Is he already regretting his impetuosity? Does he wish that he had not proposed this morning, or that I did not accept?*

Nothing in his demeanor, nor in his expression as he inclined his head to hear her mother's quip about the unexpected benefits of having an engaged daughter, hinted at the slightest disquiet. After giving instructions to his coachman, Dunnley smiled and offered his arm to her mother, then extended the other to Sarah. "With two such lovely ladies by my side, I shall be the most envied man at the ball."

The countess laughed. "I shall generate no envy, I assure you."

"Loath though I am to contradict a lady, I feel certain that Tregaron would disagree, ma'am."

Sarah smiled, pleased by her fiancé's discernment. "He would, indeed, my lord."

He turned his attention—and his smile—on her, tucking his arm close to his body—so close that the back of her hand brushed against his side as they walked. She felt the flush of color in her cheeks, knowing that Society would deem such an intimacy shockingly improper. To Sarah, though, it felt neither wicked nor indecorous; instead, she was comforted by the touch. It did, however, waken the butterflies in her stomach.

Bending toward her, he said softly but with conviction, "Just as I will disagree if you make such a statement two or three decades from now."

The color in her cheeks deepened, and the butterflies burst into flight. Unsettled by her reaction, as well as taken aback by his certainty, especially in light of her doubts a few moments ago, she dipped her head, hoping to hide her inner turmoil from his too-perceptive gaze and the *ton*'s prying eyes.

By the time they joined the throng on the stairs, Sarah had recovered a degree of equanimity. Not all of it, but she had regained as much as she was likely to command after such a tumultuous day. All too well aware that this evening would present a new set of trials, she could not help but wish that she possessed Dunnley's sangfroid. Even a fraction of it would be enormously helpful, given her current state of mind.

"Which dances have you saved for me?"

Caught up in her anxieties and unable to look at her escort while negotiating the crowded staircase, it took a moment for Sarah to realize that Dunnley was speaking to her. "Um, the two you requested—the first waltz and the supper dance."

"Excellent! I hope you will save those two dances for me at every ball we attend."

"I will, of course, if that is what you wish—"

"What I *wish*, sweet Sarah," he whispered, "is the supper dance and all your waltzes and minuets, but even an engaged couple cannot share that many dances without creating a scandal."

At that moment, Sarah could not have said whether she was pleased that Society limited a couple to two sets an evening or not. Fortunately, no response was expected as they reached the top of the stairs and greeted their host and hostess.

Before they had taken three steps inside the ballroom, Sarah, her mother, and Dunnley were surrounded by a throng of friends and acquaintances, not to mention a few quidnuncs, all of whom wanted to know if there was any truth behind the rumor that Sarah and Dunnley were to be married.

"They are indeed," the countess confirmed. "But the engagement will not be formally announced until our ball on the twenty-eighth, so how on earth anyone outside the families knew . . ." Her pretty show of confusion would have convinced anyone who did not know her well. Which, since last Season was the only one she had spent in Town since her marriage, was most of the *beau monde*.

"I proposed only this morning," Dunnley laughingly explained. "We hoped to keep the news a secret for a bit longer."

"If you wanted to keep it a secret, Sarah's brother ought not to have proposed a toast to the two of you in the middle of White's," Lady Smithson opined. In addition to being Nasty Ned's mother, she was one of the biggest gossipmongers in the *ton*.

"Where is her betrothal ring?" one man asked. "She can't be your fiancée without a ring."

Clutching the pocket of his waistcoat, Dunnley groaned—and blushed. "I can't believe I forgot!" Smiling sheepishly, he bent his head to hers and whispered, "I am so sorry, my dear. I meant to give it to you earlier so you could wear it tonight, but . . ."

When he answered the question, his reply was more of a declaration. "Ring or not, Lady Sarah and I are engaged. Surely you gentlemen can understand my plight. One look at a woman as beautiful as Lady Sarah is enough to make any man lose his head, is it not?"

Sarah blushed at that and wished, fervently but uselessly, that she and Dunnley were not the cynosure of nearly every eye in the room. But given a choice between attracting attention because of their engagement or because they had left the assembly room last night, their present circumstances, though daunting, were vastly preferable.

The crowd ebbed and flowed around them, re-forming several times. Thanks to her mother and Dunnley, who fielded nearly all of the questions thrown at them, Sarah had little to do save smile and accept a plethora of good wishes, a bit of advice, and several astonished, rather envious stares. That, and wonder how her friends would react when they heard the news. Finally, after about ten minutes—and several veiled but increasingly pointed hints about the discourtesy of keeping the ladies standing—Dunnley was able to guide Sarah and her mother to chairs at the side of the ballroom.

Several matrons followed, no doubt hoping to get more details from Lady Tregaron, and so did the Duke of Fairfax. After bespeaking a dance with Sarah, the duke turned to Dunnley and asked, in a quiet voice that hinted at umbrage, "Did you know about this yesterday at White's?"

"Yesterday?" Dunnley sounded as if he did not recall seeing Fairfax at the popular gentlemen's club the previous day. Then, his astonishment apparent, "Zounds! Was it only yesterday?"

The duke's terse nod of confirmation seemed, to Sarah, to indicate a degree of bewilderment or hurt feelings. Dunnley must have thought the same, for he offered his friend a far more detailed explanation than those he'd previously given. "I knew I wanted to marry Sarah, yes. But I did not know how long it would take me to muster the courage to approach Tregaron and ask permission to pay my addresses to her."

Even more softly, he added, "Neither of us mentioned our intentions. White's is not the place to exchange such confidences."

Sarah could not help but wonder what, exactly, they had discussed. Wondered, too, when her friends would arrive, and how explosive Tina Fairchild's reaction might be. Engrossed in plans to defuse her friend's inevitable ire, Sarah was not aware that Fairfax had departed until Dunnley asked, "What troubles you, my dear?"

Her eyes locked on the toes of his shoes, she scrambled for an explanation that was honest yet discreet. "You are, perhaps, aware that Tina Fairchild feels more than a cousinly affection for you?"

"Yes, she had a schoolgirl crush on me for several years." He swallowed audibly, clearly uncomfortable. "One that persisted after her release from the schoolroom."

Sarah's heart sank. *How can I disabuse him of the idea that Tina's infatuation is a thing of the past without betraying her confidence?* Fortunately, that organ is resilient; it bounced back into place with his next statement. "But I believe—or, rather, I hope—that is no longer the case." He recounted his conversation with Tina at Lady Oglethorpe's ball.

Smiling up at him, Sarah laid her hand on his arm. "Oh, that was very deftly done!" Then, remembering what she had learnt from her study of *Debrett's Peerage* this afternoon, she steeled herself to inquire, "Does it bother you that I am seven years younger than you are?"

"Of course not! There is a vast difference in maturity between eighteen and two-and-twenty—for both men and women."

While it was true that people learnt a great deal in those four years, Sarah felt certain that they also matured significantly between the ages of twenty-two and twenty-nine. Instead of dwelling on what could not be changed, she consoled herself with the knowledge that, even at eighteen, she had not been as giddy as Tina Fairchild. In fact, at no stage of her adolescence or childhood had Sarah ever been as capricious and volatile as her friend. Although she envied Tina's vivacity, all in all, Sarah was content with her own, more sedate demeanor.

"Does the fact that I have seven more years in my dish concern you?"

At first, Sarah thought Dunnley was teasing, but there was no accompanying twinkle in his smoky gray eyes. "Not at all," she reassured, and was rewarded with his special smile.

The almost simultaneous arrival of the Fairchild ladies and the Woodhurst twins, Lord Henry, and Lady Kesteven called a halt to Sarah and Dunnley's private conversation. Tina scurried across the room, her mother trailing in her wake, skittered to a stop in front of them with petticoats arustle and a rather indecorous display of ankle, and, in lieu of a greeting, breathlessly demanded, "Is it true?"

Uncertain of her friend's mood, Sarah shot a pleading glance at her fiancé, then greeted Tina and her mother.

"Good evening, Your Grace, Lady Tina. Is what true, you ill-mannered hoyden?" Dunnley's good-natured scold was offset by a smile.

Rolling her eyes at his obtuseness, Tina made no attempt to disguise her impatience. "Is it true that you and Sarah are engaged?"

His smile gentle yet fond, he confirmed, "Indeed it is."

Tina's squeal was as impossible to judge as her mood . . . until she threw her arms around Sarah and hugged her hard. Surprised but relieved, Sarah returned the embrace. "Thank you, Tina." The duchess offered a delighted smile and sincere felicitations, as did Lady Kesteven and Lord Henry. Deborah's joy was evidenced by the exuberant hug she gave Sarah, as well as her comment to Dunnley.

"You are a very fortunate man, my lord."

"I am, indeed, Lady Deborah. Very fortunate and very happy."

It was equally apparent that Deborah's sister did not share her feelings; both Diana's smile and her good wishes were patently insincere, and quite obviously tendered merely to satisfy the conventions. Sarah was amazed that the younger twin bothered—politeness generally did not govern Diana's actions—until she realized that they had drawn another crowd, which included several patronesses of Almack's and other leading Society matrons.

Fortunately—blessedly!—the musicians chose that moment to begin the evening's first set. Sarah's partner, Lord Howe, cut through the throng to bow in front of her, and Dunnley immediately excused himself to find his partner. Both threw Lady Tregaron a smile of apology as they departed, since she would have to deal with the siege of questions.

Theo danced the first set with the younger Miss Enderby, the second with the elder. When his hostess dragooned him into dancing with three wallflowers in succession, for pair of reels, a cotillion, and a set of country dances, he did not demur. It was as good a way as any to pass the time. None of the three was the least bit remarkable, except for the last—a young lady with a slight squint, two left feet, and far more hair than wit. Rather, if she had aught but air between her ears, she hid it well, behind a rambling discourse on the weather and the latest fashion in bonnets. *Bonnets, forsooth! What the hell did he know about bonnets?*

Although it seemed interminable, the set with Miss Left Feet finally came to an end. With more haste than grace, Theo escorted the chit back to her chaperone's side and made his escape. Then, praying that the waltz would be next, he turned his aching toes in Sarah's direction. She might not have much to say, but at least she would not subject him to foolish prattle about bonnets. Nor would she stomp on his feet.

He—and his toes—were rewarded for his chivalry and good manners. The waltz was, indeed, next. With a bow and a smile, he led his lovely fiancée to the dance floor.

More rewards were in store. Sarah chatted freely and easily, regaling him with descriptions of her first five partners' reactions to the news of their engagement. Fortunately, all were favorable, with nary a hint of gossip about their behavior last night. He, in turn, entertained her with an account of his partners, which, though it did not provoke the laugh he'd hoped, set her beautiful blue eyes to dancing merrily.

She surprised him again, in an entirely different way, once their shared mirth had faded. Peeking up at him through her lashes, she rather hesitantly inquired, "Theo, may I ask you a question?"

"Of course, my dear. You may ask anything, at any time. And you needn't request permission first."

"Is something troubling you? You were very quiet after dinner."

His initial reaction of dismay at having been so transparent was immediately followed by a surge of delight at her perception—surely a desirable trait in a wife—and her concern. It was all Theo could do to keep from hugging her, and had they been in a less public setting, he would not have restrained himself. He told her so, relishing her modest blush, as well as the speaking glance she darted at him. Even her hissed reproof was a reward of sorts, since she used his name again instead of his title.

Unrepentant, he smiled, reveling in the happy, contented feeling that warmed his heart and his soul. He drew her a little closer and explained how her family's bantering had reminded him of the interactions between himself, his brother, and his great-uncle, before Stephen was wounded. "Stephen's injury is not healing as quickly as he expected, and I am worried about him. Not just physically, but also because his spirits have been low."

"Under the circumstances, you cannot expect him to be merry as a grig."

"No, of course not. But he is behaving so oddly. Last night, instead of going out with his friends, he sat home and read a book!"

Her grin faded quickly when she saw that he did not share her amusement. Feeling like an ogre, he hastened to explain his concern. "I doubt Stephen has opened a book since he left school. For him to read for pleasure defies belief."

"His years as a soldier have no doubt changed him, perhaps in ways you haven't realized. It is quite possible that he reads more than you know."

"Perhaps, although I think it highly unlikely. And if Stephen had been reading a book of history or a military treatise, something to do with war, I daresay it wouldn't have seemed so odd. But, Sarah"—Theo paused before presenting the clinching argument—"he was reading a *novel*."

Sarah's musical laughter bubbled forth, rippling like an arpeggio. Theo stiffened, his roiling emotions a hodgepodge of hurt pride, outrage at her dismal of his concern, and disappointment. But as she spoke, his tension—and his temper—eased.

"I beg your pardon. I ought not to have laughed, but you made it sound as if he was reading the most lurid gothic tale ever written. I am not disparaging or belittling your concern, merely trying to understand it."

Aware that he had overreacted, Theo attempted to muster a smile. "It wasn't a gothic, lurid or otherwise. He was reading *Pride and Prejudice*."

"Then you must give him credit for selecting a good book. Of all the novels I have read, that one is my favorite."

"It is one of my favorites as well."

She dropped her gaze to his cravat and bit her lip, then timidly, almost warily, suggested, "Theo, if your brother is in pain, he might welcome the diversion that reading a novel—a good novel—provides."

Thinking back over the past few days, he could not deny that distraction might have motivated his brother's choice. "You may be right. Much as I wish otherwise, Stephen is still suffering. Possibly even more than I suspect."

"Instead of wondering and worrying, why don't you just ask him?"

He laughed. It was that or kiss her, and given their location, laughter was safer. Much safer. "I have tried, my dear. Many times. But he rarely gives me a straight answer. Why don't you, as his solicitous, soon-to-be sister-in-law, ask him?" It was more jest than suggestion, offered in the hope of banishing the shadows, wrought by concern, that lurked at the back of her eyes.

"Rhys might be a better choice, but since he isn't here tonight, I will. I have never met your brother, though, so you will have to introduce me."

"Sweet Sarah." Theo could no longer restrain his desire. Whirling her into a turn, he pulled Sarah close and dropped a kiss on top of her head. "Stephen isn't here tonight, my dear. He left this morning for Hampshire to escort our great-aunt to Town."

"Will they return before your dinner on Saturday?"

"Yes."

The waltz soared to its conclusion, much to Theo's regret. If he'd had his way, it would have lasted for hours, so he could spend the entire evening with Sarah in his arms.

He was pleased to discover, after escorting her back to her mother, that the feeling of euphoria and elation engendered by their waltz remained with him for the rest of the evening. Through a succession of unexceptional, mostly unmemorable partners, it stayed with him, strengthening during supper, when Sarah was at his side, and lingering late into the night.

At two o'clock, Theo took one look at Lady Tregaron's face and decided it was time to leave. She had graciously and good-humoredly borne the brunt of the questions tonight, but if her expression was any indication, the next person to importune her was likely to have his, or her, head snapped off.

She greeted his suggestion with obvious relief. Sarah, too, relaxed visibly, and he wondered if his shy little love had been hunching her shoulders against the *ton*'s intrusive inquiries since the dancing resumed after supper.

He called for his carriage, then went in search of Lord Tregaron, who had, as promised, arrived about midnight. After dancing with his daughter, his wife, and her two friends—a treat, both the marchioness and the duchess said, with which they would twit their husbands—the earl had disappeared into the card room. He was there still, Theo discovered, although not at play. Instead, Tregaron stood with his back against the wall, surrounded by half a dozen men, and appeared as much in need of rescue as his wife.

Theo was glad to perform that small service for his future father-in-law. As they left the room, the earl muttered, "Demmed bunch of jackals, the lot of them."

"They can be, at times. Your wife appears to have reached the limit of her tolerance for their questions tonight, and wishes to leave."

"Bronwen is not known for her patience, except with the children. She has probably been mumbling Welsh imprecations under her breath for the past several hours."

Although he smiled at the image conjured by the earl's words, Theo defended the countess. "I have not heard any, but I spent most of the evening on the dance floor. Lady Kesteven and the Duchess of Greenwich could give a more accurate accounting."

"Ach," Tregaron groaned theatrically. Then, with mock sternness, he inquired, "Do you mean to tell me, young man, that in addition to hearing about the rag-mannered rudesbys in the *ton* on the drive home, my wife will also treat me to a lecture on the folly of giving our only daughter's hand to a here-and-thereian who deserted her in her hour of need?"

"Possibly so." Suddenly realizing that his services as an escort were superfluous now that the earl was present, Theo suggested, "If you like, I will take Lady Tregaron in my carriage, and Sarah can ride in yours."

"Gallant, but unnecessary, Dunnley. I am quite capable of seeing both ladies safely home."

"I am sure you are, sir. I was hoping for a few minutes of private conversation with Sarah. I bought an engagement ring for her this afternoon, but I . . . um, forgot to give it to her earlier."

The earl chuckled. "Distracted, were you?"

"A bit, yes. Your daughter is very beautiful—"

"Just like her mother."

"—as well as talented and intelligent. Sometimes just looking at her, realizing what a treasure she is, is enough to drive every other thought out of my mind."

They reached the ballroom then, and in the flurry of leave-taking and the ladies' plans for the morrow, Theo feared his request would be forgotten. Or ignored. But Sarah's father was more sympathetic—and more astute—than Theo gave him credit for. As they waited for the earl's carriage, he drew Theo aside. "As long as you can contrive to remember that Sarah is not yet your wife, I have no objection to you being private for five or ten minutes."

"Thank you, sir. I won't forget."

"See that you don't. No dawdling on the drive home, either."

Sarah was a bit surprised when her father announced that Dunnley would escort her home. Not displeased, just surprised. In the close confines of the carriage as it rolled through the streets of Mayfair, she was dismayed to discover that the butterflies had returned. Even worse, they'd been joined by all their friends and relatives.

Dunnley seemed unaware of her plight, much to her relief. He kept up a spate of inconsequential chatter about the ball and the other guests. When the coachman drew rein in front of Tregaron House, they were marveling at how quickly the news of their engagement had spread.

"Speaking of our engagement"—he stepped down and turned to assist her—"your father has granted me a few minutes alone with you, so that I can give you your engagement ring."

Given the seemingly boneless state of her legs, most of Sarah's attention was concentrated on keeping her feet moving steadily forward. Preferably without falling on her face. But apparently some corner of her mind was attending to his conversation, because she not only heard him, she also remembered him mentioning a ring earlier, shortly after they arrived at the ball. "I will be honored to wear your ring, Theo." She wobbled up the front steps. "Is it a family heirloom?"

"Good evening, Lady Sarah, my lord." Jones ushered them into the entry hall—where her parents stood, awaiting her return. "Did you enjoy the ball?"

Smiling a greeting at the butler, Sarah nodded. "It was very nice but exhausting." She handed him her reticule, fan, and shawl, then realized that she needed to remove her gloves in order to don Dunnley's ring. The tiny buttons defeated her, though; her fingers suddenly seemed as rubbery as her legs. Stifling a sigh, she turned to her mother and extended an arm.

As her mother bent to the task, the earl led Dunnley into the morning room. When the last button had been unfastened and the gloves removed, Sarah and her mother followed the men.

"Ten minutes, *bach*." Though she spoke to Sarah, the countess's gaze was directed at Dunnley. "Then you will join us in the drawing room."

"Yes, Mama."

"Thank you, my lady." Dunnley gave the countess a half-bow, acknowledging her command, then offered his arm to Sarah and escorted her to the sofa.

Seating himself beside her, he resumed their interrupted conversation. "You asked me something about the ring, I believe."

"Yes. I wondered if it was an heirloom." She knew that it must be—he'd proposed only this morning and had spent most of the afternoon at White's with her father and brother—but talking with him might help her feel less . . . unsettled.

"No, my dear. I bought it for you this afternoon. Would you prefer an heirloom ring? There are several in the viscountess's collection."

"I . . . er—No, um . . ." She huffed out a breath and began anew. "I am sure that I will like whatever you have chosen. I only thought the ring must be an heirloom because you could not have had much time this afternoon for shopping."

"Not a great deal, but one can always find time—or make time—for things that are important."

"And buying me a ring was important today?" Hearing the wonder in her voice, she winced inwardly—and hoped that his ears were not so acute.

"Of course it was, Sarah." He reached for her hand, his larger, warmer one enveloping hers. "I feel like I should say something profound, something momentous and deeply meaningful, before I give you the ring, but regrettably, nothing comes to mind. I am sorry, sweetheart—my wits seem to have gone abegging."

He knelt in front of her, the movement and his resulting posture both thrilling and terrifying her. It was, of course, wonderfully romantic. What young lady would not be delighted to have such a handsome, charming, eminently eligible man so humble himself before her? Sarah doubted there was a woman in the realm between the ages of fourteen and forty who would disdain to have Dunnley at her feet. She also wondered if any of them would feel as unsettled as she did at this moment.

"Since I can think of nothing profound to say, I will simply tell you again that I love you. More and more each moment we spend together." His grip on her hand tightened. "Please, my darling, will you do me the honor of becoming my wife?"

"Theo—" She could have argued that she had only agreed

to an engagement, but there was little point. Given the depth and conviction of his feelings, not to mention his strong sense of honor, he was as likely to cry off as pigs were to fly over St. Paul's. Or the sun to rise in the west. Since she was not brave enough to end it and risk being labeled a jilt, the engagement she'd agreed to this morning would someday—probably before the end of the Season—result in a wedding. That, too, was as inevitable as night following day.

Sarah found that a daunting prospect. But even more alarming was Dunnley's utter certainty, his absolute conviction, that he loved and wanted her. Only her, for the rest of his life. The conflicting feelings he roused in her were no match for his surety, and that vulnerability frightened her.

She took a breath as deep as the butterflies would allow. "Yes, Theo, I will. I would be honored to be your wife."

"Thank you, sweet Sarah. You have made me a very happy man." His smile was wide yet gentle and sweet. "Twice today. But even more so now than this morning."

He dipped a finger into his waistcoat pocket and pulled out a ring, closing his fist around it before she caught a glimpse of it. "I was hoping to find a sapphire to match your beautiful eyes, but none of the stones were as vividly blue. Then I considered a pink diamond, but although it had a lovely hue, its color could not compare to the blush in your cheeks. In the end, I chose a ruby"—he slid the ring on her finger—"because it sparkles with the same fire that is in your heart and soul."

"It is beautiful, Theo." And it was beautiful—breathtakingly so—a brilliant ruby surrounded by smaller but equally magnificent diamonds. "But I have no fire in my heart and soul."

He clasped her hands, drawing her to her feet as he rose, then cupped her face in his hands. "You do, sweetheart. I hear it in your music when you sing or play the harp." Lowering his head, he kissed both eyelids and her cheeks, each caress soft and gossamer-light. He feathered the same soft, sweet kiss against her lips—once, twice, thrice—before drawing her closer. The next set of kisses was much the same, but each lingered longer, as if he were loath to raise his head. Then, with a groan, he wrapped one arm around her waist and tugged her against him, his other hand stroking up and down her spine. Sarah's hands, caught against his chest, slid, seemingly without volition, up his lapels and cupped the back of his neck, then tangled in his hair. Suddenly, his kisses seemed to touch her more deeply—so deeply that she trembled. By the time he pressed one last kiss on her brow and straightened, she'd begun to wonder if he might be right, because it felt like fire flowed in her veins.

And that frightened her even more.

Chapter Twelve

London, Saturday, 16 April 1814

*T*heo was normally the most even-tempered of men. Anyone who knew him, from his friends and family to the servants he employed, would attest to that.

But today was not a normal day.

He set high standards for himself, his family and friends, and his employees, as the eight previous viscounts and the fifteen barons before that had done. And like all twenty-three Middlefords of Dunnley who had come before him, as long as his family, servants, and tenants strove to attain those goals, Theo was pleased. Even if they did not quite succeed, he was satisfied with knowing they were working to achieve their objectives.

Except for today.

Today, as everyone from Price, the London butler, to the scullery maids and the boot boy would attest, trying was not enough. Perseverance counted for naught. Even scrubbing one's fingers to the bone was not enough.

Today nothing less than perfection would do.

Because tonight the future viscountess and her family were coming to dinner.

As a result, the servants had been cleaning and polishing for two days. And that was on top of all the rubbing and scrubbing done earlier in the week, tasks assigned by Mrs. Mitchum, the housekeeper, to ensure that everything looked as fine as fivepence and was as neat as a pin for the dinner party his lordship and Captain Middleford were hosting tonight.

Yesterday morning over breakfast, she'd pronounced the household ready, save for the usual cleaning and dusting done every Friday and Saturday morning.

Not two hours later, the viscount had declared the preparations woefully inadequate, and they'd all been working like demons ever since.

Or working as if they feared the wrath of their suddenly demonic viscount.

Just cleaning and polishing everything in sight wasn't enough, either. Molly, one of the upstairs maids, could testify to that. The viscount's inspection had been uncommonly thorough, encompassing *everything*—including the floor under the bed in the third-best guest chamber. Regrettably, Molly, who was wont to hurry through her work, had neglected to dust beneath the bed.

After a rare trimming by Mrs. Mitchum, who'd been informed of the lapse by his lordship, Molly had grumbled that "a bit of dust under the bed didn't matter, since her high and mighty ladyship would not step foot above stairs."

Unfortunately, his lordship overheard the impertinent remark, and as a result, Molly would likely still be dusting and scrubbing when the last trump sounded on Judgment Day. She was also the reason all the other servants were rushing about, inspecting their work and each others'. No one wanted to be the next Molly.

Especially not today.

Today, the viscount's temper was so uncertain that Lady Richard, who'd come over from Bellingham House to help with the place cards and flower arrangements, had not stayed above fifteen minutes—less time than most morning callers! Carter, the haughty valet who considered himself above the usual household grumblings, was in the dismals because his lordship had complained about the amount of starch in his cravats. Even the amiable and kindhearted bishop, who often preached about tolerance and Christian charity, was giving the viscount wide berth.

No one wanted to fall afoul of his lordship today, so all the servants were running around like a gaggle of geese with their tail feathers alight, trying to do two things at once, and occasionally getting in each other's way.

Tomorrow they would collapse into chairs and put their feet up.

If they survived tonight.

"If I survive tonight," Sarah vowed to the pale, slightly wild-eyed girl staring back from the mirror, "I will never again judge people on my first impression of them. Never complain about lack of space or the dearth of air to breathe if a hostess's ball or rout becomes a shocking squeeze. Never again go out of my way to evade meeting new people."

Pacing from one end of her bedchamber to the other, she continued her lecture. "If I hadn't been so reserved last Season, and hadn't ducked behind quite so many potted plants to avoid introductions, I might not be in this fix now."

Sarah desperately wanted to impress—favorably impress—Dunnley's relatives tonight, but she was all too well aware that she did not show to advantage in a crowd. "Very well," she conceded, nodding at the girl in the glass, who appeared quite at ease in her comfortably worn but slightly faded blue flannel dressing gown. "Nineteen isn't really a crowd, but it is still quite a lot of people."

We will sit down nineteen to dinner.

Dunnley's words came back to her, followed by a surging wave of relief. "The nineteen includes me, my family, and Dunnley, so there are only fourteen people I must impress."

Turning away from the unhelpful image, Sarah dragged her hands through her hair, realized it was still rather damp, then crossed to the hearth and plopped down on a stool to finish drying her hair.

"Perhaps less than that."

She was already acquainted with several of the remaining fourteen. "But," she informed the crackling flames, "the fact that Beth Weymouth and Karla Elston are good friends, or that Elston showed me more than passing attention last Season, or that Lord Bellingham and Lady Richard think I am a fine musician does not necessarily mean that they will deem me a suitable wife for Dunnley."

But they might approve.

Sarah did not know if the optimistic little voice came from her head or her heart, but she was grateful for its cheerful perspective.

"They might," she agreed, lowering her head to her knees and wielding her brush. "And if they do—if Beth and Weymouth, Karla and Elston, and Lord Bellingham and Lady Richard approve—then there will be only eight people I need to impress."

Frowning, she straightened, propping her elbows on her knees and her chin in her hands. "But there were only five people I hadn't met, so who are the other three?"

A minute or two later, she stood. "I can't remember, but I will learn their identities tonight."

She rang for her maid, then entered her dressing room to survey, once again, the gowns hanging in the wardrobe. Although she had known about Dunnley's dinner and Opera party for two days, she still had not selected a gown to wear. Rather, she'd made the decision half a dozen times—and chosen six different gowns. But there was no more time for dithering. No time for anything save choosing an evening or opera gown and performing her toilette. And, perhaps, a quick prayer or two.

Her decision made, Sarah carried her choice—an amaranth silk gown with blond lace trim, pleated puff sleeves, and a single flounce at the hem—into her room and laid it on the bed. Returning to the dressing room, she debated which shawl, gloves, slippers, reticule, and fan would create the most attractive ensemble.

"If I survive tonight and all goes well—or reasonably so—I vow to do everything I can to please Dunnley, and to be a perfect wife."

"If all goes well tonight, I swear that I will do everything in my power to make Sarah happy, and to be a paragon among husbands."

Theo uttered the short but heartfelt prayer to God, or to any benevolent deity that might be listening, before lathering his face to shave. He was not worried because his family and friends were overly critical and like to complain about the meal or his choice of entertainment. They were, on the whole, an amiable, fairly tolerant group. He was, however, concerned that their approbation of his chosen bride would not be given as freely and easily as it had been for past decisions. Of a certainty, they would like Sarah. She was, after all, a very lovely, well-mannered, extremely likeable young lady. But he suspected—strongly suspected—that their approval of her as his future wife would be neither as simple nor as straightforward as his arrangements for the excursion to the Opera.

As much as he loved his family—and he did, very much—Theo's primary concern was not what they would think about Sarah, but what his shy little love would think of the sometimes boisterous males and the gregarious, eternally chattering females of the Middleford and Winterbrook families. There wasn't a reticent one in the bunch, although both his cousins' wives were reserved around anyone they did not know well. Theo had recently come to realize, in the most delightful possible way, that Sarah's reserve melted over time, as she became better acquainted—and, thus, more comfortable—with people. Nice people, that is. Familiarity with Sir Edward Smithson had bred only contempt, and had increased her wariness.

"Which coat will you wear tonight, my lord?" His hands full of freshly ironed shirts and cravats, Carter bumped his hip against the door to close it.

"The black one."

The valet's long-suffering sigh echoed through the chamber. "Let me be more specific. Which of the six black evening coats hanging in the wardrobe do you wish to wear tonight?"

"You decide." Theo bent over the basin and splashed water on his face, removing the last of the lather. "Pick your favorite. Tonight I count on you to dress me from the skin out, and in the finest, most elegant style you can contrive."

Carter goggled, so rarely did he get to do the choosing. "Yes," he said faintly. Then, more strongly, "Of course, my lord." With a spring in his step, the valet directed his attention to the huge armoire.

The wry smile of amusement quirking Theo's lips faded as he turned back to the mirror and leaned forward to check for any missed whiskers.

God, please let everything go well tonight.

Chapter Thirteen

Please, Lord, let everything go well tonight.

By the time the coachman halted the carriage in front of Dunnley's townhouse on Upper Grosvenor Street, Sarah was so nervous that she feared butterflies would emerge from her mouth if she opened it. That would, of course, rid her of some of the pesky creatures, but the lepidoptera, no matter how lovely, would not embellish the image of an elegant, refined, well-mannered, competent, and confident young lady with which she hoped to win the regard of her fiancé's nearest and dearest.

Even though it was a complete sham, save for the part about her manners.

They would get her through the evening ahead, one way or another. No matter what it held in store.

Accepting her brother's assistance from the carriage, she stepped down to the pavement. Then, with her head held high and her heart racing—and a viselike grip on her brother's arm—Sarah followed her parents to the door.

Please let everything go well tonight. Please!

The butler, despite his rather formidable countenance, welcomed her with a smile. Even before Price had collected her father's and brother's hats, gloves, and canes, Dunnley stepped into the entry hall to greet her. Her family, too, of course, but his smile seemed to be for her alone.

A gracious host, he welcomed all four of them to his home, but the kiss he dropped on her cheek reminded Sarah that he had already welcomed her into his heart.

That reassured her more than a volume full of words could have, and she silently blessed him for it, despite its shockingly public setting. His soft-voiced, private greeting also bolstered her confidence.

"Good evening, my dear, and welcome to my home. You look lovelier than ever tonight, and I look forward to the day when we will greet our guests together."

Nodding to the butler to lead the way, Dunnley gestured

to an open set of double doors on the left side of the hall-way toward the rear of the house. "Although it is a bit crowded, we have gathered in the morning room, so that Lord Castleton won't have to climb the stairs."

Sarah knew that the Earl of Castleton, who walked with the aid of a sturdy cane, had injured his hip in a riding accident many years ago. She also had observed—an observation later confirmed by the earl's niece—that staircases posed his greatest, and most painful, challenge. "You are a very considerate host, Theo Middleford, as well as a very kind man."

"Thank you, sweet Sarah." Securing her hand in the crook of his arm, Theo escorted her down the hall in the wake of her parents and brother.

As she reached the doorway, Sarah saw a young man in a dark blue uniform jacket, heavily encrusted with silver braid and cording, set his glass on the mantel and, with the help of a cane, cross the room to greet her parents. Like the officers in most cavalry regiments, he wore white breeches, but his gleaming boots had silver tassels and silver trim at the top instead of the usual gold. Although he was the only military man in the room, he did not notice-ably resemble Dunnley, so she wasn't certain of his identity until he greeted her father, then bowed over her mother's hand.

"Lady Tregaron, it is a pleasure to meet you. I am Dunn-ley's brother, Stephen Middleford."

Smiling up at him, the countess returned an equally po-lite greeting, then requested, "Captain Middleford, perhaps you would be kind enough to introduce me to your relatives."

"Of course, my lady. Delighted to do it." When she moved to take his arm, he flushed and stammered, "I-I am still a bit unsteady, ma'am, so you will fare better with the earl's support."

Sarah would have been as red-faced and tongue-tied as Captain Middleford, but her mother was less easily flus-tered. Accustomed to dealing with young men and women and their insecurities, the countess, still smiling, stepped to his side and, after an arch glance at her husband, appealed to the captain's gallantry. "But Tregaron will undoubtedly talk politics with the men. I wish to meet the ladies."

"She is right." The earl's admission made it seem like Dunnley's brother would be doing both guests a favor. "I can't seem to help myself."

Captain Middleford bowed—to the inevitable and to Sarah's mother. "Be glad to introduce you, ma'am."

When Sarah and Theo stepped forward, every eye in the room slewed to the doorway. Sarah tightened her grip on her fiancé's arm and pinned a smile on her face. Then, feeling a great affinity for the early Christian martyrs thrown into the lions' dens, she advanced into the fray.

The first assault came before she'd taken three steps. And since it came from behind, she was totally unprepared. A pair of strong arms slid around her shoulders, pulling her back against a hard paunch.

"I am so delighted for you both!"

Recognizing her attacker's American accent, Sarah beat down the almost overwhelming panic that had assailed her and turned within the encircling arms to hug her friend, Beth Weymouth. Doing so required more care than it once had; Beth was *enceinte* and only two months from her confinement.

Pleased to know that one of Dunnley's relatives approved of the engagement, Sarah was shocked to see tears swimming in Beth's cornflower blue eyes. "If you are happy, why are you crying?"

"Happy tears, no doubt." Slipping an arm around his wife's expanding waist, the Earl of Weymouth bent to kiss Sarah's cheek. "Welcome to the family, Lady Sarah."

"Thank you, Weymouth."

After a whispered promise to talk more later, Sarah took Theo's arm again, feeling a bit more confident. *Two down, twelve to go.*

"You are a marvel, my dear," he complimented, leading her toward a group of three elderly ladies who were engrossed in a conversation in which their hands and mouths seemed to be equal participants. Two of the ladies, sitting side by side on a camelback sofa, were slender with silver hair; the third, a bit plump, had hair as white as new-fallen snow. "You appear as calm and composed as if we were taking the air in Hyde Park, whereas I count myself fortunate that the servants haven't quit en masse."

"*Appear* is the correct word. I fretted all afternoon and

worked myself into quite a state. I was terrified on the drive here—not so much about meeting your family, but worried that, once I did, they would not approve of me. Now, thanks to you, I am only . . . unsettled. Greatly unsettled, to be sure, but nothing worse than that."

"Pleased as I am to have been of service, I can't imagine what I did that helped."

"You were yourself," she said quietly so that no one would overhear.

One tawny eyebrow rose in inquiry, but he was unable to question her further because they reached their destination. As they'd approached, she had recognized one of the silver-haired ladies as Beth's great-aunt, Lady Julia Castleton, but Sarah did not know the other two women.

"Sarah!" Lady Julia smiled and held out a hand, tugging Sarah forward when she grasped it. "How lovely to see you again, my dear. Will you join us?"

She curtsied to all three ladies. "I am delighted to see you, too, Lady Julia. And I would be pleased to join you, if your companions do not object."

"Of course they don't object, child. They are eager to meet you." Lady Julia slid sideways, making room for Sarah, then flapped a hand at Dunnley as if to shoo him away. "You needn't hang about. We aren't going to eat her."

Unrepentant, he smiled. "I certainly hope not. I would be brokenhearted, and my chef would quit in high dudgeon. I am only 'hanging about,' as you so charmingly put it, so that I can introduce Sarah."

"I am quite capable of introducing her." Hauteur edged Lady Julia's voice.

"Of course you are, but since Sarah is my fiancée, I reserve that pleasure for myself." He smiled at Sarah and the two other women. "Aunt Meg, Lady Lavinia, may I present my fiancée, Lady Sarah Mallory." Then, to Sarah, "My dear, these ladies are"—he gestured to the woman seated on Sarah's right—"my great-aunt, Miss Margaret Middleford, and"—a nod to the lady in a nearby wing chair—"Elston's great-aunt, Lady Lavinia Symington."

Having already made her curtsy, Sarah inclined her head to each lady in turn and expressed her pleasure in making their acquaintance. Dunnley smiled again, then stepped back, warning the older women, "Much as I adore you, I won't allow you to monopolize Sarah. At least, not until after dinner. You may enjoy her company and conversation while I get her a glass of sherry, but when I return, I intend to whisk her away and introduce her to the rest of the family."

Lady Julia took him at his word and immediately launched into speech. "We were discussing embroidery, my dear. Since I know it is one of your passions, too, tell us what you have been working on since last I saw you."

Miss Middleford and Lady Lavinia nodded their approval of the topic. Delighted not to be interrogated, Sarah readily complied. "I prefer functional pieces to merely decorative ones, so I generally work chair covers, fire screens, and the like. For the last ten years, I have been working on a set of chair covers. As part of my trousseau," she explained, ducking her head to hide her blush. "Each depicts a different wildflower, all of which grow in the woods and fields around Tregaron Castle. The flower I am working on now is columbine."

"How many have you completed?" The question came from Lady Lavinia.

"Ninete—no, eighteen. Columbine is the nineteenth."

"How many were you planning to do, child?" Lady Julia inquired, sounding surprised that Sarah had done so many.

"Mama suggested twenty, so that is what I planned. She said some gentlemen might have longer tables with more chairs, but that if more covers were needed, I could do them after I was married."

Frowning slightly, Miss Middleford closed her eyes for several seconds, then shook her head. "I cannot remember if there are twenty chairs or twenty-four at Dunnley Park." She reached over and patted Sarah's arm. "No matter, though. If there are, in fact, twenty-four, I hope you will allow me to help you complete the set."

Is she offering to help because she approves of me, or because she does not? "I would be pleased to have your help, ma'am." Sarah smiled to show that her words were sincere, not just the polite response such an offer required.

"Are the covers your own designs?"

"Yes, ma'am, they are, although my younger brother,

Dafydd, helped me draw some of the flowers. He is a better artist than I am."

"Interested in botany, is he?" asked Lady Lavinia.

"No more than any other eleven-year-old boy." Remembering some of his complaints about "stupid flowers," Sarah smiled. "His real interest is architecture."

"Architecture?" Lady Lavinia's question was overridden by Miss Middleford, who said, "I understand you are a very talented musician, Sarah, both a singer and a harpist. I would ask you to play or sing for us after dinner, but I doubt there will be time before the Opera. Regrettably, we don't have a harp here, although there is a fine one at Dunnley Park."

"Are you a harpist, too, ma'am?" Sarah suspected so, since Miss Middleford had declared the harp at Dunnley's principal seat "a fine one."

"Indeed she is," Lady Julia and Lady Lavinia said in chorus, then Lady Julia added, "An excellent one."

Miss Middleford shook her head. "Not anymore. My fingers aren't as quick as they once were."

"If Dunnley will agree to cart my harp to Hampshire after we are married, perhaps you and I can play some duets, ma'am."

Sarah had not been at all certain whether Dunnley's great-aunt would like the idea, so she was delighted when Miss Middleford smiled and grasped her hands. "Oh, that would be lovely!"

Theo strolled among his guests, automatically performing his duties as host, but his eyes and his thoughts seldom left Sarah. He did not begrudge the three older ladies her company—well, yes, he did, but he knew he shouldn't. Sarah did not need his protection against a trio of sweet, kindhearted septuagenarians. Nor did she need him hovering over her all evening. But demmed if he didn't want to do just that!

She was a treasure, a far greater prize than a rakish viscount—reformed or not—deserved or should expect to win. But, amazingly, he had. She was his, at least for now. His to treasure and admire and adore. His to love and cherish. And like a miser hoarding stacks of gold coins, Theo coveted Sarah's time and attention.

Seeing her here tonight, in one of the homes they would one day share, had been a revelation. A rather painful one, since his mind and body were now riveted on images of Sarah in his life, in his home—and in his bed. She, however, was thinking nothing of the sort. Instead of imagining the days—and the nights—they would spend together here, she was torturing herself with needless worries whether his relatives would like her. As if they could do aught else but—

"Theo!"

The hand that grabbed his arm shattered Theo's reverie; his uncle's voice, slightly raised and a bit exasperated, registered a second later. Theo turned, aided by the hand on his arm, to face the Marquess of Bellingham. "Yes, Uncle Andrew?"

"I wanted to offer you my congratulations and best wishes. Lady Sarah Mallory is an admirable and utterly delightful young lady—one that any man would, and justifiably could, be proud to call his wife."

"Thank you, sir. I quite agree."

"I was a bit surprised by the timing of your proposal. Rather sudden, wasn't it?"

Theo did not particularly want his family to know the reason behind his rather precipitous proposal. Not even this man, who had guided him through adolescence into adulthood and taught him the duties and responsibilities that came with his title, and who loved him and Stephen almost as much as he loved his own sons. "Had I realized how I felt about Sarah last Season, I would have offered for her then. But it wasn't until I saw her again, earlier this week, that I truly understood how much she means to me."

Taking his uncle's arm, Theo headed for the far side of the room. Not only was the sherry decanter there, on the sideboard beside a tray of glasses, but that area was deserted. If he were going to confide the whole—and Theo rather thought he was, since his uncle wielded enormous influence both politically and socially, and would be a valuable ally—he wanted to do it in private.

After pouring a glass of sherry for Sarah, Theo told his uncle everything. Well, almost everything. He did not mention his resolution to reform, nor the reason for it, but he catalogued most of the rest, from Smithson's treatment of

Sarah to his own, quite deliberate decision to close the door of that little room at Almack's.

Bellingham said nothing for several moments. Several very long moments. "Was it the threat that Smithson poses to Sarah or the threat of scandal that led to your enlightenment?"

"My enlightenment, to use your term, was not the result of either," Theo replied in a carefully neutral tone. "It occurred shortly after I realized the extent of the threat Smithson poses, and the day before I realized that scandal was a possibility. My *enlightenment* was the realization that I would do anything, including sacrifice my life, to make Sarah happy and protect her from harm.

"I can't deny," he continued, "that the threat of scandal influenced the timing of my offer. But I already knew that I loved Sarah and wanted to spend the rest of my life with her, so I would have proposed before the end of the Season, scandal or no."

His uncle nodded. "That is the answer I expected. Thank you for indulging me and my impertinent questions. Now"—he smiled—"you'd best take your fiancée that glass of sherry before she wonders if you are having it shipped from Portugal."

Dunnley's reappearance signaled the end of Sarah's conversation with the three older ladies. As he escorted her toward a knot of gentlemen in the center of the room, he apologized for the delay and inquired how she'd fared.

"Better than I expected," she admitted, relieved to have crossed the first hurdle unscathed, "so I shan't take you to task for deserting me."

"Bowled them over, did you, sweetheart?"

"Of course not. But Lady Julia was predisposed toward me, and I think your aunt's opinion is likely to be favorable—provided I don't commit a terrible *faux pas*. I don't know about Lady Lavinia, though."

"Lady Lavinia's opinion is not important. Karla must curry her favor, but you need not."

The cluster of gentlemen, when they reached it, proved to be smaller than it had appeared. There were only four men—all those present above the age of fifty, including her

father—and Dunnley made quick work of the introduction
to the man she did not know. The gentlemen's approval
was granted even more readily than the ladies' had been,
but the reasons for their approbation varied greatly. For
Dunnley's great-uncle, the Bishop of Lymington, the fact
that she was her father's daughter and "a lovely, well-
mannered lass with a kind heart" was enough to earn his
regard. She had won the approval of the Marquess of Bellingham, Theo's uncle and Weymouth's father, and of the
Earl of Castleton, Beth's uncle, last year by staunchly sup-
porting Beth and Weymouth when they were the subject
of scandalous rumors fabricated out of whole cloth. That
esteem stood her in good stead now: Lord Castleton
praised her as "loyal and kindhearted"; Lord Bellingham
acclaimed her for those traits, too, as well as her musical
talent. All three men offered their best wishes to Sarah
and Theo, and the bishop and Lord Bellingham warmly
welcomed her to the family.

Thrown a bit off balance by their ready acceptance of
her as Dunnley's future viscountess, Sarah followed blindly
as her fiancé led toward the next group. She had lost track
of the number of people she had met, as well as her success
thus far. *Seven, I think. Possibly eight.*

"Just a moment, Theo."

He stopped on the instant, his expression concerned.
"What is it, my dear?" His hands slid up her arms, past
her elbow and the top of her glove, to the bare flesh between glove and sleeve. It was a tender, solicitous grip,
allowing him to hold her, as well as support her should she
require it.

Much as she wanted to lean forward and rest her head
on his shoulder, she could not. Not with so many people
watching. Instead, she looked down at the lovely Axminster
carpet, patterned with vines and flowers. "I just need a
minute to . . . to catch my breath."

Apparently far more concerned about her than about
appearances, he wrapped his arms around her and turned
his back to everyone in the room. Pulling her close, he
rested his cheek against her hair, sheltering her within his
embrace and, did he but know it, comforting her, too.
"Overwhelmed, are you, sweetheart? I shouldn't have invited so many people."

She tilted her head to look up at him . . . and found his lips a mere inch from hers. "It isn't the number of people—"

One tawny brow arched in disbelief, and she hastened to explain. "The number of people is daunting, but not overwhelming. What is overwhelming is your relatives' ready acceptance of me as your future wife."

Both brows soaring, he pulled back just far enough to focus on her face. "Surely you did not expect them to find you unsuitable? You are an earl's daughter."

"Yes, but he is a Welsh earl, and I am . . ."

"You are what, my dear?"

"A shy little mouse with no skill at conversation, especially with strangers."

"Even if that were true—and I would argue that you have already proven it is not—you are the shy little mouse I love. And who has some fondness for me. Those are the qualities of greatest concern to them." He dipped his head and kissed the tip of her nose. "I know that you are the perfect wife for me, and my relatives are smart enough to realize it, too."

"But, Theo—"

He placed a finger over her lips. "No more protests, my love. I will discuss this as much as you wish tomorrow or next week, but for now, you will have to trust my judgment. If we stand here much longer, your mother and brother, our friends, and all four of the aunts are going to come over, either out of concern that you have taken ill, or fearing that you have changed your mind."

Worry clouded his eyes. "You haven't, have you?"

"I have neither taken ill nor changed my mind," she reassured, not certain which possibility exercised him.

"Good." Clearly relieved, he stepped back and reached for her hand. "Are you ready to greet the rest of our guests? Most of them are already known to you."

"Yes, of course. Thank you for indulging my . . . foolishness."

"Not foolishness, and you are very welcome." Tucking her hand in the crook of his arm, he squeezed her fingers gently and smiled. "In truth, I am rather grateful for your foolish fancy, since I was able to hold you. I didn't think I would have the opportunity to do that tonight."

"Theo!" she chided, feeling the rush of color to her cheeks.

"Yes, my dear?" The twinkle in his gray eyes belied the innocent tone of his voice.

She was unable to say more—not unless she wanted the people they were approaching to hear. Her remonstrances would not upset her mother or brother, especially not Rhys, who had earned—and heard—dozens of them over the years for his teasing, but she did not want Theo's aunt or his brother to think her a termagant.

His aunt, Lady Richard Winterbrook, and Sarah's mother were ensconced on a sofa, chatting as if they had known each other for years. Which, perhaps, they had. Sarah suspected that her mother, at five-and-forty, had a few more years in her dish than Lady Richard, but it was quite possible the two women had met during the long ago Season when the newly married Lady Tregaron had accompanied her husband to Town to be presented at Court. Rhys and Captain Middleford sat across from them, talking almost as companionably. Well schooled by their mother, Rhys stood as Sarah and Dunnley drew near. Seeing Captain Middleford reach for his cane, Sarah hastened forward and pressed her hand against his shoulder, then slipped into the chair beside him.

Despite her effort to halt him, Captain Middleford rose, so Sarah did, too. As Dunnley introduced her to his brother, she looked from ginger-haired, blue-eyed Hussar to the slightly taller and leaner, tawny-haired, gray-eyed viscount but could detect no resemblance. Captain Middleford grinned. "If you are looking for some likeness between us, Lady Sarah, you won't find it. Theo looks like our mother, while I take after our father." His smile broadened. "I take it you haven't met our cousin David yet. That is where you will see a resemblance."

Sarah was not certain what he meant, but since she would, presumably, find out when she met Lord David Winterbrook, she did not inquire.

Clasping her hand between his, Captain Middleford hesitated for a moment, as if searching for words. "It is a pleasure to welcome such a lovely lady to the family. And I thank you for bringing me two new brothers, especially since one is my age."

Dunnley glanced at his brother and drawled, "My dear boy, what need have you for new brothers when you have me?" The twitching of his lips rather spoiled the effect of his mock haughty query, but Captain Middleford guffawed, as did Rhys. The ladies, however, restrained themselves to smiles. Broad smiles, to be sure, although Sarah thought that Dunnley's aunt might have muffled a giggle behind her handkerchief.

Resuming her seat, Sarah waved the men into theirs. "I hope, Captain Middleford, that you will treat me as a sister. Rhys can show you the way of it," she suggested, smiling at her brother. "It is not as simple as you might think. Younger siblings have far more respect for their older brothers than those brothers do for them."

Not unexpectedly, Rhys and Dunnley disputed her statement, but Captain Middleford was quick to agree. "That is certainly true of some older brothers, Sarah." He grinned at his brother.

"May I call you Sarah? And will you call me Stephen, please?"

"Yes, please do. I was just about to suggest it." Sarah wanted to ask him not to feel obliged to stand whenever she did, or to rise every time she entered the room, but she decided to save the request until she knew him a bit better.

Lady Richard's welcome provided the greatest surprise. "I am *very* pleased to welcome you to the family, Sarah. I spent most of last Season hoping that you would catch the eye of one of my nephews, and now you have." Like a matchmaker well pleased with her work, she smiled at Sarah and Theo.

He stared at her in amazement. Or, perhaps, astonishment. "Did you indeed, Aunt Caro?"

"She did. She even mentioned it to me," Lady Tregaron said, drawing her daughter's astounded gaze.

"You don't have your eye on any other young ladies, do you, Aunt Caro?" Stephen's nervous fidgeting made it clear that he hoped for a negative answer.

"No, not yet, but the Season has barely begun."

He muttered something that sounded suspiciously like "Lord save me," but his words were drowned by Rhys's anxious query. "Mama, you don't have your eye on any young ladies, do you?"

"No, dear," the countess assured, and Rhys sighed with relief. "But," she added, a mischievous smile quirking her lips, "as Caroline said, the Season has barely begun."

"I believe this is our cue to depart." Dunnley reached for Sarah's hand. "Sarah hasn't met David and Lynn yet, nor spoken to Elston and Karla, so we will leave you two"—he grinned at his brother and Rhys—"in Caro's and Lady Tregaron's capable hands."

"Unfair!" was Stephen's reaction.

"Not very sporting of you, Dunnley," Rhys complained.

"I have found my lady," Dunnley reminded the disgruntled pair. "I imagine Caro and Lady Tregaron will be happy to offer suggestions to help you do the same."

Glancing around the elegantly furnished room, something she had not yet had the time—or, perhaps, the presence of mind—to do, Sarah was amazed to realize that she had talked to all but four people. And the ten members of Dunnley's family with whom she'd already spoken seemed to approve of her—except, possibly, Lady Lavinia. Even so, as she strolled, hand in hand with Theo, toward the final cluster of people, a group of six gathered in front of the fireplace, Sarah could not help but wonder if his family was truly pleased with his choice, or if politeness, not to mention Dunnley's expectations, had influenced their responses. Time would tell, she supposed, but she would much prefer to know now.

The three gentlemen rose when Sarah and Theo reached them. Weymouth offered her another smile; the Marquess of Elston, a smile, his good wishes, and a kiss on the cheek. The third man, Weymouth's younger brother, Lord David Winterbrook, turned when Dunnley introduced him and his wife—and Sarah immediately understood Stephen Middleford's cryptic comment. She glanced from Lord David to Dunnley's brother, then back at Lord David.

He bowed over her hand, expressed his pleasure at making her acquaintance, and then, smiling, asked, "Did no one warn you?"

"No. Well, yes, but I didn't understand what he meant." She compared the two men again. Despite subtle differences in the color of their hair and eyes, Lord David and Stephen could easily be mistaken for twins. Lord David's hair was darker in color, auburn to Stephen's ginger; his eyes a richer

blue, like the sky on a perfect summer day. Perhaps an inch
shorter than his cousin, Lord David also appeared to be a bit
leaner, more like Dunnley than Stephen.

The ladies finished their conversation, and Karla Elston
and Lady David rose to greet Sarah. Karla with some difficulty, since she, like Beth Weymouth, was *enceinte*. Although her confinement would not be until mid-July, Karla,
perhaps because she was so petite, appeared closer to her
time than her much taller friend.

Lord David squeezed his wife's hand, then stepped away,
leaving the women to their conversation. Once again, Sarah's gaze darted from him to Stephen and back, marveling
at their almost identical appearance.

"Amazing, isn't it?" Lady David said. A very attractive
woman with beautiful hazel eyes and a hint of auburn in
her brown hair, she was only an inch or two taller than
Karla, but her figure was every bit as generous as Sarah's.
"David and Stephen look more like brothers than . . . than
most brothers do. But all four cousins are the image of one
of their parents." Turning to Dunnley, she said, "You must
show Sarah the portraits of your parents and your aunt.
George and David's mother, that is."

"If there is time after dinner, I will. Or," he suggested,
"you can show them to her while the gentlemen drink
their port."

"If you dawdle overlong, perhaps I will."

Warned by Dunnley of the need to stand close to Lady
David when speaking to her, and to face her, Sarah stepped
closer. "I understand you and Lord David are newly married. May I offer my best wishes to you now, since I was
unable to do so at your wedding?"

Lady David looked around for her husband, then back
at Sarah. "I am sorry, Lady Sarah. I could not hear you.
Would you mind if we sat down? If you sit on my right,
very close to me, I should be able to hear you."

"I don't mind at all," Sarah said, sitting in the position
Lady David indicated.

It took two tries—Sarah was not quite close enough the
first time—but she was able to convey her good wishes to
the newlyweds.

"Have you and Dunnley set a wedding date yet, Lady
Sarah?"

Since they were sitting almost in each other's laps, addressing each other by their titles seemed incongruous. "No, not yet. Will you call me Sarah, please? And may I call you by name?"

"Thank you, Sarah." Lady David's smile lit her face, vanquishing the frown that had creased her brow as she'd watched Sarah's mouth to better "hear" her. "My name is Madeline, but I prefer Lynn."

Price, Theo's butler, entered to announce that dinner was ready. Sarah repeated the message for Lynn, then stood, figuring out who her dinner partner would be. She was the lowest-ranking lady save for Lynn and Miss Middleford, and Lord David was the third-lowest in precedence of the men. She smiled as he walked toward her, but he offered his arm to his wife. The numbers were not even, Sarah realized; there were ten gentlemen and only nine ladies. She looked for her brother, but before she spotted him, Dunnley appeared at her side.

"Shouldn't you be escorting Karla?" she asked.

"If precedence prevailed, I would. But this is a family dinner, my dear, and in the Middleford and Winterbrook families that means a gentleman may choose his dinner partner. I choose you, sweet Sarah." Theo raised her hand to his lips before placing it on his arm. "You will notice that every married man here has chosen to escort his wife. And the unmarried ones, except for Castleton, have chosen ladies unrelated to them."

"Why do you suppose Lord Castleton chose his aunt?"

"Probably because she is accustomed to his rather halting pace."

Once they were seated, with Sarah on Theo's right, Lord Bellingham, the bishop, and Stephen rose, almost as one, each wanting to propose a toast to Sarah, "the lovely new member of our family." Bellingham prevailed, since he was the eldest male member of the family, but the bishop was nimble-tongued and slipped his toast in after Bellingham's. Amid the laughter at the marquess's mock indignation, Weymouth, Lord David, and Stephen quickly added their mite. Sarah's cheeks were crimson long before they finished their high-flown praises, and she wished that she might propose a toast to the members of Dunnley's family. Her father did it for her, and far more eloquently than she could have ever contrived.

Then, the toasts drunk and her acceptance no longer in question, for the first time all day, the knots in Sarah's stomach eased.

Thank you, God, for helping me survive this evening.

Chapter Fourteen

*T*heo and his brother arrived at Tregaron House shortly after noon on Sunday. Last night, the countess had invited all four Middlefords to dine with them after church, but his great-aunt and great-uncle had declined, pleading a previous engagement. As he followed Jones up the stairs, the spring in Theo's step was not because he was looking forward to spending the afternoon with the Mallorys, although, of course, he was, but because he was eager to see one particular member of that family—his betrothed, his beautiful, beloved Sarah.

Especially after the scare she had given him—given all of them—last night.

Hearing her sigh of relief after all the toasts had been drunk, he'd looked over in time to see her slump back in her chair, her eyelashes fluttering as she struggled to retain her grasp on consciousness. She had lost the battle, but he'd won a minor victory by swooping her up just before she'd hit the floor.

Never in his life had Theo moved so quickly. Nor felt such terror as when he'd held her unconscious form in his arms.

She'd come to her senses a minute or so later, although it had seemed considerably longer. More like a millennium, or an eon. Cold and terrified as he'd been, the Ice Age might well have come again before she opened her eyes and spoke.

Sarah had been mortified, her embarrassment almost a tangible thing. Theo had felt only relief that she was alive and conscious and able to experience emotion. Any emotion, even an unpleasant one.

They had all fussed over her, of course, especially her mother and all four of the aunts. She hadn't liked that—she hated being the center of attention—but she'd borne it with her usual grace and dignity.

Entering the drawing room before Jones could announce him, his brother a step or two behind, Theo's eyes quickly swept the room. As he crossed to greet his hostess, he struggled to conceal his disappointment, as well as his worry, over Sarah's absence. He did, however, manage a few moments of rather desultory conversation with Lady Tregaron and his Aunt Caro, whom he had not known would be present.

Just as he spotted his younger cousin talking to Tregaron and Llanfyllin, delighted laughter at the far end of the room spun Theo in that direction. His knees weak with relief, crossing the fine Savonnerie carpet to exchange greetings with the three men seemed akin to walking through a bog. Neither feat was particularly difficult, but one felt strangely off balance whilst accomplishing it.

But even as he spoke to the trio, Theo's gaze repeatedly drifted to the far corner of the room. And it was neither the furnishings nor his cousin's wife that drew his attention.

It was Sarah, his sweet, sweet Sarah, smiling and looking as lovely as ever. As healthy as ever. As if she had not stopped his heart and scared ten years off his life last night by swooning in his dining room.

A bark of laughter from Llanfyllin drew Theo's attention back to his companions. "Dunnley, you'd best go greet my sister and assure yourself that she is well—which she is—before you make any further attempts at conversation."

Tregaron wore an amused smile, and David and Stephen wore ear-to-ear grins as identical as in appearance as they themselves were. Loath to admit that his attention had wandered, Theo said, "I can't imagine why you think I wasn't attending."

"Perhaps," his cousin suggested, "it was the fact that when Llanfyllin asked your opinion of mangel-wurzels, you said they were very tasty."

There was no way, graceful or otherwise, to wriggle out of that. Not only had Theo never tasted the beet-like plant, he didn't even grow them for fodder. With a shrug and a smile, he confessed. "You have caught me out. I apologize for my lapse, but I worried about Sarah all night and all morning. Relieved as I am to see her looking so well, I won't be completely reassured until I have spoken to her."

"Then why are you standing here with us?" the earl asked, still smiling. "I imagine my daughter is anxious to talk to you, too."

"In that case, gentlemen"—Theo stepped back a pace and gave a mock bow—"I shall take my leave."

Appearing to nonchalantly stroll the length of a room when he wanted to run was not an easy task, but Theo gave it his best effort, all too aware that Sarah's father and brother were watching. As he approached Lynn Winterbrook and Sarah, he heard snatches of their conversation.

". . . admired ladies who play the harp," Lynn commented. "They look so delicate and graceful, and harp music sounds . . . like something angels would play."

Sarah laughed. He heard that well enough, and delighted in the sound, but the rest of her response was too softly spoken to reach his ears.

"You are very kind to offer, but it would be a waste of your time. I cannot hear well enough to give my stepdaughter lessons on the pianoforte, unless I rest my head against the lid."

". . . harp is a perfect instrument . . . head close to the strings." Sarah grabbed Lynn's hand and tugged her to her feet, then led her to the harp.

Unwilling to interrupt, especially if doing so would deprive him of an opportunity to hear Sarah play, Theo stopped, hoping that he was far enough away to be out of both ladies' sight.

Once she had persuaded Lynn to sit on the stool, Sarah positioned the harp so that the upper curve of its back rested against Lynn's left shoulder, her ear mere inches from the strings. Standing behind Lynn and slightly to her left, Sarah leaned forward and, a frown creasing her brow, began to play.

Not two measures into the piece, Lynn's face lit with

delight. "I can hear it! I can hear every note." Turning on the stool, she threw her arms around Sarah's waist and hugged her hard.

Smiling, Sarah returned the embrace. "Good. Then would you like me to teach you to play?"

"Yes!" Lynn jumped to her feet, exuberant at the prospect, and hugged Sarah again, but a moment later her smile faded. "No. There is little point in learning, since I don't have a harp."

Drawn the length of the room by his wife's excited exclamations, David, who had been standing behind Theo, crossed to Lynn and tipped her face up to his. "Sweetheart, I will gladly buy you a harp. I will buy a dozen of them, if you wish."

She searched his face, then sighed and leaned against him, resting her head on his chest. "Thank you, David. One is all I need."

He slipped an arm around her waist. "While we are in Town, there is a harp in the music room at Bellingham House you can use. It probably hasn't been played in a decade, but knowing my father, it will be in perfect tune."

Theo felt a hand—a small, delicate hand—slip into his. Raising it to his lips, he smiled down at Sarah, exulting in the fact that, for the first time, she had reached for his hand. "Good afternoon, my love. How are you feeling today?"

"I am fine. Truly," she insisted.

Schooling his features, he attempted to remove whatever trace of doubt or incredulity in his expression had prompted her final utterance. "I am very glad to hear it. You had me—and everyone—extremely worried last night."

Her gaze dropped, and she studied the toe of her slipper as it drew patterns on the carpet. "I am sorry, Theo. I . . . I don't know what . . . why . . ."

Theo had a very good idea why she had fainted, although he had not realized that she would find the prospect of meeting his relatives so daunting. Slipping his arm around her waist, he hugged her to his side. She leaned against him and peeked up at him through her lashes. "Are you very angry with me for ruining your dinner party?"

"What?" He tipped her face up to his, keeping his fore-

finger beneath her chin so that she could not avert her gaze. "Sarah, you didn't ruin anything, and I am not angry. Why in the world did you think I would be?"

"Do ladies frequently faint at your table?" Her tone was a blend of sarcasm and amusement, as if she were mocking herself. Or, perhaps, mocking him.

Hiding a smile, he pretended to consider the matter. "No. You were the first." Bending his head, he whispered, "First in my heart and first to faint at my table."

As expected, she blushed. While she was searching for a response, he led her to the chair in which she'd been seated when he arrived. Taking a place beside her, he glanced around, wondering what had become of his cousin and Lynn. He was pleased to see that they were at the far end of the room, where Lynn was talking animatedly to Aunt Caro and Lady Tregaron. Selfishly, his pleasure had naught to do with Lynn's enthusiasm, but was solely because Lynn's and David's absence afforded him a few minutes of private conversation with Sarah.

And Theo desperately needed a few private minutes, although not for the same reason as he had a few nights ago.

Not that he would refuse an opportunity to be alone with Sarah and to test the depth of her passionate nature. He would not, of course; he wasn't a fool. But at the moment, passion was not his primary concern. It wasn't even a consideration. And wasn't that an extraordinary admission for a rake—even a reformed one?

Especially since he would like nothing more than to haul Sarah in front of a parson, and then, as soon as the ceremony was over, carry her off to his bed. But he knew that she did not share his eagerness. And twenty-two days into his reformation—twenty-two and a half, to be precise—he was demmed eager. Abstinence was hard on a man, especially one whose body seemed achingly unaware of the vows his mind and his heart had made. Celibacy was like to be the death of him—if all the cold baths did not kill him first.

Just as he was losing his composure, Sarah recovered hers, along with her voice. "You cannot deny that I ruined your plans for the Opera, and I am very sorry for that. You wanted the *beau monde* to see us, and our families, together—"

Baffled by her self-recriminations, he interrupted without a twinge of guilt. Well, without any twinges for his rudeness; he felt a number of guilty pangs for subjecting her to last night's ordeal. "They saw us together at—" He bit back the word Almack's. "At the Enderby ball. Where, if you recall, the news of our engagement seemed quite well spread."

"Yes, but—"

"And while I cannot deny that I would have enjoyed attending the Opera with you and hearing Madame Grassini sing as Sabina in *Gli Orazi e i Curiazi*, I also thoroughly enjoyed spending the evening talking with you, George and Beth, Elston and Karla, and David and Lynn."

"Don't forget Stephen," she added with an impish smile.

Hoping to further lighten her spirits, he rolled his eyes and, with a dramatic flair worthy of Edmund Kean, exclaimed, "How could I possibly forget our chaperone?"

She giggled, the sound delighting him. "I enjoyed myself, too. And our families were seen together at the Opera." In a contemplative tone, she added, "Perhaps my swoon wasn't so disastrous, since it gave Beth and Karla and Lynn an excuse not to attend."

"Actually, my dear, you—and your swoon—saved me from looking like an idiot. It was stupid of me not to realize that Beth and Karla would be uncomfortable appearing in such a public forum, and that Lynn would be bored, and probably frustrated, because she couldn't hear."

"You are a man, so how could you possibly know how Beth and Karla would feel?"

"The fact that they haven't attended any social events this past week ought to have been sufficient indication. Even for a man," he appended wryly.

Damn, damn, damn! Theo closed his eyes in a feeble and quite useless attempt to halt the conflicting emotions warring inside him. Despite the rather urgent necessity of informing Sarah of the unexpected news he had received this morning and its unfortunate repercussions, he was loath to interrupt her lighthearted chatter. It pleased him, perhaps far more than it ought, that her formidable reserve had melted like snow in the sunlight of his regard.

"Theo, what is wrong?"

His eyes flew open, the brush of her hand against his

warming his heart even more than the concern in her voice. Her other hand hovered near his face, as if she'd reached to cup his cheek but halted, uncertain of his reaction. To assure her that he welcomed her touch, he captured her hand in his and carried it to his cheek, reveling in the sensation of her skin against his, then turning his head to place a kiss in her palm.

"Theo?" There was a world of surprise and several questions in that single word. She hesitated but forged ahead resolutely, venturing another question; one more direct and, thus, more difficult to avoid. "Are you unwell?"

Aye, I am sick at heart. He swallowed that retort, knowing that she would not understand it. Closing his eyes, he searched his mind—or his heart—for a different one. A better one.

"Theo?" Worry laced her tone now. But it was the balm of her touch, fingers stroking his cheek, then feathering over his forehead, that finally loosened his tongue.

"I am not ill," he muttered, but the croaking voice bore little resemblance to his normal tone, and sounded utterly unconvincing, even to his own ears.

"Please, tell me what is wrong. And what I can do to help you."

You can love me. Again he bit back the words. Love could not be requested or demanded. It could be given, but not taken. When the time came—if it ever did—she would offer her heart freely. Although the outcome had initially hung in the balance, he entertained the hope that, in time, she would grant him that wondrous, much-desired gift. A hope that grew stronger every time he saw her, nurtured by the fact that, in the past few days, her feelings had warmed from friendship to a certain fondness. Perhaps even affection.

Her hand fluttered down, her fingertips brushing his coat above his heart. Gossamer-light though it was, the touch galvanized him—into action and into speech. He caught her hand, pressing her palm over his heart and securing her hand with his own. "Sarah, I beg your pardon for being such a rag-mannered guest. I received some bad news this morning and—"

"My lady, luncheon is served," Jones intoned from the doorway.

"*Damnation!*" Theo winced; he had not been able to keep the heartfelt curse between his teeth. "I beg your—"

Sarah's finger sealed his lips. "I agree with your assessment. But, Theo, you will tell me about this after luncheon." It was neither a question nor a request; it was an order. One with which he would readily comply.

"Yes, my dear, I will," he promised.

Damnation indeed! Sarah had hoped she would be able to question Theo during luncheon, but Fate, in the guise of her mother, intervened. Since there were three male guests, the countess informed her daughter's fiancé that she intended to treat him as if he were already a member of the family and seat him in the middle of the table, giving his cousin and brother the places of honor on her right and left. A nonpareil, Dunnley was as meticulous in his manners as in his dress, so it was not surprising that he declared himself flattered to be deemed part of the family.

The surprise—and the disappointment—were Sarah's. Not only did she not have Theo sitting beside her, she was stuck on the opposite side of the table, between Stephen Middleford and her brother. Her brother! What could be more lowering than for a young lady to have her brother as one of her dinner partners? Especially since her mother could as easily have seated Sarah in the empty place on the other side of the table, between Theo and Lord David.

Sarah loved her brother dearly, and his conversation could not be faulted. He was a good table partner, too, showing her the same courtesy and consideration he showed Lady Richard, who was on his other side. But charming and well mannered though he was, Rhys was not the dinner partner Sarah wanted.

She concentrated her attention on her fiancé's brother, since she could not give it to her fiancé. Stephen answered her questions readily enough, but not at any length, making it difficult to sustain a conversation. At first, she thought his concise replies might be due to some sort of military preciseness, but by the end of the meal, her opinion was quite different. Unless she was very much mistaken, and Sarah was almost certain that she was not, Stephen Middleford, heroic captain of the Seventh Hussars, was as shy as she.

In a voice too quiet to be heard by anyone else, she put

the question to him. "Stephen, perhaps my imagination has run amok, but . . . That is, I wish you would explain to me how it is possible for a military officer—an officer whose bravery has been mentioned in dispatches on more than one occasion—to be so reserved?"

"I am not shy with my men or with other officers. Not even with Wellington. If I am in camp or on campaign, I know what is expected of me. But social situations are quite different because I can never think of anything to say, especially to ladies."

His expression and tone anxious, he asked, "Is that going to be a problem?"

"Is what going to be a problem?"

"Is my shyness going to be a problem when I am escorting you?"

Sarah blinked, wondering if she had lost another portion of her memory last night when she fainted. "Are you planning to escort me somewhere?"

Stephen muttered something she couldn't quite hear, then sighed deeply. "Theo didn't tell you yet, did he?"

It was more statement than question, but Sarah answered anyway. "He said very little in the drawing room, and he seemed . . . distracted. Then, just before Jones announced luncheon, Theo said that he had received some bad news this morning, but he has not yet told me what it was."

He nodded, then asked rather hesitantly, "Since I have already put my foot in my mouth, would you like me to tell you?"

"No. I think it would be best if Theo tells me. From what you have said, I take it that you have agreed to escort me somewhere in his stead?"

"Not just agreed, I *volunteered* to escort you." He smiled, proud of his accomplishment, and given what he'd told her earlier, it was, indeed, an achievement.

She returned his smile, even though she suspected that Stephen's reasons for offering had more to do with a desire to help his brother than for the pleasure of her company. "Even if you must escort me to a *ton* social event?" she quipped.

"Even then. Ball, rout, soiree, Venetian breakfast, whatever entertainments you wish to attend. Can't dance, though. But that is just as well. Unlike my brother, I have two left feet. Tromp on ladies' toes whenever I dance—not just my partner's, either."

The countess rose to lead the ladies from the room. As she passed through the doorway, Sarah was struck by two startling revelations. The first was that she had no idea what she'd eaten during the last half of the meal, if she'd ever lifted her fork during her attempts to draw Stephen into conversation. The second discovery was so astonishing that she could not imagine why—or how—it had escaped her notice until now. *I sat next to Theo for quite half an hour before luncheon and never once did I feel the slightest flutter. Nor were my knees the least bit wobbly.*

She recalled wondering earlier in the week—at Almack's, perhaps?—if being around him more would ease or exacerbate the strange feelings she experienced whenever he was near, but she had not expected propinquity to have such an immediate effect.

Especially after the kisses he had given her Thursday night! Not only did they heat her blood near to boiling, but also rendered her legs utterly boneless and roused the butterflies to such frantic fluttering that it was a wonder they had not worn out their wings. Indeed, if the lepidoptera hadn't been active early last evening, she might have thought they'd been frightened off by Theo's kisses. In much the same way that those kisses had frightened her— and, at the same time, thrilled her.

In all fairness, she could not say that Theo's kisses and caresses *per se* had been frightening. It was her response to them—or to him—that alarmed her. Sarah had been caught beneath the kissing bough a few times, mostly by her cousins or the scions of neighboring houses, but none of those kisses had affected her as profoundly as Theo's. Nor had those Christmas kisses ever incited her to indecorous behavior. An urge to giggle, yes; once or twice, a squirming aversion. But never before had she been tempted to respond wantonly. With Theo, she had been more than tempted; she'd thrown her arms around his neck and kissed him back.

Her face heated at the recollection, so she stopped short of the drawing room doors to allow her cheeks to cool. Fate was still proving fickle, though; Theo appeared at her side a moment later. Sarah hoped that her cheeks were not glowing crimson, but she feared their color was as fiery as it felt.

"Sarah? Are you unwell?" He slid his arm under hers, offering his support.

"No. Just a bit embarrassed."

"Embarrassed? Why?"

"It does not matter." She waved a dismissive hand—but in front of her face, hoping to cool her heated cheeks. "You wanted to talk to me?"

"Yes. I asked your father's permission, and he granted me ten or fifteen minutes alone with you, either in his study or in the morning room. Do you have a preference?"

She turned toward the stairs. "No. Do you?"

His frown was more abstracted than contemplative or aggrieved, and coupled with his lack of an answer, worried Sarah a bit. Yet when they reached the ground floor, he led her to her father's study, an indication, or so she chose to believe, that he was not as lost in thought as he'd been before luncheon.

As soon as he closed the door behind them, Theo's actions made it clear that he was not unaware of her. He slipped his arms around her, hugged her close, and rubbed his cheek against her hair, holding her as if her very presence comforted him in a way that nothing else did or could.

But as flattering as that was—and it was extremely flattering—it was also rather disquieting to think that the news he had received had so unsettled him that he needed consoling. Ignoring her fears and forebodings, Sarah looped her arms around his waist and relaxed against him, perfectly content to comfort him and be comforted in turn. And as willing as he to defer the bad news for a minute or two.

She wondered if he would kiss her. She was not altogether certain whether she wanted him to or not. Just the thought that he might caused a not unpleasant fluttering in her stomach. When he moved, however, it was only to nuzzle his cheek against hers, not to kiss her. Surprised to feel a stab of disappointment, Sarah's arms tightened involuntarily as she realized that she now knew the answer to her unformed question. She wanted him to kiss her, no matter how the butterflies reacted when he did.

She hugged him again, harder this time, hoping he would divine her thoughts. Then, feeling quite daring, she turned her head and kissed his cheek.

She'd intended the kiss as an offering of comfort and

support. And, perhaps, also as a hint. She hadn't expected a revelation. But unexpected or not, she rejoiced at the enlightening discovery: Theo's cares and concerns were of vital importance to her, not just because he was her friend, but because he was essential to her happiness.

Is love caring for a man so much that you cannot imagine being happy if he is not? If your life will seem empty and incomplete if you cannot share it with him? She might not have a name for these feelings, but that did not prevent her from experiencing them and knowing their truth. Nameless or not, they moved her so much that she kissed Theo again. Not just a quick brush of her lips against his smooth-shaven cheek, but a more lingering caress this time.

"My sweet, sweet Sarah," he murmured. His hands slid to her waist, and he stepped back.

She surged forward, a wordless protest slipping past her teeth, but his grip tightened, arresting her motion. Holding her in place, the distance between them enough to satisfy the highest of high sticklers, he smiled ruefully. "If I kiss you, my love, our time will expire before I speak a single word. Or, rather, before I speak another sensible one."

"In that case, perhaps we should sit down, so you can tell me the news you received." She crossed to the two wing chairs in front of the hearth and sat in the one her father favored, evidenced by its slightly worn burgundy leather upholstery.

Theo crossed one leg over the other, flicked an invisible piece of lint off the sleeve of his dark blue superfine coat, then uncrossed his legs, planting both Hessian-shod feet firmly on the floor. Were he any other man, Sarah would believe such fidgets an indication that he was ill at ease, but he was the Viscount Dunnley, famed for his poise and his address. By all reports, he never suffered the slightest uncertainty in any social situation. At the moment, however, he bore more resemblance to a schoolboy summoned before the headmaster than to the urbane, sophisticated gentleman whose behavior set the standard by which others were judged. And like an errant schoolboy, Theo looked as if he would prefer to be somewhere else. Anywhere else.

Every silent moment that passed increased Sarah's conviction that his news must be very bad indeed. Each one frayed her nerves and composure a bit more, until she wanted to beg him to tell her so that her imagination would cease envisioning ever more dreadful scenarios.

Finally, when she thought she could not bear it another second, he leaned forward, bracing his forearms on his legs, and caught her gaze. "This morning a groom arrived from Dunnley Park with an urgent message from my steward. All the rain we have had this spring on top of all the melted snow this winter has caused two drainage ditches to collapse, and extensive flooding. My steward is a good man, and the fact that he requested that I come immediately tells me the problem is both serious and severe."

He sighed, his eyes pleading for her to understand. "I have to go to Hampshire, sweetheart."

Sarah's heart sank, but she was the daughter and sister of landowners whose responses would be exactly the same. "Of course you do."

"The timing is damna—er, horrible. In fact, it could hardly be worse. But there is no help for it. I have to go."

"Of course you must," she reiterated. "How long will you be gone?"

"A week or so."

A week! Sarah strove to conceal her dismay.

"I will return as soon as I can, my love. Until I do, Stephen has volunteered to escort you."

She mustered a smile. "That was very kind of him. Will it be too much . . . That is, do you think he has recovered enough for that?"

"He should be fine as long as he doesn't have to stand or walk for extended periods of time." His smile a bit strained, he added, "He isn't likely to ask you to dance, either."

"I shall be pleased to have his escort, whether he dances or not." Suddenly fearful, she blurted, "Does Stephen know about Sir Edward?"

"Not yet, but with your permission, I will tell him tonight. I would also like to tell Fairfax and Blackburn. They can help Stephen keep an eye on Nasty Ned."

"Stephen needs to know, and you have my permission to tell Fairfax." She bit her lip, considering the Earl of Blackburn. She did not know him well, but he was older than Stephen and the duke, and something of a Corinthian, so he might prove to be a valuable ally. "Blackburn, too, if you think he would be willing to help."

"He will." There was not a trace of uncertainty in Theo's tone. "I would also like your permission to tell David, if he and Lynn plan to accept any invitations."

"Of course you may tell David. Lynn, too."

"Thank you, sweetheart. It will ease my mind to know that several of my friends, as well as my family, are looking out for you." He reached out a hand. When she placed hers in it, he tugged her to her feet, then into his lap.

"Theo!"

"Yes, my love?"

"I thought you wanted to talk to me."

"I do. I have been. But I am nearly finished now." He grinned. "Are you saying that you can not talk when you are sitting in my lap?"

"That," she said primly, "will depend on the subject of your conversation."

"Music" was his surprising reply. "If you have selected some songs for us to sing at the duchess's musicale, I will take the music with me and start practicing my part."

"I have several songs in mind, but I thought it would be best if we chose them together. The music is in the drawing room." She attempted to rise, but his arms banded around her, holding her in place.

"It will still be there in a few minutes." He nuzzled her cheek, then strung a line of soft kisses from her ear to her chin. "I have one or two more questions."

"Then you'd best ask them quickly, while I can still provide a sensible answer."

His head came up, a roguish smile curving his lips and brightening his eyes. "Is that so?" he drawled.

Although she blushed, Sarah met his gaze. "Yes."

"Ah, my sweet Sarah." He rested his forehead against hers. "Will you write to me while I am gone? And may I write to you?"

A strange request, since he would only be gone a week. "Of course I will, if you wish."

"I do. I will miss you, sweetheart, so I would like you to tell me what you are doing, and what is happening in Town."

She nodded. "And will you write and tell me what you are doing?"

"I will." Circling her waist with his hands, he lifted her to her feet, then rose to stand beside her.

After looking at her—very intently, as if memorizing her features—he pulled her into his embrace. When his hand began rubbing her back, she slipped her arms around his waist and leaned against him, utterly content. Gathering her courage, she lifted her head and confessed, "I will miss you, Theo."

For the next several minutes, she had neither the breath nor the wit to say more.

Chapter Fifteen

London, Monday, 18 April 1814

*D*awn was only a faint glimmer on the horizon when Theo left London on horseback. Both the time of his departure and his mode of transportation were unusual. He usually drove his curricle, or rode in style and comfort in his traveling chaise. He usually left after breakfast, arriving at Dunnley Park in midafternoon after a leisurely journey. But usually he did not start thinking about how quickly he would be able to return to Town before he even reached the first tollbooth.

Riding, he soon discovered, gave a man a great deal of time to think. Given the number and variety of the subjects competing for his attention, Theo welcomed the opportunity for quiet contemplation.

Not surprisingly, Sarah dominated his thoughts. Perhaps she always would. He hated having to be away from her just now—and perhaps that would always be true as well—but there was no help for it. He might wish that the ditches had not collapsed and flooded the fields, but wishes, no matter how fervent, would not change a thing.

Even so, he wished that he hadn't had to leave Town at this particular time. Their engagement was only a few days old. The possibility of scandalous gossip was still very real. And he was not entirely convinced that Nasty Ned would give up his pursuit of Sarah. Although he had assured her that Smithson would no longer be a problem, Theo had done so believing he would be there to guarantee that the baronet was not.

Theo knew that Stephen, Fairfax, and Blackburn, as well as Sarah's father and brother, would do everything in their power to keep her safe. And to keep Smithson far away from her. David had volunteered, too, in the unlikely event that he could persuade Lynn to accept some of the invitations they had received. But even though Theo trusted all six men explicitly, he trusted himself more. His love for Sarah would ensure that he was not distracted from his purpose, whereas the other men either did not love her or, if they did, they were more likely to be distracted.

He also feared that while he was absent, she might rebuild the walls of her formidable reserve. Having laid siege to them and successfully breached them, he would much prefer to spend his time exploring the treasures within instead of having to repeat the exercise.

And treasures there were—an abundance of them. Beauty, talent, intelligence. A kind and caring heart. A deep, abiding affection for those she loved. And a well of passion just waiting to be tapped.

Deep in his bones, in his heart and soul, Theo knew that Sarah was the perfect wife for him. And he, the perfect husband for her. She would be his friend and companion, his confidante and sounding board, and a passionate lover; he was eager to fill all those roles for her. Unfortunately, Sarah did not yet realize how perfectly matched they were.

Theo knew that her feelings for him had deepened. She had reached the point of being comfortable showing affection for him. She could—and did—touch him, reach to hold his hand, kiss him. But although he was more than just a friend, she had not yet given him her heart.

And he wanted it. Wanted it more than he'd ever wanted anything in his life.

He had done what he could to minimize the effects of his absence. All that was left was to hope that he need spend only a few days in Hampshire, that Smithson would not press scurrilous attentions on Sarah, and that her family and their friends would keep her safe if the baronet did.

And to pray that John Donne had been right when he'd written that absence joined hearts of truest mettle.

As she strolled downstairs for breakfast, Sarah wondered if Theo had departed for Dunnley Park yet. He had dominated her thoughts since the moment she'd awoken—in truth, since he and his brother had left Tregaron House last night—but it was possible that he was still in Town. How strange that she was already missing him when he might still be here.

Even though she was a bit later than usual coming downstairs, she was surprised to find the dining room empty. Her father would have eaten hours ago; her brother was probably still abed; but her mother was usually here at this hour. Sarah filled a plate from the warming dishes on the mahogany sideboard, smiling at Jones as he seated her and poured her a cup of tea.

Noting the red rosebud and the letter between her place and the countess's, Sarah realized that her mother had not yet breakfasted. Smiling at the thought of her father sending the bloom to her mother, Sarah picked up her fork— and almost choked on a bite of eggs when Jones said, "His lordship sent ye yon flower and note this morning."

When she recovered her breath, she shot a disbelieving glance at both items. "They are for me?"

"Aye, miss. His lordship's man brought them early this morning."

"Lord Dunnley's footman brought them?"

"Not a footman, Lady Sarah. 'Twas Carter, his lordship's valet, who brought them."

Apparently, in Jones's mind, there was only one "lordship" in Sarah's life. Hiding a smile, she thanked him and requested a vase. Her amusement notwithstanding, the august butler was correct: Dunnley was the only lord, other than her father and brother, of interest to her.

As she ate, she eyed the letter, wondering why Theo had sent it, or if his plans had changed. The envelope did not— could not—answer her questions. Finally, she poured herself another cup of tea, dismissed Jones, and picked up the letter.

Dunnley House
Monday, 18 April 1814

My sweet Sarah,

Four o'clock is a strange hour of the morning—too late to be the middle of the night, but not yet dawn. The house and streets are dark and quiet, making a man wonder if he is the only person in the entire city, or in the world, who is awake. Looking out at the stars, one cannot help but feel like a small and rather insignificant speck in this marvelous universe God has created, and to contemplate one's position in the Creator's scheme, as well as one's life.

As my thoughts so often do, my contemplations turned to you. You, my darling girl, have greatly enriched my life. Much as I dislike having to spend time away from you right now—and lest I neglected to say so yesterday, I dislike it excessively—it occurred to me, amidst my other musings, that we can either bemoan our separation or find ways to use it to our advantage. In the past week, there have been several occasions when we deferred conversations to a later time. Perhaps now is a good time for us to have them. Not conversations per se, but dialogues conducted via correspondence.

So, sweet Sarah, in addition to telling me about the events of your days, I hope that you will explain two things that have puzzled me greatly ever since you mentioned them. First, why do my compliments put you to the blush? Second, why does my presence sometimes disconcert you? Perhaps now that we are engaged, those things are no longer true. But if that is the case, I find myself wondering why they aren't. Have I changed in some way, or have you?

Carter (my valet) has brought my hot water, and since I ordered my horse to be saddled and ready at dawn, I'd best end this missive and prepare to depart. I shall miss you, my love.

Affectionately,
Theo

Dropping the letter from nerveless fingers, Sarah propped her elbows on the table and her head in her hands, and stared down at its pages. It was a far cry from the brief note she had expected, yet it was very typical of the warm, caring man she now knew Theo to be. His philosophical musings were a surprise—she had not yet seen that aspect of his character—but his point about using the time apart to their advantage was an excellent one. She wished, though, that he had chosen different topics for their first "conversation." She could not answer his questions until she discovered the answers to some of her own.

Isn't it time you did?

Was that chiding voice her conscience? Whatever its source, it was quite correct. It was time and past for her to seek the answers to her questions. Perhaps doing so would help her better understand her feelings for Theo. And to make sense of the way she felt when he was near—and when she was in his arms.

Carefully refolding the letter, she tucked it into her bodice, picked up the slender crystal vase holding Theo's rose, and left the dining room.

She stopped briefly in her bedchamber to place the vase on her dressing table. Determining the appropriate location for the letter took longer, but she finally slipped it into the drawer of her nightstand. For some inexplicable reason, that seemed a better place than a drawer of her writing desk. Having learnt in the past week that logic and emotions often do not go hand in hand, she accepted the enigmatic rightness of the choice with little more than a shrug.

After several minutes of searching, she found her mother in the drawing room—an unusual location for this time of day, as was the needlework with which the countess occupied herself. Bending to kiss her mother's cheek, Sarah seated herself nearby, her hands needlessly smoothing the skirt of her sprigged muslin morning gown as she wondered how to begin the conversation.

Don't wonder, just begin. Sarah would have liked to ignore the knowing, sardonic little voice, but its advice was sound. "Mama, when you were my age—" She sputtered to a stop; her mother had been married for several years by the time she was two-and-twenty. "That is, when you were younger, before you married Papa, did you ever feel shivery in a gentleman's presence? Or like there were tiny birds or a dozen butterflies fluttering in your stomach?"

A smile lit the countess's face. "Indeed I did. Whenever your father was nearby."

"*Papa* made you feel that way? B-but you love him."

"Yes, I do." She lowered her work to her lap. "Is it Dunnley who makes you feel that way?"

Too confused for words, Sarah nodded.

"Do you feel that way around any other man?"

"No. Isn't that strange?"

" 'Tisn't strange at all, dearling. In fact, it is quite wonderful."

"It is?" Bemused, she stared at her mother.

"Indeed yes." A smile twitched the corners of the countess's mouth. "What would you say if I told you that sometimes I still feel that way when your father is near, or when he looks at me a certain way?"

"It is a good thing?" Sarah gasped. "That is, you make it sound as if it is."

"Oh, aye. 'Tis a very good thing to feel that way about the man you love." Her mother's gaze suddenly seemed more intent. "You do love Dunnley, don't you?"

"I . . . I don't know. How can you tell if you love someone?" When her mother did not reply, Sarah plunged, headlong but falteringly, into an explanation. "I like Theo. I have ever since I met him. But I have always felt disconcerted in his presence." She groped for words to describe the sensations he roused in her. "Even more tongue-tied than usual and . . . skittish. That shivery, fluttering-butterflies feeling. No other man affects me so, not even those I don't know very well."

"You have felt that way since you first met Dunnley?"

"I don't remember if I did the very first time I met him, but if not, I began feeling it very soon afterward."

Her mother nodded like a sage. "Has he kissed you, *bach*?"

Sarah's cheeks flamed crimson. Ducking her head, she covered her face with her hands. *Lud, what have I gotten myself into?*

Her mother chuckled. "I shall take that blush to mean that he has. And that you enjoyed his kisses."

"Yes. He has, and I did."

"If you love someone, you want that person to be happy, and you would miss him if he suddenly disappeared from your life. You feel safe and protected and cherished when he holds you. His kisses . . . Well, there are different types of kisses. Some make you feel cherished and adored, others are more exciting—like the bubbles in champagne or the fireworks at Vauxhall Gardens."

I love Theo! Sarah jumped up to hug her mother. "Thank you, Mama. Thank you so much. I do love Theo. I thought so yesterday, but . . . Oh, I cannot believe it has taken me so long to understand my feelings. What an idiot I am!"

"Do not fret because you didn't realize it sooner. 'Tis better to be a bit cautious than to give your heart to someone who does not deserve such a precious gift."

Sarah could not help but worry that Theo might have been wondering if he had committed just such a folly. Could she tell him she loved him in a letter? *Should* she do so, or wait until he returned?

"I have only my experience with your father to judge by, but if you are like me, those fluttering butterflies haven't plagued you since Dunnley declared himself."

It was not quite a question, but she choose to treat it as one. "I noticed their absence yesterday. Before that, it is difficult to say. Thursday night and Saturday, I was so nervous that I remember little else."

Realizing that she still did not know—or perhaps had not quite understood—the answer to the question underlying her original question, Sarah asked, "Mama, what causes that quivery feeling? And why does it disappear after a man declares his love?"

She watched, astonished, as a blush transformed the countess's cheeks from alabaster to a delicate pink. "It is because you are . . . attracted to the gentleman. Not to his looks and appearance, but to him as a man. And it doesn't entirely disappear—at least, I still experience it from time to time—but once you know the gentleman is not only attracted to you, but loves you, the feeling isn't so overwhelming." A contemplative frown creased the countess's brow. "I am not certain if it lessens, or if it only seems to once we understand what causes it."

"Do gentlemen feel it, too?" Sarah had never considered that possibility.

Her mother's silvery laugh rang out. "I don't know, dearling. You will have to ask your father."

As much as she loved and admired her father, Sarah could not imagine having a discussion like this with him. A few days ago, she would have deemed it impossible to ask her mother these questions.

"Or," the countess appended, her smile mischievous, "ask Dunnley."

Considering that possibility, Sarah rose, then hugged her mother and kissed her cheek. "Thank you, Mama."

Hampshire, Thursday, 21 April 1814

Theo stretched his arms heavenward, trying to work the kinks out of his back. Picking up his coat between the tips of two fingers, he laid it between the pommel and his horse's neck, then hauled his tired, begrimed self into the saddle. As he headed for home, he told himself that he would not hope for a letter from Sarah.

He lied.

Despite his disappointment the past two days, he hoped for just such a missive. The way things were going, he desperately needed something to boost his spirits, and a letter from his love might well be the only thing that could accomplish the feat.

At the stables, he sluiced off the worst of the mud under the pump, then crossed the lawn to the house. Carter would have a bath waiting for him. The cook would be preparing a fine meal, which Worth, the butler, would serve promptly at six o'clock. But his household's attentions notwithstanding, Theo was not certain that he could get through another day without some word from Sarah. Or word of her.

God, I miss her!

By the time he descended the stairs, looking and feeling more like himself, Theo was fretful but resigned. Or so he told himself. That, too, was a lie, as his eager acceptance of Worth's offer to bring him the post proved. Sorting through the small stack of mail, it was all Theo could do to hold back a shout of exaltation when he espied the letter from Tregaron House, its superscription penned in a precise but delicately feminine hand. With a sigh of relief, he set the thick missive aside, preferring to savor it with his after-dinner brandy in the solitude of his study.

Tregaron House
Tuesday, 19 April 1814

Dear Theo,
As a contrast to your early morning letter, I return this one, written at almost the same hour, but late at night. (The date should, in fact, be Wednesday, although it seems like Tuesday night.) Your brother has been an admirable escort, but I am looking forward to your return. Stephen and I have little in common, save love for you . . .

The pages slipped from Theo's fingers. With a hand that was not quite steady, he reached for his brandy. His heart seemed intent on thumping its way out of his chest, even as his mind questioned his interpretation of that last sentence. Leaning his head back against the wing chair's soft leather, he wondered if he was reading too much into Sarah's words, imbuing them with the meaning he wanted to have instead of whatever she'd intended. Knowing that there was only one way to find out, he picked up the letter.

. . . Stephen and I have little in common, save love for you and affection for your cousins and their wives, and it isn't easy for two shy people to sustain conversations—especially when one of them answers every query with the fewest possible words!
Despite our conversational difficulties, your brother deserves praise. Although I know he has been bored at times, he has not uttered a word of complaint about spending two afternoons at Bellingham House, Monday evening at Lady Moreton's rout (a sad crush with abominable refreshments and horribly overheated rooms), and tonight at Lady Sherworth's ball (a lovely affair with everything from the decorations to the music to the supper a testament to the countess's exquisite taste). He is, however, quite adamant in his refusal to attend Almack's, so Rhys will escort Mama and me. (Stephen cites misplacement of his voucher as his rea-

*son, but I suspect there is more to it than that, espe-
cially since he is well aware that Sir Edward Smithson
usually attends.)*

Smiling at Sarah's perspicacity even as he worried
whether Rhys could deter Nasty Ned, Theo skimmed over
her account of Lynn's first two harp lessons, which had
prompted a similar interest in her sister-in-law. His search
for the crux of the letter was rewarded near the bottom of
the second sheet.

> *Your request to resume our deferred conversations
> accounted for a rather embarrassing discussion with
> my mother. An enlightening one, to be sure, since I
> learnt—or, rather, confirmed—something very impor-
> tant, as well as obtained the answers to several ques-
> tions of my own, but had I known beforehand that
> it would provoke so many blushes, I might not have
> embarked on it. (No teasing about my blushing, please;
> I daresay you blushed, too, if your mother ever asked
> if you'd been kissed!)*

Theo chuckled, and not only because she was right. He
would give a great deal to know exactly what Sarah and
her mother had discussed, and how Lady Tregaron had
come to ask that particular question.

> *While I am on the subject of blushes, I shall attempt
> to answer your questions. I do not know why your
> compliments put me to the blush. Most compliments
> do, except for obviously insincere ones, so it is proba-
> bly simply that they make me uncomfortable. It is a
> bit off-putting when someone says you are beautiful
> (handsome, in your case), since it is something over
> which a person has no influence. They ought to be
> singing the praises of my parents and ancestors, not
> me. If I am to receive a compliment, I would much
> rather it be on my manners, my intelligence, my musi-
> cal talent, or my skill at needlework, since those are
> things that I have worked to develop.*
> *(Note, dear sir, that I only promised answers, not
> sensible ones.)*

Chuckling again, Theo wondered why he had never before noticed Sarah's wry wit. Had he been so blinded by her beauty that he had not completely comprehended her words? Or had she never before allowed him to see it? He preferred the latter explanation, not because it was more flattering to him, but because he chose to believe that Sarah was more comfortable with him now and, therefore, more likely to reveal heretofore hidden aspects of her character.

As for why your presence sometimes disconcerted me (and that seems to be a thing of the past)— Oh, I am blushing already, and I have not yet begun to explain. The answer to that question was one of the revelations during the conversation with my mother. No doubt you will think me quite foolish, Theo, but ever since we met, I have felt tongue-tied and skittish in your presence—sort of shivery and as if there were dozens (sometimes hundreds) of butterflies in my stomach fluttering their wings. No other gentleman made me feel that way, so I thought it was a strange kind of nervousness. But, according to Mama, it was not. That is, part of it may have been nervousness, but mostly it was because I was attracted to you as a man. I still am, of course, but now that I know you love me—and, presumably, are attracted to me—the feeling is not so overwhelming. (Mama said that she still feels that way sometimes when she sees my father!)

Theo was amazed at the amount of wonderful news in that one paragraph, the best being that Sarah was attracted to him. Also, since Sarah was very like her mother, it was encouraging to know that Lady Tregaron was still attracted to her husband after more than twenty-five years of marriage, although Theo suspected that the countess would blush to know that her daughter had passed that tidbit on to him.

The other revelation from my conversation with Mama wasn't truly a revelation, but more a confirmation of something I had already realized, although, regrettably, not in time to tell you before you left. I daresay it is not comme il faut *to tell you in a letter,*

*but since I feel like the veriest goosecap already, I am
going to tell you, even if it breaks every rule of proper
correspondence. I love you, Theo. So much that I cannot imagine not sharing the rest of my life with you.*

*No doubt you will think me the greenest of green
girls for not having realized it sooner—and you are
quite right. But I have never been in love before, nor
loved a man who wasn't related to me, and that kind
of love—familial love—is a very different feeling than
my love for you.*

*I hope that the work at Dunnley Park is proceeding
apace, and that you will soon return to Town. I miss
you.*

Your loving Sarah

A letter to savor, indeed! Theo did just that, reading the
last two pages again, more slowly this time. Then he sat
for a few minutes, silently exulting, before crossing to his
desk to pen a reply.

London, Friday, 22 April 1814

Sarah was surprised—and rather taken aback—when
Jones entered the drawing room in midafternoon, interrupting her harp practice.

"Lady Sarah." He extended a silver salver on which a
letter rested. "Lord Dunnley's groom has just ridden up
from Hampshire with this message from his lordship. The
groom said to tell you that he will carry your reply to Lord
Dunnley. I am to send a message to Price, the butler at
Dunnley House, when your letter is ready."

Fearing that something was terribly wrong, Sarah requested a tea tray, then curled up in her favorite chair to
read Theo's missive.

*Dunnley Park
21 April 1814*

*My darling Sarah,
I cannot find words to tell you how pleased I was
to receive your letter, and to read the gladsome tidings*

therein. They were a most welcome change from the news here.

Matters have gone from bad to worse since I arrived. On Monday afternoon, the dam that forms our largest lake gave way, resulting in even more flooding and causing two more ditches to collapse. Even worse, my steward, who was checking the dam at the time, broke his leg. The doctor has set it and says Herndon (the steward) will be fine, but until his leg mends, or until I find a temporary replacement, I must do his work as well as my own.

Repairing dams and ditches is dirty, backbreaking work. Satisfying, in its way, but filthy and exhausting. In the middle of a summer drought, it might be less grimy, but during a spring flood, it is naught but muddy drudgery. There is but one advantage to spending most of the day standing waist-deep in cold water, but I seem to be the only man who appreciates the distraction. I have not come home so covered in muck since the day I measured my length on the bank of the lake while fishing with my father. I was five or six years old at the time and thought it quite a lark then.

Sweet Sarah, do not lambaste yourself for not understanding your feelings sooner. As I told you when I proposed, it took me a while to realize mine, too, and for the same reason. Looking back, I can only wonder at my failure to comprehend them, and how I could have been so oblivious, but things, be they events or emotions, always seem much clearer in retrospect.

Comme il faut or not, I am glad—ecstatic, in fact— that you told me about your revelation. I shan't tease you about your blushes, nor consider you a slowtop, if you will grant me the same leniency. I wish I were in London so that I could show you how very much your news pleased me.

Unfortunately, my darling, it will take a few more days to finish shoring up the ditches. (The dam has already been repaired.) I promise to return in time for your mother's ball—and sooner if at all possible.

All my love,
Theo

P.S. I am going to send one of my grooms to Town

*in the morning to deliver this letter. I shall instruct him
to wait at Dunnley House until he can bring back your
reply. I am too impatient to wait an extra day for the
post, my love, so whenever you have a message for
me, please have Jones notify Price, who will instruct
one of my grooms to act as your messenger.*

Disappointed as she was to realize that Theo's sojourn
in the country would be longer than he had expected, Sarah
was delighted by his response to her revelations. Indeed,
the height of her gratification was almost enough to balance
the depth of her disappointment. And she looked forward
to the demonstration of his pleasure when he returned.

Given all that he had on his plate right now, she wished
that she had not written—or, rather, had not sent—that
second letter, the one she'd written in the early hours of
Thursday morning after this week's assembly at Almack's.
When questioned, Jones confirmed that it had been sent in
yesterday's post and would have arrived at the receiving
station nearest Dunnley Park this morning. Was it foolish
to think Theo might have been reading her letter while she
was reading his? Yes, of course it was. He had flooded
fields and four or five collapsed ditches to deal with, and
since his steward was unable to direct the workers and tenants, Theo was undoubtedly out in the fields. He would not
know about her letter until he returned home his evening—
perhaps not even then, unless one of his servants went to
the receiving office today.

Climbing the stairs to her bedchamber and her writing
desk, Sarah realized that if she replied to Theo's letter now,
his groom, no matter how devoted, would not set off for
Hampshire until morning. That being the case, she could
respond to Theo's letter now, then later tonight add any
news garnered at Viscount and Lady Lorring's ball, or a
report of Sir Edward's most recent antics.

Hampshire, Friday, 22 April 1814

Despite the exertions of the day, and they had been
many and frustrating, Theo returned to the house in almost
the same good humor he'd left it this morning—a continua-

tion of the exultant mood in which he'd gone to bed last night. Perhaps even enhanced a bit by his dreams of Sarah. The welcome tidings of another letter from her lent a spring to his step as he climbed the stairs to his chamber to bathe, and kept a smile on his face through his solitary dinner.

But not three seconds after he opened her missive, the smile was replaced by a scowl.

> *Tregaron House*
> *20 April 1814*

> *Dear Theo,*
> *When Mama, Rhys, and I left the house tonight to go to Almack's, I found it difficult to believe that only a week had passed since the last time we attended. So much has happened in the past seven days, all of it wonderful save for the flooding and collapsed ditches at Dunnley Park.*

> *Unfortunately, almost from the moment we arrived in King Street, Sir Edward Smithson did his best to bring about a recurrence of the loss of composure I suffered last week. Oh, he is the most vile, loathsome, odious man!!! I cannot imagine why the patronesses have not long since denied him entry. Surely they must know what kind of man he is! Or do they not care that he is a repulsive, obnoxious toad?*

> *One would think, after the slight you dealt him last week, that he would have given me wide berth. But no, not he! In addition to all his other horrible qualities, he is stupid as a stump. After I refused to dance with him, he had the gall to ask Lady Jersey to present him to me as a suitable partner! Fortunately, I already had a partner (Fairfax) for that dance because I could not have borne a waltz with Nasty Ned.*

> *After that, Rhys and Fairfax took pains to ensure that I had partners for every dance—all chosen well in advance. I believe Lord Blackburn may have helped, too. All told, I refused Nasty Ned five times tonight. Five! Even so, he managed to catch me alone once, so I was forced to listen to his disgusting scurrilities. He is despicable!*

I apologize for carrying on so, but you are the only person who understands how much I abhor Sir Edward. Rhys was even more vigilant after that, but much as I love my brother, I do not feel as safe with him as I do with you. We are attending the theater tomorrow night, so I won't have to worry about unexpected encounters with Nasty Ned.

On a more pleasant note, I am beginning to believe that Fairfax has a tendre *for Deborah Woodhurst. I think they are very well suited, don't you? Unfortunately, Diana seems intent on creating mischief. She tried to usurp the duke's waltz with Deb tonight. (I recall you telling me she attempted the same thing at Lady Oglethorpe's ball.) Fairfax mentioned tonight that he is expecting his cousin—Walsingham is his name, I believe—to arrive in Town soon. I had the impression that the duke is hoping Diana will be smitten by his cousin, although I am not certain why he believes she will be.*

I hope that the repairs and such are going well and that you will soon return to Town.

Your loving Sarah

Duty warring with desire, Theo stomped around his study, cursing Smithson, his ancestors, and his future progeny·in English, French, Latin, and Greek. The vituperation helped to vent Theo's outrage, but it did little to ease his frustration. He wanted to be with Sarah, to protect her and care for her. Duty, however, demanded otherwise.

"To hell with duty!" Theo slumped against the window frame, the responsibilities of his family, his dependents, and his title weighing on him more heavily than since he'd inherited the title as a grief-stricken boy of twelve.

Devil take it! He had a duty to Sarah, too.

Calling for his horse, Theo paid a visit to his steward, then to the tenants of the Home Farm. Late that night, his brain seething with conflicting schemes and strategies, Theo refined his plan.

And prayed that it would cover all possible contingencies.

Chapter Sixteen

London, Tuesday, 26 April 1814

*E*ven before she found a seat at the side of Lord and Lady Abernathy's ballroom, Sarah wished that she had given in to her initial impulse and stayed at home. So many people were crowded into the small room that it was impossible to imagine how a set with only five or six couples could be formed. Not without crushing everyone else against the walls like pickled beets in a jar. Shaking out the skirts of her new, ice blue silk ball gown, which were creased from making her way through the crowd, Sarah looked around, searching for her friends. Unfortunately, all she could see were the backs of a group of gentlemen in front of her, none of whom was the man she most wanted to see.

Beside her, Rhys and Stephen debated the merits of attending a mill on Saturday. One of the pugilists—Sarah was not certain if it was the challenger or the champion—was called "the Welsh Bruiser," and Rhys seemed convinced, perhaps solely because of his nationality, that the Bruiser would triumph. Stephen, however, believed the Welshman would be beat all hollow, which, she assumed, meant that he didn't have a chance of winning. Not having the slightest interest in boxing, she interrupted their friendly squabble without a qualm.

"Do either of you see Tina or Deborah? Or their mothers?"

Stephen shook his head. "Can't see a blessed thing in this crush, unless it is under your nose."

"Lady Abernathy must have an inflated sense of the size of her ballroom," Rhys opined. "Or perhaps she was set on having the most shocking squeeze of the Season. How is a man supposed to find his partners? Or get to them, if he does spot them?"

"You may have to dance every set with me," she teased.

"Dance with my sister? Heaven forfend!"

"She, at least, won't stomp on your toes," said Stephen.

My word, a compliment and a complete sentence from the reticent captain! Sarah smiled at her future brother-in-law. "Thank you, Stephen." Shooting a glare at her brother, she added, "I might tromp all over them, since he finds the prospect of dancing with me so horrid."

"Bickering already, children?" their father inquired, having finally escorted his wife safely through the crush.

Sighing, Lady Tregaron sank onto the chair beside her daughter's. "We ought to have gone to the Opera instead."

"Perhaps." Sarah feared that even if Theo returned to Town in time to attend—and the chances of that were slight, at best—he would never find her in this crowd. But she could, and did, look forward to seeing him tomorrow. He had promised that he would be back in time to escort her on the jaunt the Woodhurst twins had planned to Richmond, and having given his word, Sarah knew that Theo would move heaven and earth to keep it.

Tina Fairchild arrived at a more decorous pace than usual, her mother at her side. No doubt it was the size of the throng, not a sudden loss of spontaneity, that accounted for Tina's seemingly increased propriety.

"Lud, what a crush!" Tina dropped onto the chair next to Sarah's, while the Duchess of Greenwich took a seat beside Sarah's mother. The gilt spindle-back chairs were so close together that their skirts brushed. The countess wore mauve satin; the duchess, lavender.

Idly smoothing a hand over the wrinkles in her ivory muslin gown, Tina declared, "It is a good thing you chose to sit so near the entrance, otherwise we never would have spotted you. Anyone who attempts to reach the far end of the room will likely disappear and not be found until morning."

Glancing in the direction her friend indicated, Sarah agreed.

Her father bent to speak to the duchess. "Greenwich did not accompany you?"

"He is in the card room. One peek at this crowd, and he beat a hasty retreat."

The earl cast a longing look at the doorway, but made no move to depart. Sarah suspected that no matter how bored he became, her father would not stir far from her side. Sir Edward Smithson's brazenness at Almack's, and again two nights later at Viscount and Lady Lorring's ball, had compounded the earl's alarm. Sarah knew that her father's increased protectiveness was not because he did not trust Rhys and Stephen, but an additional safeguard—a palladium to ensure his only daughter's safety.

"Where is Deborah?" Tina asked, gazing around the room.

Sarah shrugged. "Still trying to get inside, perhaps. Or maybe the Woodhursts arrived before we did and ventured farther into the room. If that is the case, they are probably wondering where we are."

"Are you excited about going to Richmond tomorrow? It seems an age since I rode my mare at more than a sedate trot. Once we get to Richmond—and probably on the way, too—we can *gallop*."

"I am looking forward to the excursion, but I won't be riding. I—"

"*What?* Why not?" Tina demanded. "You are an excellent rider, and you must be longing for a gallop."

"Thank you. I would enjoy a gallop, but Dunnley is driving his curricle, and he asked me to ride with him."

Judging by Tina's wrinkled-nose grimace, she did not consider that an acceptable reason for not riding. Although Sarah did not feel that she had to defend her decision, neither did she want to be deemed poor-spirited. "I have not seen him for more than a week!" *Nine days, to be exact.*

Tina rolled her eyes, but was distracted by the arrival of the Woodhurst twins, Lord Henry, and their mother. Lady Kesteven sank gracefully onto the chair beside the duchess, plying her fan to cool her flushed cheeks. Glancing from her blue watered-silk gown to her friends' ensembles, she smiled wryly. "Had you told me that purple was the color of the day, I would have worn my lilac crepe."

Taking the seat next to Tina, Deborah exclaimed, "What a horrible squeeze! How are we supposed to dance in this crush?" Sarah knew the twin speaking was Deborah only because Diana would stand all night rather than sit next to Tina. Although both had a bent for impulsive, sometimes indecorous behavior, the two girls cordially despised each other.

With a sniff of disdain, Diana took the far chair. The twins wore blush pink silk ball gowns, but the flowers embroidered on the bodice and puff sleeves of Deborah's gown were white, while Diana's were dark pink.

In an attempt to draw both twins into the conversation, Sarah said, "Tina and I were discussing the trip to Richmond tomorrow. We are looking forward to it."

"Are you indeed?" Instead of her usual air of ennui, Diana wore a sly smile—one which undoubtedly boded ill for someone. Sarah wondered who the unfortunate victim was, but knew better than to ask. Diana held no great opinion of the members of "The Six," possibly because they felt the same about her.

"Should be fun." Lord Henry propped himself against Diana's chair, displaying a waistcoat of startling crimson. Sarah much preferred the subdued elegance of her brother's black and white evening attire, or the glittering yet restrained array of braid on Stephen's uniform.

Rhys readily agreed with the young dandy, but Stephen's response was an unintelligible mutter. He had not ridden such a distance since he was injured, and would make the trip only if his brother did not return in time to escort Sarah.

Leaning over Tina, Deborah spoke quietly but with some urgency. "I need to talk to you later."

Sarah nodded her agreement, wondering what troubled her friend. It was quite possible that her concern was related to her twin's gleeful smirk.

The musicians began tuning their instruments, the notes barely audible over the din of dozens of conversations.

Stepping behind Sarah's chair, Stephen bent down and asked, "Do you already have a partner for the first dance?"

"Only if it is a minuet, a waltz, or a country dance. And only if my partner can find me in this crush."

"Not likely unless he has toured the perimeter and knows where all the young ladies are seated."

"An excellent idea, Captain, assuming it is possible." Rhys smoothed a hand over his cravat. "If I am not back in half an hour, send out a search party."

When the minuet was announced, Sarah scanned the room for Lord Blackburn, who had bespoken it. Taller than most men, with a distinctive silver streak in his hair, the earl stood out in a crowd. But, unfortunately, not in this horde. Beside her, Tina chattered contentedly, apparently unconcerned about the absence—or lack—of a partner. Deborah, on the other hand, glanced around, obviously looking for someone.

"Do you see Fairfax?" she inquired, after a minute or two of fruitless searching.

Sarah shook her head. "No, nor Blackburn, either."

A few moments later, Tina elbowed Deborah. "Fairfax just arrived." Then, frowning, she added, "Or is that his cousin?"

Despite her growing friendship with Fairfax, who was Theo's best friend and had taken on the mantle of protector during his absence, Sarah was not certain of the gentleman's identity, either. She had met the duke's cousin, Sir Frederick Walsingham, the previous afternoon, and the two men looked remarkably alike—even more so than Stephen Middleford and David Winterbrook. The duke and his cousin were the same height—average—and shared the same rather plain features, brown hair, and blue-green eyes. The only difference Sarah had discerned was that the baronet lacked the duke's presence, and if Walsingham's slightly worn clothing was an indication of the state of his purse, his pockets were not as well-filled as his cousin's.

"Whether it is Fairfax or Sir Frederick, his cousin is greeting Lady Abernathy now." As the pair approached, she decided the man slightly in the lead was the duke.

Much to her surprise, the second gentleman increased his pace and brushed past his cousin to stand in front of Deborah. After greeting everyone, he bowed over her hand. "I beg your pardon for my late arrival. We can still join the dance, um . . . Unless you would you prefer to sit it out?"

Smiling, Deborah rose. "I would much rather dance."

"Then dance we shall."

Sir Frederick Walsingham glanced from Sarah to Tina to Diana. When his gaze returned to Sarah, perhaps because she was the oldest, she shook her head slightly to indicate that she already had a partner. He smiled, then bowed in front of her friend. "Would you honor me with this dance, Lady Christina?"

"Me?" Tina popped out of her chair like a jack-in-the-box.

"Yes, you," Walsingham confirmed. "Unless you are not dancing this evening?"

"No . . . Yes . . . I mean, I would like to dance, thank you." She looked at her mother, awaiting the duchess's nod of permission, then took the baronet's arm.

Sarah leaned back in her chair, feeling a bit foolish. Sitting on the edge of the seat would not speed her partner's progress through the overcrowded ballroom—if he was even here. Although she wondered about Blackburn's absence, she was not overly concerned. Her brother had not yet returned from his stroll around the room, so she assumed that other men were having the same difficulty navigating through the crush. A political debate might prevent the earl from claiming his dance, but little else would cause him to behave so discourteously. And since her father, the Duke of Greenwich, and a number of other peers, both Tory and Whig, were present, Sarah felt quite certain that affairs of state had not delayed Blackburn.

Their hostess's foolishness, possibly, but not political concerns.

Lord Durwood and Sir Kenneth Peyton approached and, after bowing to the older women, asked Diana and Sarah to dance. Although Diana accepted the baron's invitation, the curl of her lip indicated she was not best pleased with her partner. Feeling both awkward and gauche, Sarah thanked Sir Kenneth, then explained, "I am promised to Blackburn for this dance, but I do not even know if he is here."

"Indeed he is. I saw him shortly after I arrived. No doubt he is trying to find you, Lady Sarah, but maneuvering through this crowd is a bit like swimming in treacle."

She laughed at the image conjured by his words. "It can be done, but not easily?"

"Exactly so." With a boyish grin that made him look much younger than his thirty-odd years, he nodded. "Since my friend has already claimed this dance, will you grant me one later this evening?"

"The second country dance?" she suggested.

With a bow, he accepted. "Perhaps—Ah, here comes Blackburn."

Looking harried but determined, the earl wove his way through the clusters of people packed into the space between the wall and the dance floor, speaking a few words to anyone who greeted him, but not allowing himself to be drawn into conversation. In much the same manner, he greeted her parents, the duchess, Lady Kesteven, and Stephen. Bowing over Sarah's hand, he smiled ruefully and apologized for his tardiness, then explained, "I began my search on the other side of the room, so I made almost a complete circuit. It is my good fortune that you are a kind-hearted lady, and the minuet, a forgiving dance—one we can join in progress."

He offered his arm. "Do you wish to dance, Lady Sarah? Or would you prefer to promenade?"

"Let's dance. I have no wish to risk life or limb by attempting to promenade."

After a short wait at the edge of the dance floor, they joined the line of couples. Blackburn was an excellent partner—tall, confident in his moves, and graceful in the way that most Corinthians, their muscles honed by years of sporting activities, seemed to be.

She soon had cause to be even more grateful for his grace and skill. As they made the turn at the top of the room, he bent his head and whispered, "Are you aware that Smithson is here tonight?"

Sarah froze, terrified by the thought of another confrontation with Nasty Ned. Her paralysis was short-lived, not much more than the space of a heartbeat, but Blackburn's deft, sure movements covered her lapse and propelled her into a turn. Her feet moving by rote, she fought to regain her composure. She would not allow the mere mention of the baronet's name to frighten her. *She would not!*

Blackburn's calm, level gaze helped to steady her, much as Theo's had the night of his dinner party. She did not feel the same comforting protectiveness with the earl as with Theo, but even so, his presence settled her. With something of a start, she realized that Blackburn possessed the same quiet, gentle strength Theo had. Not that it was an unexpected quality in the earl—he was, after all, several years older than Dunnley and a force to be reckoned with in government—but it was not a trait most people would expect, or even recognize, in Theo, a man famed for his address and as a fashion leader of the *ton*. The real surprise was that she had not, until now, realized that Theo did possess it. She'd reaped its benefits, more than once, without understanding their source. Nor that it was one of the qualities she most admired in him.

Thinking of Theo, of his quiet strength and his love, calmed her. And bolstered her. If he could be strong yet gentle for her, then she would be gentle and strong for him. And for herself, too.

She found her resolve in the nick of time: Smithson was standing not more than ten feet away, leering as usual. Taking a page out of Theo's book, Sarah deliberately looked away. Not as effective—nor as overt—as the cut direct, but Sir Edward would understand the slight, even if no one else did. Especially since there was nothing in the center of the room save the floor.

"Brava!" Blackburn's whispered compliment was as enthusiastic as those shouted at the Opera.

Warmed by his admiration, Sarah felt a certain pride that she had battled her fear and had, if only in a small way, stood up to Nasty Ned. It was more than she had ever done before. And it was far, far better than falling apart.

Once her father, her brother, and Stephen knew that Sir Edward was present, Sarah was edged about for the rest of the evening. The three of them formed a protective guard around her—a gauntlet that would daunt most men. In addition, Blackburn, Fairfax, and, surprisingly, Sir Frederick joined them between sets, lending their presence, consciously or unwittingly, to the barricade. Perhaps some of her prospective partners found it too formidable a barrier to attempt to breach, or maybe they could not find her in the crowd. Whatever the reason, for the first time ever, Sarah sat out several dances. And she did not mind a whit. Given the paucity of space on the dance floor, the increasing heat, and the dearth of fresh air, she would have happily sat out a few more.

She was, however, bothered by the fact that her protectors' vigilance had, for all intents and purposes, rendered Deborah mute. Not that Deb didn't speak; she did, of course, but not about whatever was troubling her. After two hours of watching her friend fret, Sarah suggested a visit to the ladies' retiring room, hoping they would be able to talk there. Unfortunately, she failed to take into account her protectors' determination to foil any possible attempt by Sir Edward to importune her. All six of them deemed it the height of folly for Sarah to stroll from the room with only Deborah as companion. Or, as Stephen put it, "trouble begging to happen."

Deborah's puzzled frown indicated her bewilderment when Rhys and Stephen escorted them to the ladies' retiring room. Sarah knew that her friend would question her the moment they were alone, but she was far more interested in learning what troubled Deborah than in explaining her own problems.

Three older ladies were there before them, but Sarah was determined to wait them out. "Sit down, Deb, and I will pin your flounce."

Tina would have immediately insisted that she had not torn a flounce, but Deborah understood Sarah's intent. Her blue eyes dancing with merriment, Deb chose a chair in the corner of the room. "I cannot imagine how I came to be so clumsy."

"I daresay it was your partner's fault, not yours." Pulling a packet of pins from her reticule, Sarah knelt at her friend's feet and pretended to pin the flounce.

The moment the door closed behind the older women, Deborah burst into speech. "Sarah, what is going on?"

Rising, Sarah pulled a chair close so that she and Deb could have a comfortable coze. It would have to be a short one, though; Stephen and Rhys were waiting for them. "You said earlier that you wanted to talk to me."

"Yes, I do, but that isn't what I meant."

Sarah mustered a smile. "I know, but we can't stay here long, so tell me what is troubling you."

"Well, there are two things now. No, three."

"Let's deal with them one at a time. What was—or is—the first one?"

"I fear—no, I am certain—that Diana is up to something. I don't know what, though. She has been acting strangely—sly and secretive—for several days, and this morning I heard her muttering about 'just desserts.' I am worried that someone will be hurt by whatever she is planning."

An all too likely possibility, Sarah knew, having seen examples of Diana's malice the previous year. "Something more than insidious comments against a rival?"

"I don't know!" Deborah all but wailed. "But I think it is something worse."

"Has Diana mentioned one young lady more than others? Or one gentleman?"

"Not really. She has mentioned you—your engagement to Dunnley—a few times, but I can't recall her talking much about any other girl."

The knowledge made Sarah feel rather queasy. If Diana was jealous of her because she was engaged to Dunnley, then she might be Diana's next victim. Jealousy was an unlikely motive, though; Diana seemed determined to catch the highest title and biggest fortune she could, and Dunnley, although wealthy, was only a viscount.

But if she wasn't Diana's target, then who was?

"The man she has talked about most is Fairfax."

She will catch cold at that! During the past week, Sarah had become increasingly convinced that Fairfax had a *tendre* for Deborah. Thinking of the duke caused something that had been niggling at the back of Sarah's mind all evening to rise to the fore. "Speaking of Fairfax, does he seem . . . different tonight? Or is it just my imagination? It may well be. I have mistaken him for his cousin all evening."

"I have as well. Strange, isn't it?" Deborah's laugh sounded a bit forced. "Perhaps it is a trick of the light."

Sarah thought that unlikely; for all its faults, the ballroom was well lit. But since neither she nor Deborah had previously had difficulty identifying the two men . . .

The thought splintered as an elderly dowager pushed open the door. Although a high stickler, she was also a notorious gossip, so Sarah rose to return to the ballroom. Deborah followed, but more slowly, as if she were reluctant to put period to their coze.

Before they left, Sarah stopped and, in a quiet voice that could not be overheard, did her best to comfort and advise her friend. "Deb, I doubt there is anything you can do to prevent your sister from doing whatever she plans. Unless, of course, you can find out what she intends and either put a stop to it or warn her intended victim."

"That is what I thought, but I wondered—I was hoping there was a solution I'd overlooked."

Although they left several problems unsolved, they knew each other well enough to know that they would tackle the others as soon as they could. In perfect accord, they stepped into the hallway.

A short distance down the corridor, Stephen and Rhys were engrossed in conversation with Lord Howe and two military men: one in a red jacket as braid-encrusted as Stephen's; the other, dark green and slightly less dazzling. Loath to interrupt their discourse since Stephen looked happier than Sarah had ever seen him, but equally unwilling to wait until the conversation reached its natural conclusion, Sarah linked arms with Deborah and smiled as she passed the men, pretending not to understand Rhys's "come here" gesture.

"Sarah, *what* is going on?" Deborah whispered. "Your father and brother . . ."

"I can't tell you here"—Sarah gestured at the people clustered in the hallway like knots on a rope—"but I will explain tomorrow."

"I will hold you to that promise." A hint of steel edged Deborah's quiet voice, but her eyes held only concern.

Outside the entrance to the ballroom, they were hailed by Diana. With some reluctance, Sarah allowed herself to be drawn into the conversation, which concerned the arrangements for tomorrow's excursion to Richmond, but as soon as she could politely do so, she made her escape.

Unfortunately, in doing so she stepped from the frying pan into the fire.

Sir Edward Smithson lay in wait for her just inside the ballroom. Almost before she realized what was happening, he cornered her, crowding her against the wall and blocking her view of the room.

And blocking her from the sight of everyone in the ballroom.

His hand clamped her arm like a vise, thwarting her attempts to sidle away as easily as he ignored her hissed demands that he release her. Her gaze darted frantically from side to side, but there was no one in sight. Even as she prayed for rescue, Sarah stiffened her spine, conjured Theo's image in her mind's eye for courage, and turned a deaf ear to Nasty Ned's lewd remarks. Determined not to let him see her fear, even though inside she quivered like a blancmange, she tapped her foot as if impatient.

Interrupting him in mid-spate, she inquired, in tones of deepest ennui, "How much longer do you intend to keep this up?"

"Eh?" He jerked back, inadvertently loosening his grip, and she slipped past him. Under other circumstances, his poleaxed expression might have been comical.

She raked him with a contemptuous gaze, then turned away, saying over her shoulder, "I merely wondered how long you intended to prattle. I have a partner for the next set."

Then, praying that her shaking legs would not fail her, and that she could maintain her composure until she reached her parents, Sarah made her second escape.

Theo reached London shortly before midnight, weary to his bones. He had been up since dawn, spent twelve hours helping his tenants repair the last ditch, then, after a quick bath and an even quicker meal, he'd ignored the objections of the entire household and ridden back to Town. The trip, which usually took about three and a half hours, had been two hours longer tonight because his horse had thrown a shoe three miles outside of Farnborough.

Now, sitting in his study, warm and dry again, wearing his favorite maroon brocade dressing gown over biscuit kerseymere pantaloons and a loose-fitting white linen shirt open at the throat, with his boots propped on the polished brass fender and a snifter of brandy at his elbow, Theo flipped desultorily through the mail that had accumulated during his absence. His breath caught when he espied the letter in his fiancée's now-familiar hand, and he grabbed it from the pile, his heartbeat accelerating.

Breathe, idiot! It is probably a "welcome back to Town" note. If anything had happened to Sarah, Stephen would know about it, which means Price would know, and he would have told you as soon as you arrived.

Despite his lecture—and a restorative sip of brandy—Theo's hands were not quite steady as he opened Sarah's letter.

> *Tregaron House*
> *Tuesday morning, 26 April 1814*
>
> *Dear Theo,*
> *I hope all of the repairs at Dunnley Park are fin-ished and that you had a pleasant journey back to Town. I am very glad you are back,* cariad; *I have missed you sorely. If you return early and decide to*

gratify one of Society's hostesses by gracing her enter-
tainment with your handsome, charming presence, I
hope you will choose the Abernathy ball. My family
and I will be there, as will Stephen. If you aren't able
to join us this evening, then I hope that, if you don't
have a prior engagement, you will call tomorrow
morning. We can discuss wedding plans . . .

"Wedding plans." Exultant, Theo surged to his feet.
"Sarah is going to be my wife!" Closing his eyes, he sent
a prayer of thanks winging heavenward. In her letters,
Sarah had told him that she loved him, but she had not
specifically said that she would marry him. He had hoped,
though. Lord, how he'd hoped! With two simple words, she
had granted his most fervent wish, turning dreams into real-
ity, and he felt . . . Theo was not quite sure what he felt,
but he wanted to shout the news from the rooftops, so all
of London would know that Lady Sarah Mallory was going
to marry him.

Struck by the foolishness of such an action, he chuckled.
Since the Enderby ball, the *ton* had believed that he and
Sarah planned to marry; only the two of them had known
that their engagement might not end with a wedding. His
eyes on the leaping flames, Theo wondered if he could persuade her to marry him in a few days, or a few weeks,
instead of at the end of the Season.

"Only one way to find out," he told himself, picking up
the letter.

. . . We can discuss wedding plans, or practice our
songs for the Greenwich musicale, or just talk. Any
time after nine o'clock would be fine. (If you come at
nine, you can join Mama and me for breakfast.) Soci-
ety would deem that an unsuitable hour—probably
also an uncivilized one—and for most callers, I would
agree. But not for you. It seems an age since I saw you.
                              With all my love,
                              Sarah

Breakfast with Sarah was a lovely thought. God willing,
he would share forty or fifty years of breakfasts with her.
But he was not sure whether tomorrow should be the first.

He would prefer that their reunion be a private one—*God, how he longed to hold her again!*—but they did need to discuss wedding dates and plans, and they also needed to rehearse their songs for the duchess's musicale, which was only a fortnight hence.

Folding the missive, he slipped it into the pocket of his dressing gown, knowing that he would read it again before he went to sleep. Probably several times. He had read all her letters so often that he could quote them from memory.

Resuming his seat, he sipped his brandy and flipped through the rest of the mail. Near the bottom of the pile, a familiar feminine script again caught his gaze. This time, it was not his breathing that hitched, but his insides.

Why has Jani written now? Tapping the edge of the letter against his thigh, Theo pondered the vagaries of fate. It was the fifth or sixth letter he'd received in the months she had been away, but since he'd just been thinking of Sarah and their wedding, it seemed wrong—almost a sin—to read a note from his ex-mistress, even if she was in Yorkshire and did not yet know that she had been relegated to that status. He had hoped to wait until she returned to give Jani her *congé*, but he'd become increasingly uncomfortable about having, at least technically, a mistress and a fiancée.

Should I read this note or throw it in the fire unopened? Tossing it into the air like a coin, he watched it flutter back to earth. *Superscription up is heads.* It landed face up in his lap—heads indeed, but he had neglected to decide if that meant that he would read it or throw it away.

"To hell with it!" He grabbed the letter, crumpling it in his fist—then suddenly realized that it had been sent from London, not Yorkshire. The possibility that Jani was in Town was enough to change his mind. He would feel much better, and his conscience would be greatly eased, if he could break off his relationship with her before he saw Sarah again. After smoothing out the letter's creases, he broke the seal.

> *Half Moon Street*
> *22 April 1814*

> *My dear Theo,*
> *No doubt you wondered if I had grown roots in Yorkshire. I wondered, too, at times, but I am back in*

*Town, at least for a while. Mother is feeling much
better, although she is still quite weak. I finally finished
the new book, and I have written about half of the
clean copy. I hope to take it to John Murray on Monday. He has been very understanding about the delay,
but I don't want to test his patience any further than I
already have.*

*I would very much like to see you, my dear. Would
you please call on me at your earliest convenience?
Morning (after ten o'clock) or early afternoon would
be best.*

Your Jani

A strange letter, but a timely one. He could formally
sever his ties with Jani before he saw Sarah. After that, he
need only hold to his resolution—his penance, as it were,
for past sins—until he and Sarah were wed. Then he would
receive his reward.

Thinking of the love and passion inherent in that reward,
he drank the last of his brandy, then stood and crossed to
the door. As he climbed the stairs, a snippet from one of
Sarah's letters came to mind, about her love of boating.
Theo smiled, envisioning giving Jani her *congé* as the last
shoal he had to navigate. After that, it would be smooth
sailing for him and Sarah.

Chapter Seventeen

London, Wednesday, 27 April 1814

"*W*ell, hell!"
     Dropping his razor, Theo grabbed a towel and
pressed it to his bleeding chin. He could not remember the
last time he'd cut himself while shaving—it had been years
ago—but this morning he was so ham-fisted that he'd
nicked his jaw twice. And he was only half finished.

The fact that he felt like the worst sinner since Cain and was finding it difficult to face himself in the mirror probably accounted for a large part of today's clumsiness. Not that he was contemplating murder, but sinning, whatever form it took, was wrong. While it might be comforting to believe that some sins were worse than others, all were breaches of faith.

And a man who returns after nine days in the country and refuses an invitation to have breakfast with his fiancée in order to visit his soon-to-be ex-mistress was surely committing a sin. Not to mention a number of breaches of decorum.

The knowledge that he was doing wrong in order to do right did not ease Theo's conscience. Nor did the fact that he could name a number of married and betrothed men who kept mistresses or took lovers—some of them other men's wives—seemingly without feeling a twinge of guilt. How could a man of honor promise before God, family, and friends to be faithful to his wife and then not keep that vow? What was honor, but doing what was right and keeping one's word once it was given?

Knowing that nothing would change his opinion, Theo looked his image in the eye. "Yes, seeing Jani is a breach of my vow to Sarah, but today's meeting is merely a formality. And since I made the decision not to give Jani her *congé* via the mail before I saw Sarah this Season and realized my feelings for her, there is no insult to her. Sarah has been the sole object of my interest and affections since I vowed to reform, and she will hold that position until the day I die."

Then, feeling a bit better, he picked up his razor and resumed shaving. Fortunately, he completed the task without doing himself further injury, despite his valet's muttering that two such singular occurrences in one morning were a bad omen.

Two hours later, when he halted his curricle and pair in front of Jani's house on Half Moon Street, Theo was feeling less sanguine. He had spent so much time worrying about the rightness or wrongness of this visit that he'd given little thought to the meeting itself, aside from deciding that it should take place in the drawing room. Now, however, he wished that he had spent some of that time thinking about what to say. *How the devil does one tell a woman who has been a dear friend that she has been supplanted in his affections by another lady?* He was fond of Jani, though he'd never been in love with her, and he did not want to hurt her.

Tossing the reins to his tiger, he jumped down from the vehicle. "No need to walk them, Tom. I won't be long."

"Aye, my lord."

The moment Theo's hand left the knocker, Watson, Jani's elderly but spry butler, opened the door and ushered him inside.

"Good morning, Watson. Is Mrs. Brooks at home?"

"Yes, my lord, but she is working."

Theo nodded, well aware of Jani's habits, including the fact that she almost always spent the morning writing. "She asked me to call, so I believe she is expecting me. I will wait in the drawing room while you ascertain if she can spare me a few minutes this morning."

"Very good, my lord."

Too restless to sit, Theo paced the small drawing room from fireplace to window and back. Just when he began to wonder if he would have to go through the morning's anguish another day, a footman came in and kindled a fire. "Mrs. Brooks will be with you in a few minutes, my lord."

Smiling, Theo inquired, "Is it a page or a paragraph she wants to finish?"

The manservant's demeanor was too proper to permit an answering smile, but his eyes brightened. "I don't know, my lord."

Theo dismissed the footman, then crossed to the fireplace. His arm propped on the mantel, he gazed into the flames, occasionally touching his pocket, which held his parting gift for Jani. Deep in a reverie of his reunion with Sarah, he was not aware that Jani had entered the room until she spoke.

"Good morning, Theo. I am sorry I kept you waiting."

As she crossed the room to greet him, he smiled. Wearing a pretty but ink-stained morning gown of buttercup yellow, she looked much the same: slender, slightly above average height, with dark brown hair, hazel eyes, and fair but freckled skin. But something was different. After sev-

eral moments' scrutiny, he realized what it was. Although
she had always looked younger than her thirty-seven years,
now Jani seemed to glow from within, like a young girl in
the throes of first love.

Clasping her outstretched hands, he bent and kissed her
cheek, then stepped back to admire her. "You are looking
wonderfully well for woman who spent almost five months
in the wilds of Yorkshire."

"Thank you. You look quite well, too." She tilted her
head to one side and studied him. "Happy, but worried
about something. Has your brother suffered a setback?"

"No. His recovery hasn't been as rapid as he hoped, but
the doctors at Horse Guards are pleased with his progress."

"Good." With a hesitant smile, she suggested, "Let's sit
down, shall we? I have some news for you."

"I have some news for you, too." As he led her to the
sofa, Theo wondered what Jani wanted to tell him, and why
she seemed so concerned about his reaction. When they
were seated, he said, "As a gentleman, I must defer to you.
What news, my dear?"

"I . . . um . . ." After that tentative beginning, her words
tumbled out in a rush. "While I was in Yorkshire, I met a
man. I am getting married, Theo—although some days I
find it hard to believe—and so I must end our relationship.
I hope that, in time, you can be happy for me."

Surely it cannot be this easy? With some apprehension,
Theo waited for the catches and conditions, but none were
forthcoming. "That is wonderful news, Jani, and I am very
happy for you. He is a good man, your Yorkshireman?"

"He is," she averred. "He knows about my relationship
with you, and although we have been engaged for about a
month, Henry didn't object when I refused to break the
news to you in a letter."

Had he not felt so uneasy, Theo might have laughed at
the parallels in their situations. "I appreciate your
kindness—and his—but I would not have minded overmuch. Your happiness is paramount. And I do wish you
every happiness, my dear." Reaching for her hand, he
squeezed it, then leaned over and kissed her cheek.

His chuckle was more nervous than amused. "Perhaps
there was something special in the winds of Yorkshire and

London a month ago, for I, too, made the decision to marry then, and also not to break off our relationship in a letter."

"Theo, that is wonderful!" Jani was so excited that she bounced in her seat before throwing her arms around him and hugging him. "Do I know, or would I know of, your fiancée?"

"She is Lady Sarah Mallory, one of Weymouth's wife's friends."

"She is one of 'The Six,' isn't she? The Welsh harpist?"

Amazed by Jani's ability to remember detailed information about the people in his life, it took him a moment to find his voice. "Yes. The bachelors of the *ton* call her 'The Welsh Beauty.' "

"I have seen her at the theater, and she is, indeed, beautiful." Smiling delightedly, she grabbed his hands, squeezing them. "Theo, I am so happy for you!"

"Thank you, Jani. Our engagement won't be formally announced until tomorrow night at her parents' ball, but it has been generally known for almost a fortnight."

Freeing one hand, he reached into his pocket and pulled out Jani's gift. "I have something for you, dear—a final token of my regard and admiration. Your Henry will not object, I hope?"

"I don't believe so, once he knows the reason behind it." She held the slim blue velvet case in her hands for several moments before opening it. "Oh, Theo!" With hands that weren't quite steady, she lifted the sapphire and diamond bracelet from the satin-lined box. "It is Mrs. Thompson's work, is it not?"

"I thought her name was Mrs. Ragland. But yes, it was made by the lady jeweler at Ragland and Thompson—the daughter of one of the original partners who married the son of the other."

"She was Miss Ragland, but is now Mrs. Thompson," Jani explained distractedly as she attempted to fasten the bracelet.

"Here." Brushing her hands aside, Theo made quick work of the clasp, then rose, drawing Jani to her feet. "I don't want to earn your Henry's ire, so I will take my leave." Leading her to the door, he said with all sincerity, "I wish you all the best, dear Jani. I hope that you and Henry will be as happy as Sarah and I."

Following him outside, she smiled up at him, then, overcome with emotion, wrapped her arms around his waist and hugged him tightly. Stepping back, she said, in a voice thick with tears, "You are a very good man, Theo Middleford, and I wish you and your Sarah great joy and every happiness."

"Thank you, Jani." Bending, he kissed her cheek, then, smiling at her over his shoulder, he strode down the walk to his curricle.

Returning home after the final fitting of her gown for tomorrow night's ball, Sarah was almost thrown into her maid's lap when the coach halted abruptly. Before she regained her position and her voice, the coachman opened the trap and apologized. "Beg pardon for the rough stop, Lady Sarah, but some cove in a high-perch phaeton ran into a brewer's dray, and there are kegs all over the road. I am going to turn down Half Moon Street, so's I can get to Curzon Street. It is a more roundabout way, but I'll get you home to Hertford Street, never fear."

"Take whatever route you think best, Evans."

Looking out the window as the carriage turned, Sarah could see nothing of the accident, only a hodgepodge of vehicles of every description. Turning to face forward again, her eye was caught by a familiar curricle, drawn by an equally familiar pair of perfectly matched bays, parked in front of a house farther down Half Moon Street. Theo had sent a note informing her of his return, but regretfully declining her invitation to breakfast because of a previous engagement. Although disappointed that she would not see him until this afternoon, she had known when she'd sent her letter yesterday that he might not be able to accept her impromptu invitation. Now, seeing his curricle, she wondered who'd had the pleasure of his company this morning.

As they approached the house, Theo emerged. Drinking in the sight of his beloved form, Sarah did not notice the lady who followed him out until she hugged him. When he bent and kissed the woman, Sarah gasped as her heart—and her trust—shattered.

"Is something wrong, my lady?" Marged asked. "Or have you remembered an errand we forgot to do?"

Closing her eyes to hide her pain from the old Welsh-woman's perceptive gaze, Sarah shook her head. "Neither."

He lied. He lied. He lied. The words echoed through her mind—or her heart—in time to the horses' hoofbeats. *He promised that he would be faithful to me, but he lied. He refused my invitation this morning and spent the time kissing another woman.*

She had been *such* a fool! She'd believed his words of love, his promises to be faithful to her—and she'd ignored the gossip that he was a rake. *Foolish, foolish girl!*

When they arrived at Tregaron House, Sarah could not reach the haven of her bedchamber fast enough. She checked her headlong flight to order Jones to have her mare, Cwthwm, saddled along with Llanfyllin's horse. Unaware that she'd been pressing her hand over her heart, and equally oblivious of the consternation she'd left in her wake, she threw herself on her bed and wept.

When Marged entered an hour later to help her dress for the outing to Richmond, Sarah was huddled in bed with a cold cloth over her red-rimmed eyes.

"I will wear my blue velvet habit, Marged."

"That isn't what you told me this morning, miss. I pressed a carriage dress."

Sarah sat up. "I changed my mind."

The old woman snorted, then remonstrated, "If you are driving in Lord Dunnley's curricle, you should wear a carriage dress, not a habit."

"I am going to ride with my brother and the others. I am not certain Lord Dunnley will attend."

Mumbling under her breath, the old woman went to the dressing room for the habit and its accoutrements, but she said nothing more until Sarah was dressed and seated at the dressing table to have her hair styled. "I suppose you wuz crying because Lord Dunnley mayn't be able to go to Richmond."

"Something like that."

"Just because his lordship cannot go doesn't mean he doesn't love you, *bach.*"

Unwilling to be drawn into a discussion, Sarah merely nodded and handed Marged the hairbrush. In the twinkling of an eye, the jaunt to Richmond had been transformed from a pleasant, greatly anticipated excursion to one fraught with peril. What if Dunnley did go and continued to profess his love for her? Would she find it difficult to resist his blandishments, even after seeing proof of his faithlessness?

Lud! If not for the accident on Piccadilly this morning, Evans wouldn't have driven down Half Moon Street, and I wouldn't have learnt of Dunnley's perfidy. Yesterday she and her mother had discussed wedding plans, but today . . .

Suddenly becoming aware that she was twisting her engagement ring round and round, Sarah jerked it off, clutching it in her fist so that Marged would not see it. A few moments later, after realizing that if she did not wear it, she would spend a fair part of the afternoon explaining why, Sarah reluctantly returned it to her finger.

"You are pretty as a picture." Marged placed the shako hat on her mistress's head, then patted her shoulder, signaling that she was finished.

Mustering a smile for the maid, Sarah rose. After pulling on her gloves, she picked up her crop and went downstairs to face the first round of questions—her brother's.

Arriving at Tregaron House a few minutes before noon, Theo was greeted by the astonished butler. "Lord Dunnley! We weren't expecting you."

"Weren't you?" Theo's smile of greeting faded. "Did Lady Sarah not receive my note?"

"She received it, my lord." Jones frowned, emotions ranging from puzzlement to concern and anxiety flashing across his usually austere countenance. Finally, rather hesitantly, he said, "I don't know what happened, my lord, but after reading your note this morning, Lady Sarah was in high spirits and looking forward to riding with you to Richmond. Later, though, when she came back from the dressmaker's, she ordered her horse to be saddled with Lord Llanfyllin's. They left ten or fifteen minutes ago. When the young master asked her why she was riding, she said she didn't believe you would go to Richmond."

"*What?* Did she give a reason why she thought I wasn't going?"

"No, my lord, she did not."

At Kesteven House in Hanover Square, Theo's reception

was much the same. Questioning the grooms gained him the information that Sarah was riding a gray mare, her brother a chestnut gelding, and that the Mallorys were in the second of the three groups of riders, along with Lady Deborah, Fairfax, and his cousin. Tina, Howe, and Blackburn were in the third group; they'd left a few minutes later and had announced their intention to catch up to the others. Theo didn't ask about the first group, since his quarry was in the second one, but as he remounted his curricle and picked up the reins, one of the helpful grooms ticked off its members. Theo heard only the first two names: Lady Diana and Sir Edward Smithson; the crack of his whip drowned out the rest.

Icy terror clenching his insides, Theo threaded his rig through London's congested streets with more haste than grace. *What the hell is Nasty Ned planning?* Pleasant excursions to the countryside were not his usual choice of entertainment, so something—or someone—had compelled him to attend. Theo feared that Sarah was Smithson's compelling reason.

Finally reaching the outskirts of the city, he set his horses to a ground-eating canter. Questions pounded his mind in rhythm with his pair's hoofbeats. *What made Sarah think I wasn't going to Richmond? And why, in the name of all that is holy, had she not returned home when she realized Nasty Ned was one of the party?* He had not been on the original guest list, Theo knew; Sarah had listed its members in one of her letters.

After a frantic half hour, he spotted a group of riders ahead of him. A shiver, like a cold finger tracing his spine, racked him when he realized they were stopped, and that all had dismounted. As he approached, he recognized Fairfax, Tina, and one of the Woodhurst twins, but there was no sign of either Mallory. Nor of Blackburn.

Theo knew, with dreadful certainty, that something had happened to Sarah.

Drawing his rig to a halt behind them, he braced himself for the bad news. Tina stood some distance from the road, trying to calm a horse—a gray horse. One of the twins and Fairfax knelt beside someone lying on the ground. Not Sarah, though; the other twin. But Lady Diana was supposed to be in Smithson's high-perch phaeton.

"What the hell happened?" Theo did not realize he had voiced the question until he received an answer.

"Diana tried to ride Sarah's horse and was thrown." Lady Deborah's face bore evidence of recent tears, but she looked angry as well as frightened.

The same was true of Tina, who led the horse over when she saw Theo arrive. "Dunnley! Thank God you are here. Sir Edward Smithson kidnapped Sarah."

Dear God! "What happened?"

Tina glared at him and shouted, "I just told you—Sir Edward kidnapped Sarah," before bursting into tears.

Wrapping an arm around her shoulders, he hugged her, then handed her his handkerchief. Lady Deborah attempted to explain, but since her account consisted mostly of exclamations of "Poor Sarah!" and "He tricked us!" interposed between bouts of hand-wringing, it was not particularly helpful.

Fairfax, his ever-reliable best friend, provided a coherent explanation: "Smithson set up a clever ambush. His phaeton was stopped at the side of the road when we rode up, and he said that Lady Diana wasn't feeling well. Deborah and Tina dismounted to ask her what was wrong, and after a minute or so, Diana, with much moaning and groaning, asked them to lead her to those"—he pointed—"bushes."

"And while everyone was watching the three of them, Smithson pulled Sarah off her horse, threw her into his rig, and took off." Disgust was rife in Theo's voice.

"Yes," Fairfax admitted, chagrined. "Sarah's brother, Blackburn, and Walsingham—my cousin—set off in pursuit. As they rode off, Blackburn yelled that we should go on, and they would catch up to us later."

Before Theo could ask which way Smithson had gone, the duke continued his tale. "After Smithson and the others left, Diana, who had to have been in on Smithson's scheme, made a miraculous recovery. She acted as if nothing had happened and said she'd ride Sarah's horse. Tina warned her that the gray took exception to almost every rider save Sarah and her mother, but Diana said she could ride anything with four legs. She stayed on," he said on a laugh, "at most, ten seconds. She has a broken arm as a reward for her perfidy."

Theo crossed the grass to Lady Diana in three quick strides. "Where is Smithson taking Lady Sarah?"

"To Gretna Green."

Over my dead body. "He can't reach Gretna in a day. Where is he planning to stop tonight?"

"I don't know." More weakly uttered than her previous remark, which had been laced with a smirking, spiteful glee, it didn't ring true.

He brushed the toe of his boot against her arm—the broken one. In a pleasant, conversational voice underlaid with steel, he said, "I daresay you will remember if I step on your arm. Shall we try it and see?"

Her eyes flew open. "I don't know for certain, but possibly his hunting box."

Both the distance and the location were perfect for what Smithson had in mind. Theo turned on his heel and returned to Fairfax, Deborah, and Tina, for whom he had a few more questions.

"How long since Smithson took Sarah?"

"An hour" was Tina's implausible answer. They hadn't left London an hour ago.

"No," Deborah contradicted. "Twenty or thirty minutes."

Fairfax shook his head. "More like fifteen or twenty minutes."

"Smithson went west?" Theo asked the duke.

"Yes. Lan—er, Sarah's brother, Blackburn, and my cousin were in pursuit a minute or two later, but they are riding."

Theo understood the duke's unspoken implication: Smithson, driving a pair, would have the advantage initially, but unless he changed horses, he would lose it. "But they didn't know where he was going. Did they plan to split up at crossroads?"

"They may have made plans as they rode." Fairfax's level tone was belied by the scornful "what a stupid question" look that Theo remembered from their days at Eton.

He nodded, conceding the point. He held out his hand for the gray to nuzzle, wishing he had an apple to offer as a bribe, since he wanted the horse with him. "Who and where are the chaperones?"

"My mother, Sarah's mother, and Tina's mother. No

doubt by now they are at the Star and Garter," Deborah said, naming the inn in Richmond where they were to eat. "Probably wondering where we are."

"Where are Howe and the others?"

"Diana said the others were ahead of them when she and Sir Edward stopped." A scathing look at her sister accompanied the words.

"I sent Howe to the Star and Garter," Fairfax reported. "To alert the chaperones and send a carriage for Lady Diana."

Theo nodded, grateful for his friend's presence. "What is Sarah's horse's name?"

The question garnered looks of disbelief. With mounting impatience, he explained, "I want to take the mare with me, so I need to know her name."

Tina shrugged and handed him the reins. "She has a Welsh name."

"It sounds like 'Kuthum' or 'Koothoom'." Deborah's ear for languages was obviously better than his cousin's.

Thanking her with a smile, Theo reassured, "I *will* rescue Sarah."

He look his leave of Deborah and Tina, then, with a nod indicating that Fairfax should follow, led the horse to his rig. As he tied her reins to the tiger's seat, Theo asked, "I don't suppose you have a pistol with you?"

His friend's eyes nearly popped from their sockets. "No." Then, after a noticeable hesitation, "Are you going to call Smithson out?"

"Perhaps." Theo would make that decision after he found the baronet, and after he learned what the rotter had done to Sarah.

The duke held out his hand. "Good luck and Godspeed."

Sarah had never been so terrified in her life. She could not seem to draw air into her lungs, yet her chest rose and fell rapidly. Too rapidly. If she did not calm her frantic breathing—and her racing heart—she would likely faint. And unconsciousness was *not* a desirable state for a lady in the presence of a libertine like Sir Edward Smithson.

She prayed that her brother and one of the other men, preferably Blackburn, were giving chase. Prayed that Rhys or the earl would catch up to them soon. But her heart, her foolish heart, hoped that Theo would swoop down like an avenging angel and rescue her.

Yet he was, indirectly, the cause of her present peril, although Sarah knew that she had only herself to blame. Well, herself and Sir Edward. Knowing that he was nearby, she ought to have been more vigilant than usual, but instead she had been thinking of Theo, wondering if honor had compelled his proposal, if he'd lied about loving her. And wondering about the woman he'd kissed.

Now she was paying the price for her folly. But she had learnt from her mistake, and she would not make it again. She was alert—as alert as a very frightened young lady could be—and she was not submitting tamely to her fate. She'd screamed for help when they passed another carriage, and she'd been slapped, then gagged because of it. Later, she'd tried to throw herself from the phaeton; that had earned her a clout on the temple and bound hands and feet. She did not know where Nasty Ned was taking her, nor what he planned, but she had stood up to him last night, and she could do it again.

Or so she kept telling herself, in between her prayers for rescue.

Theo pushed his pair, promising they would never have to pull a carriage again and could spend the rest of their days frolicking in Dunnley Park's paddocks, if they would give their all to help him find Sarah. An hour before sunset, he did.

He was so intent on the road ahead of him that he almost did not see Smithson's phaeton parked in the yard of a small inn. As it was, his mind did not recognize what his eyes had seen until he'd driven past. Backing his rig down the road and into the innyard had gained the attention—and admiration—of the grooms, who rewarded him with the information that Smithson had arrived about ten minutes earlier, his lady passenger bound and gagged.

"The lady is my fiancée and the Earl of Tregaron's daughter. Smithson abducted her earlier today. Needless to say, his intentions are not honorable."

"Here's what ye do, my lord," the oldest groom, a short, wiry man of forty-some years, advised. "We'll take ye in through the kitchen, so's ye can tell Mr. Johnson about that rum cove. Mr. Johnson'll take a bottle of wine or sommat into the parlor, and the four of us"—he gestured to Theo, himself, and the other two grooms—"will follow him in. You take care of the lady. We'll handle the blighter."

Theo eyed the groom's nose, which had been broken more than once. "Handle him carefully enough that he will be able to talk to the magistrate this evening."

Although they grumbled that he was spoiling their sport, they agreed, then led him across the yard to the kitchen door. Mr. Johnson, a former infantry sergeant invalided out four years ago, "but still right handy with me fives or a pistol," was eager to lend his assistance. And his pistol. A plan was quickly formed, and weapons dispersed—the pistol to Theo, a bottle of wine and a heavy tray for Johnson, and knives or cleavers for the grooms. Johnson was in his element as he led his makeshift troop to the inn's sole private parlor to engage the enemy.

Please, God, keep Sarah safe, so she and I can live and laugh and love together.

Heartened by Mrs. Johnson's obvious distrust of Sir Edward, Sarah explained her plight as the innkeeper's wife escorted her upstairs to a chamber, so she could wash her face and hands before dinner. Loath though she was to rejoin Sir Edward, she dared not linger too long, for fear of further provoking his wrath. Free of her bonds and buoyed by Mrs. Johnson's promise to send for the magistrate, Sarah gritted her teeth and returned downstairs. *Half an hour until the magistrate arrives. You can endure another thirty minutes of Nasty Ned's company.*

The innkeeper met her at the bottom of the stairs. "Everything will be all right, my lady," he assured her quietly, then escorted her down the hall to the private parlor.

"Please, send for the magistrate." Her whispered plea could not have been heard by Sir Edward, even if he had his ear against the heavy oak door.

"I already have." Opening the door, he bowed her inside.

Looking over her shoulder and wondering what kind of magic Smithson had worked on Mr. Johnson in her absence, Sarah froze at the sound of her name.

The speaker rose from a settle by the fireplace and

walked toward her. Sarah's eyes widened in disbelief. "Theo? What are you doing here? Where is Sir Edward?"

"I have come to rescue you, my darling girl. Smithson is trussed up and locked in the innkeeper's parlor, awaiting the arrival of the magistrate. After their conversation, Smithson will depart for the Indies, where he plans to live for the next few years."

"I am glad you rescued me—very glad—but I don't understand."

He smiled at her—his special smile. "What don't you understand, my love? You are safe from Sir Edward. He will never bother you again. In fact, he probably won't ever dare to speak to you again." His hands cupped her shoulders, then slid down her back to pull her into an embrace.

Sarah braced her hands against his chest, resisting the tug. Theo frowned, obviously perplexed by her refusal. "Sarah? What is wrong?"

"I saw you." It was all she could think to say.

His frown deepened. "When or where did you see me, sweetheart?"

Deep inside, Sarah began to tremble, but she did not know if it was in relief at being rescued from Nasty Ned or in fear of the coming confrontation with Theo. "This morning. On Half Moon Street. You kissed a woman."

He closed his eyes and whispered, "Oh, my sweet Sarah."

"You lied. You told me you loved me, and promised to be faithful, but you lied."

His eyes, which had snapped open at the first accusation, locked with hers. "I did not lie. Despite what you saw—and I am sorry for that—I did not lie. I do love you, Sarah, and I have not betrayed your trust or broken the promises I made to you."

Her tremors increased, and she wrapped her arms tightly around her waist in a vain attempt to still them. "I saw you. She hugged you, and you kissed her."

"Are you cold?" Scooping her into his arms, he carried her to the wing chair in front of the fire. He sat down, settled her on his lap, then wrapped his arms around her, enveloping her in the warmth and protection of his embrace. She resisted the urge to lay her head on his shoulder, but despite what she knew—what she'd seen—it was more difficult than she expected.

"Sarah, what you saw this morning was two old friends wishing each other well in their forthcoming marriages."

"Do you kiss all your *old friends* when you wish them well?"

"Jani—the lady you saw me kiss *on the cheek* this morning—is the only old friend I have." She felt rather than heard his sigh. "I promised you honesty, Sarah, so honesty you shall have. Jani was my mistress for many years, but she has been in Yorkshire since before Christmas, taking care of her mother, who was ill. She returned to Town a few days ago and sent me a note, asking me to call. Since I have wanted to end my relationship with her for more than a month, but didn't want to do it in a letter, I called on her this morning. We sat in her drawing room, told each other of our upcoming marriages and our desire to end our liaison, and wished each other joy and happiness in the future.

"Yes, I kissed her on the cheek. Twice—no, three times: when I arrived, when she told me she was getting married, and when I left. But that, and talking, was all I did. It was as proper as a morning call could be."

He laughed but there was no amusement in it. "It is really quite ironic. I wanted to sever my relationship with her before I saw you again, yet I felt guilty as hell for visiting her this morning instead of you. I was trying to do the right thing—"

"I believe you, Theo." And she did, she believed every word. His sincerity was evident in his expression, the tone of his voice, even his posture. "Thank you for explaining, and for your honesty." She kissed his cheek, the location deliberate. "I think you did the right thing." Sarah was delighted that he had, for all intents and purposes, ended the relationship before he proposed to her.

He hugged her, hard. "Thank *you*, sweet Sarah."

"Theo, if we are going back to Town tonight—"

"You need to make a choice, my love." He brushed a featherlight kiss against her lips.

"A choice about what?"

"You need to decide if we should stay here tonight or if we should risk our necks, and my horses, traveling over possibly ill-kept roads on a relatively moonless night to make our way back to Town." He smiled his most charming smile. "If you choose to stay, we will be married tomorrow—"

"We can't get married tomorrow!"

"Indeed we can. I have a special license."

"You do?"

"Yes. I got it the day after I proposed to you—with a bit of help from your father and Uncle Michael. Besides," he added, after another kiss, "don't you think your parents would be even more pleased to announce our wedding at the ball tomorrow night than our engagement?"

"Theo? There is one thing that worries me."

"What, my love?" He kissed her again, a deeper, more lingering kiss. "I told your brother that we might not be able to come back to Town tonight. He knows you are with me, and he will tell your parents."

"When—?" She shook her head. It did not matter when Theo had seen Rhys, only that he had.

"Are you asking when I am going to marry you?" He punctuated the question with a series of kisses. "I am still waiting for *your* answer."

"I cannot answer that question until I know the answer to two others."

"Ask your questions, sweetheart."

Frowning, she wondered how to ask. "I have heard it said that you are a rake. How do I know that I can make you happy? Or that you will love me forever?"

"Sarah, you know that you have made me happy today, don't you?"

"Yes." Her frown eased, its disappearance aided by the kiss he placed there.

"Do you believe that I love you today?"

"Yes, I do."

"Don't worry about forever, sweetheart. Forever is just a lot of days strung together like the pearls of your favorite necklace."

Sarah rewarded her fiancé's wisdom with a kiss. Several of them. He rewarded her by saying, "Besides, I am no longer a rake. I reformed more than a month ago, and you, sweet Sarah, have been—and will always be—my redemption."

Epilogue

On Thursday, the twenty-eighth of April in the Year of Our Lord 1814, the members of the *beau monde* flocked to Tregaron House. Ostensibly they were there to dance, to gossip, and to see and be seen. Most, however, had another reason—one related to the expected announcement of the engagement of Lady Sarah Mallory to the Viscount Dunnley. The men came to pay tribute to "The Welsh Beauty," and to envy Dunnley's good fortune in winning her. Most of the ladies were compelled by curiosity. Was the rakish, handsome viscount really going to step in parson's mousetrap? Quite a number of them, both married and unmarried, hoped that he would not.

At the beginning of the ball, when the Earl of Tregaron announced that his daughter Sarah had married the Viscount Dunnley that morning, exclamations of surprise (and some of dismay) were heard in every corner of the ballroom. Every corner save that occupied by Dunnley's relatives, the Duke of Fairfax, and Lady Deborah Woodhurst, all of whom had been present at the ceremony.

Dunnley and his bride led the first dance—a waltz. The waltz tune that Sarah had deemed interminable a little more than a fortnight ago, now seemed remarkable for its brevity. When she said as much to her husband at the conclusion of the dance, he kissed her. In the middle of the dance floor, in full view of the high sticklers, the patronesses of Almack's, and most of the *ton*.

When the absence of the bride and groom was noticed, less than an hour after the earl's announcement, no one was very surprised. They were, after all, newly wed, and Dunnley quite the rake.

No one saw Dunnley and his bride again for a fortnight, when they reluctantly left Dunnley Park and returned to Town to honor the promises they had made, individually and as a couple, to sing at the Duchess of Greenwich's musicale. Dunnley performed with his usual octet, which sang two madrigals. The new viscountess played her harp and sang two Welsh songs. For the finale, they performed one song together—*Llwyn On* or *The Ash Grove*, singing two verses in English and one in Welsh.

Although the song had not required the number of rehearsals Dunnley originally intended, no one but he knew. He had discovered more pleasurable ways to spend time with his lady.

He was, after all, a rake. A reformed, one-woman rake, but a rake all the same.

About the Author

Susannah Carleton discovered Regency romances at the ripe old age of thirty-three and promptly fell in love, since life among the *ton* in Regency England is such a diverting change from that of an engineer. She lives in Florida with her husband and teenage son, and when she isn't reading or writing, she enjoys solo and choral singing and needlework. Visit her Web site at www.susannahcarleton.com.